Dom Casmurro

A.R.

Cornell Univ.
7/3/57

Dom Casmurro

A NOVEL BY

Machado de Assis

TRANSLATED BY HELEN CALDWELL

WITH AN INTRODUCTION BY WALDO FRANK

The Noonday Press, Inc.
New York, 1953

Introduction

THERE IS a slight short story (barely more than a sketch) by Machado de Assis, about a male nurse who is called to a residential suburb of Rio de Janeiro to take care of a retired army officer, a rich old bachelor with an abominable disposition. More than once, although the pay is good, the nurse decides to quit. One night, as he leans over the patient's bed to give him his medicine, the sick man strikes him, and the nurse chokes him to death. Until dawn, beside the silent body, he meditates on the form of his confession. But, before he can speak, the doctor finds the death natural: the old man's heart has been tottering for a long time; the townsfolk praise him for his long-suffering patience; and when the will is read and it is learned that the nurse is the old man's sole heir, praise rises to a paean; for once, virtue has been rewarded. The nurse, now old and dying, having with manageable remorse enjoyed his legacy for years, tells the tale. To whom? To his priest? To the world? *He tells it to his heir*. And so ends the inconspicuous story. Presumably the narrator dies, saying: "Blessed are they who possess, for they shall be consoled"; and the inheritor inherits—not only the money but the guilt, each of which will know how to take care of the other.

The irony of this bitter-sweet little tale, its hedonistic elegance, reveal something of Machado de Assis. The structure of his art, beneath its flat surface, is always contrapuntal.

Within the quiet, courses a complex fugue: innocence cruelly punished and revealed as guilt; pleasure pleasurably crushed; the "good" and the "beautiful" on the wrack and dissolving into their contraries. The blood, indeed the core, of the fictive world of Machado de Assis is ambiguity—ambiguity raised to a principle and a substance.

The genetic critic would explain this by the man's life. Joaquim Maria Machado de Assis was born in a poor *carioca* district of Rio de Janeiro in 1839. His father, a humble house painter, was a mulatto and, according to the critic, Americo Valerio, an alcoholic and a syphilitic. His mother, a lowly Portuguese, died early and the child was raised by his stepmother, a mulatto like her husband. At fifteen, he was a printer's boy and, like most Brazilians, writing verse. The corner baker taught him French, and he taught himself English. At twenty-one, he was a reporter; at twenty-five, he was beginning to be known in Rio for his plays, his literary reviews and his political columns. He loved the works of Swift, Sterne, Mark Twain—above all, *Tristram Shandy;* he detested the Naturalists and Emile Zola, rising star of the literary heavens. Long before he had written a page of intrinsic value, his critical pieces called for a "national sensibility." He was undersized, myopic, rachitic, epileptic. And at thirty (1869, when the Brazilian Empire had still twenty years to go) he married Carolina Xavier de Novaes, daughter of Dona Rita de Cassia Calazans Rodrigues of the great house of the Barons of Taquarí. His wife's sisters, for obvious reasons, frowned on the alliance, but her mother and her lofty friend, the Countess de S. Mamede, supported her choice. She was five years older than her husband, and their wedded life was happy.

Before he died in 1908, this sickly man of color had become
president of the Academy of Brazil and the acknowledged
leader of Brazil's men of letters. Despite his successes and his
responsible government posts in the Republic, which peacefully replaced the Empire in 1889, Machado de Assis kept
growing as an artist. When he wrote his masterpiece, *Dom
Casmurro* (here admirably translated), he was sixty.

Yes: the geneticist-psychologist critic has plenty of what he
would call data for his thesis: conflicts of blood, conflicts of
class, conflicts of sickly body and imperious brain . . . never
resolved, making for the basic ambiguity of the artist's cosmos.
But I suspect that such polarities, tensions, irresolutions, exist
in every son and daughter of Adam and Eve, exposed as we
all are, to Eden and Earth, to the Serpent and to God. We
shall come, I believe, a little—only a very little—closer to a
specific relevance, if we consider Brazil. There was, of course,
race prejudice in Brazil. Gradually, peacefully, by a long series
of laws, both State and Federal, and over a long course of
years, slavery was done away with—finally in 1888. But the
children of color were predominantly the poor, drawers of
water, hewers of wood; and where does not money discriminate
in favor of money? Nevertheless, the feeling in Brazil's upper
classes against color was never allowed to stratify as it has in
the United States. The sons of slaves were *Brazilians,* not
Negroes, and a deep religious culture, old as the Colony, gave
substance to that meaning. If in the loose economy of the vast
land (larger than our States; probably richer in resources), a
man with African blood by luck or skill rose to an eminence, he
filled his place as a Brazilian. A school with a preponderance
of white children (because the district rents were high) might

have a colored principal. A physician of African blood might
be able to charge high fees because he was skilled, and hence
would have a white clientele, because whites could best afford
him. Colored men of the professions were invited to the Imperial balls, danced with the Imperial ladies. A Brazilian chose
the location of his house according to his economic status, not
his color. There was even a colored President of the Republic
—a mediocre president, to be sure, like most of the white ones
in that republic—and ours. Brazil's liberty of spirit was broad
and deep. And one basic cause was the truly pervasive spirit
of the Church, which underlay and nourished even the agnos-
tic liberals and the atheist positivists of Brazil's nineteenth
century culture. Already, in colonial days, the attitude of the
Brazilian master toward his slaves had been distinct from
that of our own South. But all this would take us too far afield.
Suffice it to say that in Brazil, despite economic injustice and
social discrimination, all races and all mixtures subtly came
to feel that they could *breathe.* All bloods circulated freely in
the nation's body, each element contributing to the whole
what it had to give and receiving . . . culturally, spiritually
. . . what it needed.

Whatever mystery produced the elements born in the great
Brazilian sculptor, O Aleijadinho,[1] son of a slave woman, or
born in Machado de Assis, *these elements could grow:* could
make of O Aleijadinho the American world's greatest plastic
artist: could make of Machado de Assis the herald of a novel-
istic art familiar to us in the works of Proust and Kafka. Ambiguity as the essence of human life may inspire a French
aristocrat or a Czech bourgeois Jew, as well as a *carioca* colored

[1] 1730-1814.

man. It might also conceivably have inspired a mulatto born to Charleston, South Carolina in 1700, 1800 or 1900. But, in our South, would elements potential of great art in a man segregated as a *Negro* have flourished? The Brazilian suffered from the ironic contrasts of his flesh and spirit. His world of Brazil let the elements of his nature live, and grow into a literary art of unsurpassed precision.

* * *

Dom Casmurro, which appeared in 1900, is a deceptive book—and means to be. The language is limpid and light; far indeed from the heavy-laden voices of the nineteenth century masters: Balzac, overfreighted with mass material; Flaubert static and hard as burnished gems; Pérez Galdós, open like the parabola of a comet; Zola, turgid with choking fires. The language of Machado de Assis resembles the simplicities of the eighteenth century, whose various rump-rationalist schools were fondly certain that the beheading of kings, the mechanics of constitutions balancing property with the rights of man, and the advance of science, would presently exile injustice and terror from the earth. The design of the book at once recalls Laurence Sterne: there is a similar play of tiny chapters, digressions, parentheses, cut-backs, verbal jests; the same discursiveness and casualness and innuendo, by which Tristram Shandy, gentleman, mirrored the expansiveness and the security of his class in William Pitt's England. Why this form in a novel of Brazil? Is there perhaps an analogy between the still expansive Britain of the Great Commoner— its loose, relaxed *largesse*—absorbing into urbanity the Seven Seas, and Brazil, a century later, beginning from its Atlantic seaboard of 4,000 miles to invade the infinitude of its rivers and its forests? A long essay could be written on that question. The Sternean style of *Dom Casmurro* and *Memórias Póstumas de Braz Cubas* * lends itself to the conveying of an obsessive spatiality, a human lostness within it, making men and women huddle close together: an emotion that belongs to Brazil and which Brazil's second great master of prose, Euclides da Cunha, author of the epic *Os Sertões,* achieved by a totally distinct stylistic method.

But the Sternean whimsy has here a deeper purpose: *to deceive.* Machado de Assis aims to entice us lightly to a storm center; to drift us into it, lazily lulled, beyond any eighteenth century scope, to a depth that we do not grow aware of until we find that our feet have lost bottom!

The book is a treacherous stroll. Each detail on the way, casual and slight, is perfect, leading us on. We know these characters as closely—and as little—as if we were sipping coffee with them. We idle onward. Suddenly, behind us, the tide has come in! We must swim to get back!

. . . those eyes of Capitú's. I can find no image—without breaking the dignity of my style—to convey what they were and what they did to me. Eyes like the tide? Yes, like the tide. That's what they were. They had some mysterious and force-giving fluid that drew everything up into them, like a wave that moves back from the shore when the undertow is heavy. In order not to be swept under, I grasped at other, neighboring parts, her ears, her arms, at her hair that was spread over her shoulders; but as soon as I sought the pupils of her eyes again, the wave that came from them kept growing, cavernous, dark, threatening to engulf me. . . .

With what consummate skill this early metaphor is woven into the ultimate catastrophe!

* Translated as *Epitaph of a Small Winner.*

And the humor: is it like Sterne's? Enough like, to make
one ask: is a box containing a bright kaleidoscope like the
telescope which makes the eyes touch the infinite black spaces
between stars?

I wish I could be sure that this Introduction will not be
read at all (the usual fate, I am informed, of introductions)
or read only after the book. I should then feel free to discuss
the central ambiguity of *Dom Casmurro:* Capitú's innocence
or guilt, without harming the innocence of the reader's stroll
from chapter to chapter. What exquisite details he will find
as he meanders! The delicious wit of the sonnet whose twelve
middle lines are never written; and the shift of the last line
from *Life is lost, the battle still is won!* to *Life is won, the
battle still is lost.* Or the sudden apparition of the leper boy,
Manduca. Or the sadism of the cat-and-mouse episode. Or the
scene where the "dependent," José Dias, sententious and
lovable, pedantically refers to the boy as a "son of man," rousing a mysterious storm. Or the superbly deft handling of the
episode of the poisoned coffee. . . . I must refrain from
discussing the final question, since the reader should first
encounter it *on his stroll.*

But when he has come out of it all—*swum back,* the reader
will understand that the true answer of Machado de Assis to
the great question, as to all the others, is *that he has no answer.*
Ambiguity is the book's texture and life vision. And this no-
answer is built with a happiness of detail that the reader can
only truly relish upon a second reading. The ambiguity begins, indeed, with the first pages. Bento's mother has vowed
a bargain with God: if He will vouchsafe her a second son
(her first has died), she will dedicate him to God's service as a

priest. By all the powers of the Church and of logic, the mother is absolved. *But is she?* Isn't Bento's life proof that they are not absolved, and that the vow *is* broken? And must one not generalize? Are we not all of us broken, because of a Vow, implicit in our birth, which our respectable lives dishonor?

Dom Casmurro is no mystery story about a marital triangle; no psychological novel about jealousy. This much can be said. Bento cites *Othello*. But Othello was not jealous; he killed from conviction and certainty of justice. There is no triangle in *Othello;* the duologue is between evil and virtuous folly. Bento is also convinced. But the stuff of his life is *the ambiguous;* and the author shares it. Whatever conclusion the reader comes to about the superbly drawn heroine and the friend and the boy, Machado will not disagree; He "knows the answer" no more than we do. What he knows is Ambiguity. This is not enough: he limns it with the sure hand of the master goldsmith.

* * *

At the turn of the last century, a Brazilian writes a novel that presages Proust and Kafka. A profound religious culture gave to all three artists insight into man's tragic marrow; but all three had lost the revelation and the subsequent faith that resolve tragedy into Wholeness. A psychologist of today has written: "As an animal, man is a poor thing." But what if he has lost the knowledge to be man? Time and space and personality will melt. Clairvoyance will be bitter. Elegance will bravely cover chaos. As Bento says: "A lottery prize fades, but death does not." The spirit of death becomes the sole remaining desperate preservative of the loved elements of chaos: woman, and comrades, and nature. Proust sang his hymn to

Ambiguity in a vast novel; Machado de Assis in a short one. Of the two, it could be that the Brazilian's will be read longer. For, according to Anatole France, a book to reach posterity must travel light. (Who today reads even excerpts from the great huge memoirs of the Duc de Saint-Simon, who equalled Tacitus except in brevity?)

The fact that this little masterpiece, now so featly englished, was composed by the epileptic son of a poor mulatto: what does it prove about the relevance of race and disease to genius? Precisely nothing.

WALDO FRANK

1952

Dom Casmurro

1. The title

ONE NIGHT not long ago, as I was coming from the city to Engenho Novo, * on the Brazil Central, I ran into a young man from here in the neighborhood, with whom I have a bowing acquaintance. He spoke, sat down beside me, talked of the moon and the government, ended by reading me some verses. The trip was short, and the verses may not have been entirely bad. It happened, however, that as I was tired, I closed my eyes three or four times—it was enough to make him stop reading and put the verses in his pocket.

"Go on," I said, rousing myself.

"I've finished," he muttered.

"They are very fine."

I saw him make a gesture to take them out of his pocket again, but it did not pass beyond a gesture. He was offended. The next day he said some hard things about me and gave me the nickname *Dom Casmurro*. The neighbors, who do not like my taciturn, recluse-like habits, took up the nickname: it stuck. This did not make me angry. I told the story to my friends in the city, and they, in fun, call me by it and write to me: "Dom Casmurro, I am coming to have dinner with you Sunday." "I am going to my old place at Petropolis, Dom Casmurro. See if you can't tear yourself away from that cave in Engenho Novo and come spend a couple of weeks with me." "My dear Dom Casmurro, don't imagine that you are going to escape my theater party tomorrow night. You can

* "The New (sugar) Mill," a suburb of Rio de Janeiro.

stay overnight in the city. I promise you a box at the theater, tea, and a bed. The only thing I don't promise you is a girl."

Don't consult your dictionaries. *Casmurro* is not used here in the meaning they give for it, but in the sense in which the man in the street uses it, of a morose, tight-lipped man withdrawn within himself. The *Dom* was for irony: to impute to me aristocratic airs. All for dozing off! Well, I have found no better title for my narrative; if no better occurs, let it stand! My poet of the train will know that I do not bear him a grudge. And, with a little effort, since the title is his, he will be able to decide that the work is his. There are books which owe no more to their authors; some, not so much.

2. The book

NOW THAT I have explained the title, I will proceed to the book. First, however, let us go over the motives which placed a pen in my hand.

I live alone, with one servant. The house in which I live is *mine*. I had it built specially, to satisfy a desire that is so personal I am ashamed to print it—but here goes. One day, a number of years ago, I decided to reproduce in Engenho Novo, the house in which I grew up on old Rua de Matacavallos. It was to have the same appearance and plan as the other house, which had disappeared. Builder and decorator understood my instructions. It is the same tall structure with three windows across the front, veranda at the back, the same rooms upstairs and down. In the living room, the decoration of ceiling and walls is more or less identical: garlands of tiny flowers steadied, from space to space, by the beaks of stout birds. In the four corners of the ceiling, are the figures of the seasons; and in the center of the walls, the medallions of Caesar, Augustus, Nero and Massinissa, with their names beneath. . . . The reason for these personages eludes me. When we moved to the Matacavallos house, it was already decorated with them; they were from the previous decade. Perhaps it was the taste of that day to introduce a classical flavor and ancient figures into American paintings. The rest of the place is in the same mood. I have a small estate with flowers, vegetable garden, a casuarina tree, a wellpool and washing stones. I use old china and old furniture. And now, as formerly, there is the same contrast between the life within, which is tranquil, and that without, which is noisy and restless.

My purpose was to tie together the two ends of my life, to restore adolescence in old age. Well, sir, I did not succeed in putting back together what had been nor what I had been. If the face is the same, the expression is different. If it were only the others that were missing, no matter. A man consoles himself more or less for those he has lost, but I myself am missing, and this lack is essential. What is here may be likened to dye on hair and beard: it barely preserves the outer *habit,* as they say in autopsies; the inner structure will not take dye. A certificate stating that I am twenty years old might deceive a stranger, like any forged document, but not me. The friends I have left are of recent date; the old ones have all gone to study the geology of holy ground. As for my lady friends, some date back fifteen years, others less, and almost all believe in their own youthfulness. Two or three would have others believe in it, but the language they speak often obliges one to consult a dictionary, and such intercourse is wearisome.

Still, a different life does not mean a worse life; it is just not the same. In certain respects, that old life now appears stripped of much of the enchantment I found in it; but it has also lost many a spine that made it painful, and in my memory I keep some sweet and charming recollections. Now, I go out little; I seldom talk to people. Rare distractions. Most of my time is spent working in the garden and reading. I eat well and I do not sleep badly.

But, as everything wearies one, this monotony too finally exhausted me. I wanted change. What if I wrote a book? Jurisprudence, philosophy and politics suggested themselves; but they did not bring with them the necessary energy. Then I thought of making a *History of the Suburbs,* something less dry than the memoirs of Padre Luiz Gonçalves dos Santos concerning our city; it would be a modest work, but it would demand documents and dates as preliminaries—a long dull business. It was then that the busts painted on the walls spoke to me and said that since they had failed to bring back the days gone by, I should take my pen and tell over those times. Perhaps the act of narration would summon the illusion for me, and the shades would come treading lightly, as with the poet, not the one of the train but Faust's: *Ah there, are you come again restless shades?*

I was so happy with this idea that the pen still trembles in my hand. Yes, Nero, Augustus, Massinissa, and thou, great Caesar, who incit'st me to compose my commentaries, I thank you for your advice, and I will put on paper the memories that come crowding. In this way I will live what I have lived, and I will strengthen my hand for some work of greater scope. Let us commence the evocation with a notable afternoon in November, which I never forgot. I had many others, better, and worse, but that one never faded from my spirit— as you will discover by reading.

3. The information

I WAS about to go into the living room when I heard my name mentioned and hid behind the door. It was the house on Rua de Matacavallos, the month November, the year— the year is a trifle remote, but I am not one to change the dates of my life just to please those who do not like old stories —the year was 1857.

"Dona Gloria, are you going ahead with your idea of putting our Bentinho in the seminary? It's high time, and even now there may be a difficulty."

"What difficulty?"

"A great difficulty."

My mother wanted to know what it was. José Dias, after several instants of hesitation, came to see if there was anyone in the hall; he did not notice me, went back and, lowering his voice, said that the difficulty was in the house close by, the Padua family.

"The Padua family?"

"I've wanted to say this for some time, but I didn't have the courage. It doesn't look right to me for our Bentinho to be always getting into corners with the daughter of old *Turtleback*. And this is the difficulty, for if they should start making love, you'd have a struggle on your hands to separate them."

"Oh, no! Getting into corners?"

"It's a manner of speaking. Whispering in secret, always together. Bentinho almost never leaves that place. The girl is a scatterbrain. Her father pretends not to see; he'd just as soon things went so far that . . . I understand your gesture;

you don't believe that there are people so calculating, you think that everyone has a frank, open nature. . . ."

"But, Senhor José Dias, I've seen the youngsters playing, and I've never seen anything to make one mistrust—their age alone—Bentinho is barely fifteen. Capitú had her fourteenth birthday last week. They're two babes. Don't forget, they were brought up together, ever since the big flood ten years ago, when the Paduas lost so much; that was what started our intimacy. And am I to believe . . . ? Brother Cosme, what do *you* think?"

Uncle Cosme answered with an "Aw!" which, translated into the vulgar tongue, meant: "José Dias and his imagination! The youngsters amuse themselves! I amuse myself! Where is the backgammon board?"

"Yes, I believe that you are mistaken, senhor."

"Perhaps so. God grant that you are right; but, believe me, I spoke only after much careful observation. . . ."

"In any case, the time is drawing near," interrupted my mother, "I must see about entering him in the seminary as soon as possible."

"Good, if you have not given up the idea of making him a priest, that's the main thing. Bentinho is bound to comply with the wishes of his mother. And then too the Brazilian church has a noble destiny. Let us not forget that a bishop presided at the Constituent Assembly, and that Padre Feijó governed the empire. . . ."

"Governed like the fool he was!" cut in Uncle Cosme, giving way to old political rancors.

"Beg pardon, doctor, I am not defending anyone, I am merely citing cases. What I want to say is that the clergy still plays a big role in Brazil."

"What you want is a capot; get the backgammon board. As

for the boy, if he has to be a padre, of course it's better for
him not to commence saying Mass behind doors. But look,
Sister, is it really necessary to make a priest of him?"

"It's a promise; it must be kept."

"I know that you made a promise . . . but a promise like
that . . . I don't know . . . I believe that, when you come
to think of it . . . What do you think, Cousin Justina?"

"I?"

"The truth is that each one knows best for himself," continued Uncle Cosme. "God is the one who knows what's best
for all. Still, such an old promise, made so many years ago.
. . . But what is this, Sister Gloria? You're crying! Oh, now,
is this anything to cry about?"

My mother blew her nose without answering. I believe
that Cousin Justina rose and went to her. There followed a
deep silence during which I was on fire to go into the room;
but another, greater force, another emotion . . . I could
not hear what Uncle Cosme was saying. Cousin Justina was
comforting my mother: "Cousin Gloria! Cousin Gloria!"
José Dias was excusing himself: "If I had known, I would
not have spoken, but I spoke because of my respect, and
esteem, because of affection, to perform an unpleasant duty,
a *most* unpleasant duty. . . ."

4. A most unpleasant duty

JOSÉ DIAS loved superlatives. It was a means of giving a
monumental aspect to his ideas; when he had no ideas, it
served to prolong his phrases. He went to fetch the backgammon board, which was in another part of the house. I

flattened myself against the wall, and watched him walk past in his white starched trousers which strapped under the shoe, his cotton jacket and the patent cravat. He was one of the last to wear such trousers in Rio de Janeiro, and perhaps in the world. He wore his trousers short so that they were stretched tight. The black satin cravat, with the steel spring inside, immobilized his neck; it was the fashion. The simple jacket of printed cotton seemed like a full-dress coat on him. He was thin, drawn, and had a bald spot. He walked off with his usual slow step—not the dragging slowness of a lazy man, but a calculated, deliberate slowness, a complete syllogism, the major premise before the minor, the minor premise before the conclusion. A *most* unpleasant duty!

5. The dependent

HE DID not always walk with that slow, stiff step. At times he gave way to excited gestures, was often swift and gay in his movements, as natural in this as in the other style. And he laughed loudly, if need be, a great hollow laugh, but infectious: to such a degree did cheeks, teeth, eyes, the whole face, the whole person, the whole world seem to laugh in him. In grave situations, *most* grave—*gravissimo*.

He had been our dependent for many years. My father was still on the old plantation at Itaguahy, and I had just been born. One day *he* appeared, representing himself as a homeopathic doctor; he carried a *Manual* and a case of medicines. There happened to be an epidemic of fevers at the time; José Dias cured the overseer and a female slave, but would not accept remuneration. My father proposed that he stay on, at the plantation, with a small salary. José Dias refused. He said it was his duty to bring health to the thatched hut of the poor.

"Who's keeping you from going anywhere? Go where you like, but live with us."

"I'll come back in three months."

He was back in two weeks. He accepted food and lodging without other wages, except what they gave him as presents. When my father was elected deputy and came to Rio de Janeiro with his family, he came too, and had his room at the rear of the estate. Once when fever was again raging in Itaguahy my father asked him to go look after our slaves. José Dias was silent, sighed, and finally confessed he was not a doctor. He had taken the title to help spread the doctrines of the new school, and he had not done it without a great deal of study; but his conscience would not permit him to accept any more patients.

"But you cured the others."

"Perhaps so; but it would be more just to give the credit to the remedies prescribed in the books. They performed the cures; yes, they—with God's help. I was a charlatan. . . . Don't deny it. It may be that my motives were the highest; homeopathy is Truth, and to serve Truth I lied; but it is time to set everything straight."

He was not sent away, as he requested: my father could no longer get along without him. He had the gift of making himself welcome and indispensable; one felt his absence as one did that of a member of the family. When my father died, his grief was enormous, that is what I was told, I do not remember. My mother was very grateful, and would not hear of his leaving his room on the estate. On the seventh day, after the Mass, he went to take leave of her.

"Stay, José Dias."

"If it is your wish, senhora."

He received a little legacy in the will, a gilt-edged security and four words of praise. He copied off the words of praise, had them framed, and hung them in his room, over his bed. "These are the best gilt-edged securities," he used to say. With time, he acquired a certain authority in the family, was listened to at least. He did not presume; he knew how to give his opinion and yet defer. In short, he was a friend, I won't say the best, but not everything is best in this world. And do not imagine that he had the soul of a toady: his bowing and scraping were calculated rather than natural. His clothes lasted forever. Unlike those who ruin a new suit the first time they put it on, he wore the old one brushed and unwrinkled, smooth-seamed, buttoned-up, with a poor and modest elegance. He had read, carelessly, but enough to be amusing of an evening or over dessert, or to explain some phenomenon, to speak of the effects of heat and cold, of the north and south poles and of Robespierre. He often told about a trip he had made to Europe, and he confessed that if it had not been for us he would have returned there long ago; he had friends in Lisbon, but our family, he said, next below God, was everything.

"Below or above?" asked Uncle Cosme one day.

"Below," repeated José Dias reverently.

And my mother, who was religious, was glad to see that he placed God in the proper place. She smiled her approval. José Dias thanked her with an inclination of the head. My mother used to give him small sums of money from time to time. Uncle Cosme, who was a lawyer, entrusted him with the copying of legal papers.

6. Uncle Cosme

UNCLE COSME had lived with my mother ever since she be-
came a widow. He was already a widower at the time, like
Cousin Justina: it was the house of the three widowed folk.
Fortune, many times, changes the intentions of Nature.
Formed for the serene functions of capitalism, Uncle Cosme
did not get rich in the law courts: he made a living. He had
an office in old Rua das Violas, near the courthouse, which
was in the abandoned Aljube prison. He was in criminal law.
José Dias never missed Uncle Cosme's speeches to the jury.
He was the one who helped him on and off with his robes,
and paid him many compliments as they left the courtroom.
At home he reported the arguments. Uncle Cosme, for all he
tried to appear modest, could not help smiling a little.

He was a fat, heavy man, short of breath and sleepy-eyed.
One of my earliest recollections was watching him mount,
every morning, the mare that my mother had given him and
which carried him to his office. The slave who had brought
the beast from the stable held the bridle while he lifted his
foot and set it in the stirrup; there followed a minute of rest
or reflection. Then he gave an impulse, the first; his body
threatened to go up, but it did not; second impulse, equal
effect. Finally after several long instants, Uncle Cosme gathered together all his forces, physical and moral, gave a final
leap from the earth and this time landed on the saddle. It was
seldom that the mount failed to show by a gesture that she
had just received the world. Uncle Cosme adjusted his flesh,
and the animal went off at a trot.

I have not forgotten either what he did to me one afternoon. Though born in the country (I left there when I was two) and despite the customs of the time, I did not know how to ride, and was afraid of a horse. Uncle Cosme grabbed me one day and threw me astride his beast. When I saw myself up high (I was nine), alone and forsaken, I began to yell desperately: "Mamma! Mamma!" She came to the rescue, pale and trembling, thinking they were killing me. She took me down, petted me, while her brother asked:

"Sister Gloria, a boy that size afraid of a gentle animal?"

"He's not used to it."

"He'd better get used to it. Even if he's a padre, if he's a country vicar he'll have to ride horseback; and here in the city, though he's not yet a padre, if he wants to cut a fine figure like other young fellows and doesn't know how to ride, he'll blame you for it, Sister Gloria."

"Then he'll have to blame me; I'm afraid."

"Afraid! Aw, afraid!"

The truth is I did not learn until much later, and then less from taste than because I was ashamed to admit I did not know how to ride. "Now he is really going to take an interest in the girls," they said when I started the lessons. The same could not be said of Uncle Cosme. In his case, it was a habit and a necessity. He no longer went in for love affairs. They say that, as a young man, he was a devil with the women, besides being a hotheaded partyman. But the years had taken from him most of his ardor, both political and sexual, and his fat had put an end to the rest of his ideas, public and specific. Now he merely performed the duties of his job, and without love. In his hours of leisure he looked on, or played backgammon. Now and again he made a witty remark.

7. Dona Gloria

MY MOTHER was a good soul. When her husband died—
Pedro de Albuquerque Santiago—she was thirty-one years
old and might have returned to Itaguahy. She chose to remain near the church in which my father was buried. She
sold the plantation and slaves, bought others whom she
rented out or sent into the streets to earn her money. She
bought a dozen or so buildings, a certain number of government securities, and kept on living in the Matacavallos house,
where she had lived the last two years of her married life. She
was the daughter of a mistress of a plantation in Minas
Geraes, descendant of another plantation owner from São
Paulo, of the Fernandes family.

Well then, in that year of grace, 1857, Dona Maria da
Gloria Fernandes Santiago was forty-two years of age. She
was still pretty and girlish, but she stubbornly concealed the
remnants of her youth however much Nature sought to preserve her from the action of time. She lived encased in an
eternal dark dress, without adornments, a black shawl
doubled in a triangle and fastened at the breast by a cameo.
Her hair was brought back straight on either side and caught
up at the nape of the neck with an old tortoise shell comb;
sometimes she wore a white cap with a frill. Like this she
plodded quietly back and forth in her plain old Cordovan
shoes, watching and supervising the work of the whole house,
from morning to night.

I have her portrait there on the wall, beside that of her
husband, just as they were in the other house. The colors
have darkened, but still give an idea of both of them. I do not

remember anything of him, except vaguely that he was tall
and wore his hair long; the portrait shows round eyes that
follow me everywhere, effect of the painting that terrified me
when I was little. His neck rises out of a black cravat of many
folds, the face is shaven except for a little patch by the ears.
The portrait of my mother shows she was beautiful. She was
twenty then and held a flower between her fingers. In the picture she seems to offer the flower to her husband. What you
read in the face of both is that if conjugal felicity can be
compared to the grand prize in a lottery, they had won it with
the ticket they purchased together.

I conclude that lotteries should not be abolished. No one
holding a winning ticket has yet charged them with being
immoral, just as no one has found fault with Pandora's box
because Hope remained at the bottom of it; she has to stay
somewhere. Here I have them, the two of them, happily wed
in the long ago, the loving ones, the lucky ones, who went
from this to the other world to continue a dream, most likely.
When I grow weary of the lottery and Pandora, I raise my
eyes to them, and I forget the blanks I have drawn, and the
cursed box. They are portraits that could pass for originals.
The one of my mother, holding the flower toward her husband, seems to say: "I am all yours, my gallant cavalier!"
That of my father, looking out at us, makes this commentary,
"See how the girl loves me. . . ." If they suffered annoy-
ances, I know nothing of them, just as I know nothing of
their sorrows. I was a child and I commenced by not being
born. After his death, I remember that she wept bitterly. But
here are the portraits of both, and the foul hand of time has
not smudged the first expression. They are like snapshots of
felicity.

8. It is time

BUT IT is time to go back to that afternoon in November, a bright cool afternoon, tranquil as our house and the stretch of road on which we lived. Actually it was the beginning of my life; all that had gone before was like the making-up and putting on costume of those about to go on stage, like the turning up of the lights, the tuning of the fiddles, the overture. . . . Now I was to commence my opera. "Life is an opera," that is what an old Italian tenor who lived and died here, used to tell me. . . . And one day he explained his definition in such a way that he made me believe in it. Perhaps it is worth the trouble to give it: it is only one chapter.

9. The opera

HE NO longer had any voice, but he persisted in saying he had. "Lack of practice is my trouble," he would add. Every time a new company arrived from Europe, he would go to the impresario and recount all the injustices of heaven and earth: the impresario would commit one more, and the old tenor would go away exclaiming against his unfairness. He still wore the mustachios of his roles. When he walked, in spite of his age, he looked as if he were paying court to a princess of Babylonia. At times, without opening his mouth, he would trill over some fragment older than he, or as old; voices muffled like that always hold possibilities. He came here to dine with me a number of times. One night, after a good deal of Chianti, he repeated his customary definition, and when I said that life was no more an opera than a voyage at sea or a battle, he shook his head and replied:

"Life is an opera and a grand opera. The tenor and the baritone fight for the soprano in the presence of the basso and the second voices, when it is not the soprano and the contralto who are fighting for the tenor, in the presence of the same basso and the same seconds. There are numerous choruses, many ballets, and the orchestration is excellent. . . ."

"But, my dear Marcolini. . . ."

"Why not?"

And after taking a long drink of wine, he set down the glass, and revealed to me the story of creation, in the following words, which I will condense a little.

"God is the poet. The music is by Satan, a young maestro with a great future, who studied in the conservatory of heaven. Rival of Michael, Raphael, and Gabriel, he could not endure the priority those classmates enjoyed in the distribution of the prizes. It may be, too, that their overly sweet and mystic music was boring to his genius, which was essentially tragic. He started a rebellion, which was discovered in time, and he was expelled from the conservatory. The whole thing would have ended there, if God had not written a libretto for an opera, and thrown it aside, because he considered that type of amusement unsuited to his eternity. Satan carried off the manuscript with him to hell. With the idea of showing that he was a better musician than the others —and perhaps to effect a reconciliation with heaven—he composed a score. As soon as he finished it, he took it to the Eternal Father.

" 'Lord,' he said to him, 'I have not forgotten what I

Excellent!

learned up here. Take this score, hear it, emend it, have it performed, and if thou find it worthy of the heavenly heights, admit me and it at thy feet.'

" 'No,' retorted the Lord, 'I will hear nothing.'

" 'But, Lord . . .'

" 'Nothing! nothing!'

"Satan went on supplicating with no better luck, until God, wearied and full of pity, consented to have the opera performed, but outside the precincts of heaven. He designed a special theater, this planet; and created a whole company with all the parts, first and second, choruses and ballet dancers.

" 'Hear some of the rehearsals!'

" 'No, I'll have nothing to do with rehearsals. It's enough to have composed the libretto; I am quite willing to split with thee the author's royalties.'

"That refusal was probably a mistake: from it resulted certain incongruities which a hearing would have detected and a friendly collaboration prevented. Indeed in some places the words go to the right and the music to the left. And there are those who say that this is the beauty of the composition and keeps it from being monotonous, and in this way they explain the trio of Eden, the aria of Abel, the choruses of the guillotine and of slavery. Not infrequently the same plot situation is used over again without sufficient reason. Certain motifs grow wearisome from repetition. There are obscure passages; the maestro makes too much use of the choral masses, which often drown out the words with their confused harmony. The orchestral parts, however, are handled with great skill. At least this is the opinion of the unprejudiced.

"The friends of the maestro would have it that a better score would be hard to find. Occasionally one of them will admit that there are rough spots, certain gaps here and there, but with the continued run of the opera no doubt these will be filled in and smoothed over, since the maestro does not refuse to emend his work where he finds it at variance with the sublime thought of the poet. The friends of the latter take a different view. They claim that the libretto has been sacrificed, that the score corrupts the sense of the words and that although it may be fine in some passages and contrived with art in others, it is absolutely unrelated, and even contrary, to the spirit of the drama. The ridiculous, for example, does not exist in the text of the poet: it is an excrescence in imitation of the *Merry Wives of Windsor*. This point is contested by the Satanists with some appearance of reason. *They* say that at the time young Satan composed his grand opera neither this farce nor Shakespeare had been born. They go so far as to affirm that the English poet did nothing more than copy down the book with such art and felicity that he seems himself to be the author of the work; but, manifestly, he is a plagiarist.

"This piece," concluded the old tenor, "will last as long as the theater lasts—and there's no telling when *it* will be demolished as an act of astronomic expediency. The success of the production is increasing. Poet and musician receive their royalties with punctual regularity, but not in the same coin. The law of division is that of the Scriptures: 'Many are called, few are chosen.' God gets paid in gold, Satan in paper."

"Very witty. . . ."

"Witty?" he shouted. Then he calmed himself: "My dear Santiago, I am not witty; I have a horror of wit. What I say is the truth, pure and ultimate. One day, when all the books have been burned as useless, there will be someone, maybe a tenor, most likely an Italian, who will teach this truth to

men. All is music, my friend. In the beginning was the *do*,
and the *do* became *re*, etc. This wineglass (he was filling it
again), this wineglass is a brief refrain. You don't hear it?
Neither do you hear wood or stone, but they're all part of the
same opera. . . ."

10. I accept the theory

WHICH IS slightly more than enough metaphysics for a single
tenor. But the loss of his voice explains everything; there are
philosophers who, when all is said, are nothing more than un-
employed tenors.

I, friend reader, accept the theory of my old Marcolini, not
only because of its verisimilitude—which is usually all that
truth is—but also because my life fits his definition. I sang a
tender *duo*, then a *trio*, then a *quatuor*. . . . But let us not
get ahead of the story; let us get back to that first afternoon
when I found out that I had already begun to sing, for when
José Dias informed against me, my dear reader, it was
primarily to me that he gave his information.

11. The promise

AS SOON as I saw our dependent disappear down the hall, I
left my hiding place and ran to the veranda at the back. I did
not bother about the tears nor the reason my mother shed
them. The reason for them was probably her ecclesiastical
projects and the cause of these is what I am about to relate,
for it was even then an old story, and went back sixteen years.

The projects were formed at the time I was conceived. Because her first child was born dead, my mother made a pact with God that the second might win out: she promised that if it should be a male, he would enter the Church. Perhaps she was hoping for a girl. She said nothing to my father, either before or after bringing me into the world: she counted on doing it when I started school, but she became a widow before then. As a widow, she dreaded the day of parting from me; but she was so devout, so Godfearing that she tried to get witnesses to her obligation by confiding her promise to relatives and members of the household. Only, that we might be parted as late as possible, she had me taught at home, my first letters, then Latin and religion by Padre Cabral, old friend of Uncle Cosme, who used to come to our house of an evening to play backgammon.

Long terms are easily subscribed to: imagination makes them infinite. My mother waited for the years to roll by. Meanwhile I was being accustomed to the idea of the Church: children's toys, devout books, images of saints, conversations at home, everything converged on the altar. When we went to Mass, she would always tell me it was to learn to be a priest and that I should watch the padre, that I should not take my eyes off the padre. At home, I played Mass—somewhat on the sly, because my mother said that Mass was not a matter for play. We would arrange an altar, Capitú and I. She acted as sacristan and we altered the ritual in the sense that we divided the host between us; the host was always a sweet. During the time that we used to play this game, it was quite common to hear my little neighbor ask: "Mass today?" I recognized what that meant, answered in the affirmative, and went to ask for the host under another name. I would come back with it, we would arrange the altar, mumble the Latin and rush through the ceremonies. *Domine, non sum dignus.* . . . I was supposed to say that three times but I believe that I actually said it but once, such was the gluttony of the padre and his sacristan. We drank neither wine nor water: we did not have the first and the second would have taken away the savor of the sacrifice.

And after a time they no longer spoke of the seminary, to such a degree that I supposed the matter forgotten. If a boy does not feel the call, at fifteen, he asks rather the seminary of the world than that of St. Joseph. Sometimes my mother gazed at me like a lost soul or caught hold of my hand for no reason at all and squeezed it hard.

12. On the veranda

I CAME to a halt on the veranda. I was dizzy, stunned, my knees wobbled. It seemed that my heart was trying to leap out through my mouth. I could not go down to the grounds and cross over into the next yard. I commenced to walk back and forth, stopping short at intervals to steady myself, then I would walk again, and again stand still. Confused voices repeated the words of José Dias:

"Always together. . . ."

"Whispering in secret. . . ."

"If they should start making love. . . ."

Bricks that I trod and retrod that afternoon, yellowed columns that passed me to the right and to the left, depending on whether I was going or coming—it was you who shared my crisis, the sensation of a new pleasure which enfolded me within myself, then made me diffuse and scattered me into a thousand pieces, that caused me to shiver and shed through my being some strange, inward balm. At times I found myself smiling, a kind of satisfied grin, which belied the abomination of my sin. And the voices were heard again, mixed up:

"Whispering in secret. . . ."

"Always together. . . ."

"If they should start making love. . . ."

A coconut palm that saw me perturbed and divined the cause murmured from the top of its crown that it was not unseemly for boys of fifteen to get into corners with girls of fourteen; on the contrary, adolescents of that age had no other occupation, nor corners any other use. It was an old coco tree, and for myself, I believed in old coco trees, even more than in old books. Birds, butterflies, a grasshopper that was practising his summer music, all the living folk of the air, were of the same opinion.

Then was I in love with Capitú, and Capitú with me? It was true that I clung to her petticoats, but I could think of nothing between us that was really secret. Before she went away to school it was all childish pranks and mischief. After she returned from school, the old intimacy was not immediately reestablished, perhaps, but it returned little by little, and in the last year, completely. The substance of our conversations, however, was the same as it had always been. Capitú sometimes called me handsome, her fine, big strapping boy, a darling; at other times she took hold of my hands to count my fingers. I began to remember these and other gestures and things she said, the pleasure I felt when she passed her hand over my hair and said she thought it beautiful. I, though I did not do the same to hers, told her that it was far more beautiful than mine. Then Capitú would shake her head with a look of disillusion and melancholy, the more amazing in that she had hair to really rouse admiration; but I retorted by calling her crazy. When she asked me if I had dreamed of her the night before, and I said "no," she told how she had dreamed of me, extraordinary adventures, how we went to the top of Corcovado through the air, danced on the moon, and then angels came to ask us our names to give them to other angels that had just been born. In all these dreams we went hand in hand. The dreams I had of her were never like that: they merely reproduced our familiar life together, and many times did not go beyond a simple repetition of the day before, some phrase, some gesture. I told them to her anyway. Capitú, one day, remarked on the difference: she said her dreams were finer. After a certain hesitation, I told her that they were like the person who had dreamed them. . . . She turned the color of a pitanga.

It was only now that I understood the emotion which these and other confidences aroused in me. The emotion was sweet and new, but the cause had eluded me and I had not searched it out, or even suspected it. The silences of the last few days had meant nothing to me. Now I felt them to signify something, and the same with the half-words, the curious questions, the vague answers, the solicitude, the delight in recalling our childhood. I was aware too that it was a recent phenomenon to wake up with my thoughts on Capitú, and to hear her voice from memory, and tremble at her step. If they spoke of her at our house I paid more attention than before, and, as it was praise or criticism, so I felt a more intense pleasure, or displeasure, than before, when we were only companions in mischief. I had even begun to think of her during Mass that month, intermittently it is true, and yet to the exclusion of other things too.

All this was now presented to me through the mouth of

José Dias, who had informed upon me to myself. I pardoned him everything—the evil he had spoken, the evil he had done, and all that might come from one and the other. In that one instant, Eternal Truth was not worth more than he, nor Eternal Goodness, nor all the rest of the Eternal Virtues. I loved Capitú! Capitú loved me! And my legs walked to and fro, they halted, quivering, eager to bestride the world. This first pulsating of sap, this revelation of consciousness to itself —I have never forgotten it. I have never known any similar sensation to compare with it. Probably because it was mine; because it was the first.

13. Capitú

SUDDENLY I heard a voice call out from inside the house close by:

"Capitú!"

And in the garden:

"Mamma!"

And again from the house:

"Come here!"

I could not hold myself. My legs carried me down the three steps which led to the grounds, and made straight for the yard next door. It was their custom in the afternoon, and mornings too. For legs are also persons, scarcely inferior to arms, and watch over themselves when the head does not guide them with its ideas. Mine arrived at the foot of the wall. There was a communicating gate in an opening which my mother had had made when Capitú and I were little. The gate had no key nor latch: it opened by being pushed from one side and pulled from the other, and closed by the weight of a stone hanging on a cord. It was almost exclusively ours. As children we paid formal calls by knocking on one side and being received on the other with many bows. When Capitú's dolls fell sick, I was their doctor. I went into her yard with a stick under my arm to imitate the cane that Dr. João da Costa carried. I would take the patient's pulse and tell her to stick out her tongue. "She's deaf, poor child!" Capitú would exclaim. Then I would scratch my chin, like the doctor, and end by prescribing leeches or an emetic: these were the doctor's habitual therapeutics.

"Capitú!"

"Mamma!"

"Stop making holes in the wall! Come here."

Her mother's voice was now closer, as if it came from the back door. I wanted to go into the yard, but my legs, just now so lively, clung fast to the ground. I made an effort, I shoved the gate and went in. Capitú was near the wall on the other side, turned toward it, cutting in it with a nail. The noise of the gate made her look around. When she saw me, she put her back to the wall, as if to hide something. I walked toward her. Probably I wore a new expression, for she came to me and asked uneasily:

"What's the matter with you?"

"With me? Nothing."

"No, no, there *is* something."

I wanted to insist that there was nothing, but I could not move my tongue. I was all eyes and heart, a heart that would this time for sure, leap out of my mouth. I could not take my eyes from that creature—fourteen years old, tall, blooming, clasped in a calico dress that was half-faded. Her heavy hair hung down her back in two braids with their tips tied together, in the fashion of the time. She was dark, with large, clear eyes, long straight nose, delicate mouth and rounded chin. Her hands, in spite of rude tasks, were lovingly cared for: they did not smell of fine soaps or lotions, but, washed with well water and common soap, were without blemish. She had on cloth shoes, cheap and old, to which she herself had given a few stitches.

"What's the matter with you?" she repeated.

"Nothing," I finally stammered.

And I added, "It's a piece of news."

"News of what?"

I thought of telling her I was going to enter the seminary and note the impression it made on her. If she should be downcast, it was because she really loved me; if not, it would mean she did not love me. But all this calculation was obscure and rapid. I felt that I could not speak clearly; my eyes somehow . . .

"Well?"

"You know . . ."

Then I looked at the wall, at the place she had been cutting with the nail, writing, or making holes in it, as her mother called it. I saw some broad strokes, and I recalled the gesture she had made to cover them. I decided to look closer, and took a step. Capitú grabbed me, but, either because she was afraid that I would get away, or to prevent me in another manner, she ran ahead and started to rub out the writing. It was the same as adding fuel to my desire to read what was written there.

14. The inscription

ALL THAT I related at the end of the last chapter was the work of an instant. What followed was still more rapid. I bounded forward, and before she could scrape off the wall, I read our two names, carved with a nail and disposed thus:

BENTO
CAPITOLINA

I turned toward her; Capitú had her eyes on the ground. She raised them, slowly, and we stood staring at each other. . . . Confession of children, thou art easily worth two or three pages, but I must hurry along. The truth is, we said nothing: the wall spoke for us. We did not move. It was our hands that stretched out, little by little, all four of them, catching hold of each other, tightening their grasp, melting one into the other. I did not mark down the exact hour of that gesture. I should have. I feel the want of a note written that very night, which I might place here with its errors in spelling. But it would have none. That was the difference between the student and the adolescent. I knew the rules of writing, without suspecting those of loving; I had had orgies of Latin, and was a virgin in women.

We did not let go our hands, nor did they fall, tired and forgetful. Our eyes met, then looked away, and after wandering near by returned to sink into the depths of each other. I, future padre, thus stood before her as before an altar, and one side of her face was the Epistle and the other the Gospel. Her mouth the chalice, her lips the paten. It only remained to say the new Mass, in a Latin that no one learns, and that

is the catholic language of men. Do not hold me sacrilegious,
my devout reader; purity of intention washes away whatever
may be slightly uncurial in my style. We stood there with
heaven in us. Our hands united our nerves, and made of two
creatures one—and that one a seraph. Our eyes continued to
say infinite things, only the words in our mouths did not
attempt to pass our lips; they returned to the heart, silently
as they had come. . . .

15. Another sudden voice

ANOTHER SUDDEN voice, but this time the voice of a man:
"Are you playing 'Wisdom?' "
It was Capitú's father: he was at the back door, beside his
wife. We dropped our hands quickly and stood confounded.
Capitú went to the wall and, with the nail, and a casual air,
rubbed out our names.
"Capitú!"
"Papa!"
"Stop ruining the stucco on my wall."
Capitú scratched over the scratches to thoroughly efface
the writing. Padua came out into the yard to see what was
going on, but his daughter had already begun something
else, a profile, which she said was a picture of him; and it
could as easily have been of him as of her mother. It made
him laugh; that was the main thing. Besides, he came up to
us without anger, all mildness, in spite of the dubious, or
less than dubious, attitude in which he caught us. He was a
short, thick man with short legs and arms, and stoop-shoul-
dered; hence the nickname *Turtleback* which José Dias had

given him. No one else at our house called him that, only
our dependent.

"Were you playing 'Wisdom?' " he asked.

I looked at an elderberry shoot near by. Capitú answered
for both of us.

"Yes, senhor; but Bentinho laughs right away, he can't
keep a straight face."

"He wasn't laughing when I saw him."

"He laughed the other times; he can't help it. Would you
like to see, Papa?"

And with a serious expression, she turned her gaze on me
and invited me to the game. Fright is naturally serious; I was
still under the effect of that caused by Padua's arrival. I
could not laugh, no matter how much I should have, to make
Capitú's answer legitimate. She grew tired of waiting, turned
her face away, and said that I did not laugh this time because
her father was there. Even then I did not laugh. There are
things that one learns late. One must be born with them to
do them early. And, naturally early is better than artificially
late. Capitú, after a couple of turns, went to talk to her
mother, who was still at the door, and left us, her father and
me, enchanted with her. Her father, looking after her and
then back to me, said in a voice full of tenderness:

"Who would think that this little girl is fourteen years old?
She looks seventeen. Mother well?" he went on, giving me
his entire attention.

"Yes."

"I haven't seen her for several days. I'd like to give the
doctor a capot, but I haven't been able to—with all the work
I bring home from the office. I've been writing every night.
It's enough to drive a man to desperation—matter of a report.

Have you seen my gaturamo? It's inside there. I was on my
way to get the cage. Come see."

That my desire was nil may be easily believed, without my
being required to swear by heaven and earth. My desire was
to go after Capitú and tell her now of the trouble that lay
ahead of us; but her father was her father, and what is more
he particularly loved little birds. He had them of various
species, colors, and sizes. The court in the center of the house
was surrounded with cages of canaries that made a racket of
all hell let loose with their singing. He swapped birds with
other fanciers, bought them, caught some in his own yard by
setting traps. And if they became ill he cared for them as if
they were people.

16. The interim administrator

PADUA WAS an employee in a department of the War Min-
istry. He did not earn much but his wife spent little, and
living was cheap. Besides, the house in which he lived, with
two stories like ours (though smaller), was his own property.
He bought it with the grand prize that he won with a half-
ticket in a lottery, ten whole contos.* Padua's first idea, when
he won the prize, was to buy a blooded horse, a diamond
necklace for his wife, and a perpetual family burial plot, order some birds from Europe, etc. But his wife, that Dona
Fortunata who was there at the back door talking to her
daughter—tall and blooming like the daughter, the same
head, the same clear eyes—it was his wife who told him the
best thing would be to buy the house and keep what was left

* Conto = 1,000,000; in all 10,000 milreis.

over for a rainy day. Padua hesitated for a long time; in the end he had to give in to the urging of my mother, to whom Dona Fortunata had appealed for help. It was not the only time that my mother had stood them in good stead: once she saved Padua's life. Listen, the story is short.

The administrator of the department in which Padua worked had to go north on a commission. Padua, either by regular right of succession or by special appointment, was made acting administrator, with the respective honorariums. This change of fortune induced in him a certain dizziness. It was before the time of the ten contos. He was not content with reforming his wardrobe and his table service. He threw himself into superfluous expenditures: gave jewelry to his wife, killed a suckling pig on holidays, was seen at the theater, even went so far as patent leather shoes. He lived in this manner for twenty-two months, on the supposition of an eternal interimity. One afternoon he came to our house, downcast and bewildered. He was going to lose his position: the regular administrator had returned that morning. Padua asked my mother to watch over the unfortunates that he was leaving; he could not endure this calamity, he was going to kill himself. My mother spoke gently to him, but he listened to nothing.

"No, senhora, I will not submit to such humiliation. Drag down my family, go back . . . I have decided: I'll kill myself! How tell my wife and child of this poverty? And the others? What will the neighbors say? And my friends? And the public?"

"What public, Senhor Padua? Stop all this. Be a man. Remember that your wife has no one else . . . and what will become of her? Well, a man . . . Be a man, come!"

Padua wiped his eyes and went home, where he lived pros-

trated for several days without saying a word, shut up in his
room, or else in the garden, near the pool formed by the
well, as if the idea of death persisted in him. Dona Fortunata
scolded him:

"Joãozinho, are you a baby?"

But he talked so much of death that she was afraid and one
day ran to beg my mother to see if she could save her husband
from committing suicide. My mother found him beside the
well and told him that he must live. 'What foolishness was
this to think that he would be ruined because of one less gra-
tuity and the loss of an interim position? No, senhor, he
should be a man, a father of a family, imitate his wife and
daughter . . .' Padua obeyed; he said that he would try to
find strength to comply with the wish of my mother.

"My wish, no! It is your obligation."

"Well then, obligation; I am not unaware that it is so."

In the days that followed, he continued to flatten himself
against the wall as he entered or left the house, and to keep
his eyes on the ground. He was not the man who had worn
out his hat taking it off to the neighborhood, gay, head high;
he was not even the same man as before the interim administration. Weeks went by: the wound was healing. Padua commenced to take an interest in things around the house, to take
care of his little birds; he slept tranquilly at night, and afternoons, he chatted and noticed what was going on in the
street. His serenity returned; with it came cheerfulness one
Sunday, in the form of two friends who came to play three-
handed whist for small stakes. Soon he was laughing, joking,
wore his customary air: the wound was healed.

With time came an interesting phenomenon. Padua began
to speak of his interim administration, not only without regrets for the honorariums or humiliation at their loss, but

even with self-conceit and pride. His administration came to
be a hegira from which he reckoned forward and backward.

"During the time that I was administrator . . ." Or:

"Ah, yes, I remember, it was before my administration, one
or two months before. . . . Now wait; my administration
commenced . . . That's right, a month and a half before;
it was a month and a half before, not more." Or again:

"Just so, I had been administrator for six months. . . ."

Such is the posthumous savor of interim glories. José Dias
claimed that it was his everlasting conceit; but Padre Cabral,
who referred everything to the Scriptures, said that neighbor
Padua illustrated the lesson of Eliphaz to Job: "Despise not
the chastening of the Almighty; He woundeth and He maketh
whole."

17. The worms

"HE WOUNDETH and He maketh whole!" Later, when I
came to know that the lance of Achilles also cured the wound
it made, I had a fleeting desire to write a dissertation on this
problem. I went so far as to pick up old books, dead books,
buried books, open them, compare them, in order to track
down the text and the meaning, and discover the common
origin of the pagan oracle and the Israelite thought. I tracked
down the very worms in the books that they might tell me
what was in the texts they gnawed.

"My dear sir," replied a long fat worm, "we know absolutely nothing of the texts we gnaw, nor do we choose what
we gnaw, nor do we like or dislike what we gnaw: we gnaw."

I did not get any more out of him. All the others, as if they had passed the word along, repeated the same refrain. Perhaps this discreet silence on the texts they gnawed was still one more way of gnawing the thing gnawed.

18. A plan

NEITHER FATHER nor mother came to disturb us when Capitú and I, alone in the living room, talked of the seminary. With her eyes on me, Capitú wanted to know what the news was that bothered me so. When I told her, she turned the color of wax.

"But I will not," I assured her quickly, "I will not enter any seminaries. I won't go, it's useless for them to insist; I won't go."

At first Capitú said nothing. She withdrew her eyes, turned them inward, and let them remain with the pupils vague and unseeing. Her mouth was partly open. She was as one without life. Then, to give force to my affirmations, I began to swear I would not be a priest. In those days I swore a stout oath, with life and death in it. I swore by the hour of my death— that the light might fail me in the hour of my death if I would go to the seminary. Capitú did not appear either to believe or disbelieve: she did not appear to hear. She was like an image made of wood. I wanted to call her by name, to shake her, but courage failed me. This creature who had played with me, romped, danced, I believe even slept with me, now left me with my arms tied and cowardly. At length she returned to herself, but her face was livid, and these words of fury burst from her:

"She's a pew warmer! popeholy! church louse!"

I was stunned. Capitú was so fond of my mother, and my mother of her, that I could not understand such an explosion. It is true that she loved me too, and naturally more, or better, or in another way—reason enough to explain the resentment a threat of separation caused her; but the abusive epithets, to call her such ugly names, and especially to revile religious customs which were her own. She too went to Mass, and three or four times my mother had taken her in our old chaise, and had given her a rosary, a gold cross and a book of *Hours*. . . . I wanted to defend her, but Capitú gave me no chance, she continued to call her pew warmer and church louse in so loud a voice I was afraid her father and mother would hear. I had never seen her so angered; it was as if she was determined to tell everything to everyone. She clenched her teeth, shook her head. . . . In my fright and anxiety I kept repeating my oaths, I promised to go that very night and announce that nothing in this world could make me enter the seminary.

"You? You will enter."

"No, I won't."

"You'll see whether you will or not."

She fell silent. When she began to speak again she had changed; she was not yet the usual Capitú, but almost. She was serious, untroubled, she spoke quietly. She wanted to know the conversation that had taken place at our house. I told her the whole thing, except the part that referred to her.

"And what interest has José Dias in bringing this up?" she asked at length.

"None that I know of; it was only to make trouble. He's a vile character; but just you wait, he'll pay for this. When I'm master, he'll be kicked out in the street. You'll see, I won't let him stay a minute. Mamma is too good to him; she gives him too much consideration, even cried apparently."

"José Dias?"

"No, Mamma."

"Cried? What for?"

"I don't know; I only heard them tell her not to cry, that there was nothing to cry about. . . . He finally said that he was sorry, and came out of the room; then I left my corner so that I wouldn't be caught, and ran out on the veranda. But just you wait, I'll make him pay for it!"

I shook my fist, and uttered other threats. As I recall them, I do not find that I was ridiculous: adolescence and childhood are not, in this respect, ridiculous; it is one of their privileges. That disease, or danger, commences in early manhood, increases with maturity and attains its greatest degree in old age. At fifteen, there is even a certain grace in making many threats and carrying out none.

Capitú was reflecting. Reflection was not a rare thing with her; one could recognize it by the narrowing of her eyes. She asked for some more of the circumstances, the exact words of this one and the other, and the tone in which they were said. As I was unwilling to tell the starting point of the conversation, which was herself, I could not convey to her its whole significance. Capitú's attention was now directed to my mother's tears; she could not understand them. Meanwhile she admitted that it was surely not wrong of my mother to wish to make me a padre; it was a promise of long standing, and she, being God-fearing, had to keep it. I was so relieved to see that she thus voluntarily atoned for the insults which had burst from her a little earlier, that I caught her hand and pressed it hard. Capitú laughed and did not pull it away. Then the conversation began to nod and fall asleep. We had come near the window. A Negro pedlar, who for some time had been crying his coconut sweetmeats in the street outside, stopped and asked:

"Sinhazinha want *cocada* today?"

"No," replied Capitú.

"*Cocadinha* so good."

"Go 'way," she said gently.

"Give 'em here!" said I, and reached down my hand. I bought two, but I had to eat them both myself; Capitú refused. I saw that, even in the middle of a crisis, I kept a nook in my soul for *cocadas;* this might as easily be a perfection as an imperfection, but it is not the moment for such definitions. My ladylove, though well balanced and lucid, refused to hear of sweets, let us leave it at that, and she was very fond of sweets. The pedlar song that the man was chanting down the street, the song of bygone afternoons, familiar to our neighborhood and to our childhood:

> "Cry, little girl, cry
> Cry 'cause you haven't any penny."

appeared to annoy Capitú. It was not the melody, for she knew it by heart and from the old times used to repeat it in our childish games, laughing, jumping and exchanging roles with me, now selling, now buying a sweet that was not there. I believe that it was the words, intended to prick the vanity of children, which now irritated her, because she said to me a little later:

"If I were rich, you would run away, you would board a ship and go to Europe."

After she said this, she watched my eyes, but I believe they told her nothing, or only thanked her for the good intention. The impulse was so friendly that I overlooked the strangeness of the venture.

As you see, Capitú, at fourteen, already had daring ideas—much less so than others which came to her later; but they were daring only in conception. In practice they were apt, sinuous, unobtrusive, and accomplished the end proposed, not at one leap but by a series of little leaps. I do not know if I make myself clear. Imagine a great plan executed by tiny means. Thus, not to abandon her vague and hypothetical desire of sending me to Europe—Capitú, if she were able to accomplish it, would not have me embark on a steamship and flee: she would throw out a string of canoes from here to there, over which I, seeming to go to Fort Lage * on a pontoon bridge, would really go to Bordeaux, and leave my mother waiting on the sands. Such was the peculiar nature of my little friend's character. It is not to be wondered at that she should oppose my projects for open resistance, and resort rather to blander methods—the slow action of intercession, pledges—gentle, daily persuasion—that she should examine beforehand the persons on whom we might count. She rejected Uncle Cosme. He was an idler; even if he did not approve of my ordination he was not capable of taking a step to prevent it. Cousin Justina was better than he, and better than either would be Padre Cabral, because of his authority, but the padre could not be expected to work against the Church, unless I should confess that I did not feel the call. . . ."

"I *will* confess . . ."

"Yes, but that would be to come out in the open, and it's better the other way. José Dias . . ."

"What of José Dias?"

"He might be a help."

"But he was the one who reminded . . ."

"It doesn't matter," continued Capitú, "he will now say

* In the harbor of Rio de Janeiro.

something else. He is very fond of you. Don't be meek with him. The whole thing is for you not to act timid, show him that you will be master one day, show him that you are determined. Give him to understand that it is not a favor. Praise him too; he loves to be praised. Dona Gloria pays attention to what he says; but that is not the main thing. The main thing is that he, because he is to be dependent on you, will speak with much more warmth than anyone else."

"No, I don't believe it, Capitú."

"Then go to the seminary."

"No, never."

"What will you lose in trying? Let's try; do as I say. Dona Gloria may give up her scheme; if she doesn't, we'll do something else—there is still Padre Cabral. Remember how you happened to go to the theater the first time, two months ago? Dona Gloria was against it, and that should have been enough for José Dias; but *he* wanted to go, and he made a speech—remember?"

"I remember: he said that the theater was a school of manners."

"Yes, and he talked so much that your mother finally gave in and paid the way for both of you. . . . Go on, ask, order. Look, tell him that you are willing to go to São Paulo to study law."

I shivered with joy. São Paulo was a fragile screen which could one day be set aside, in place of the thick wall of the spiritual and eternal. I promised to speak to José Dias in the proposed terms. Capitú repeated them, and accentuated some as of first importance; then she quizzed me on them to make sure that I had understood and would not mix them up. And she insisted that I should ask politely but casually as one requests a glass of water of a person who is obliged to bring it. I relate these minutiae to explain what the morning of my little friend was like; soon will come the afternoon, and of the morning and of the afternoon will be made the first day, as in Genesis, where seven were made in succession.

19. Without fail

WHEN I arrived home it was night. I walked fast; not so fast, however, that I did not have time to ponder the terms in which I would speak to the dependent. I formulated the request in my head, chose the words I would use and the tone in which I would say them—something between dry and kindly. In the garden before going into the house, I repeated them to myself, and then aloud, to see if they were adequate and if they complied with Capitú's instructions: "I must speak to you tomorrow, without fail. Choose the place, and let me know later." I uttered them slowly, and still more slowly the words *without fail,* as if to underscore them. I repeated them again and found them too curt, almost brusque, and really impertinent from a boy to an older man. I considered choosing others, and I paused.

Finally I told myself that the words would serve; the important thing was to say them in a tone that would not offend. And the proof is that when I repeated them once more, they came out almost supplicating. It was only necessary not to bear down too much nor be too gentle, a middle term. "And Capitú is right," I thought. "The house is mine, he is only a dependent . . . but clever, he can work very well for me, and upset Mamma's plans."

20. A thousand paternosters and a thousand Ave Marias

I RAISED my eyes to the heavens, which were becoming over-cast, but it was not to see whether they were cloudy or clear. It was to the other heaven that I raised my soul; it was to my refuge, to my friend. And then I said within myself:

"I promise to pray one thousand paternosters and one thousand Ave Marias if José Dias arranges for me not to go to the seminary."

The sum was enormous. The reason is that I was already loaded down with unfulfilled promises. The last was for two hundred paternosters and two hundred Ave Marias if it would not rain on a certain afternoon of an outing to Santa Theresa. It did not rain but I did not say the prayers. From the time I was a little boy, I had been accustomed to ask heaven for its favors in consideration of prayers that I would say, if they were granted. I said the first ones, the others were postponed, and in proportion as they mounted up they were forgotten. I arrived at the numbers twenty, thirty, fifty. I entered on the hundreds and now into the thousands. It was a mode of bribing the divine will by the quantity of prayers; besides, each new promise was made and sworn to with the idea of wiping out the old debt. But how destroy the sloth which a soul brings from the cradle and does not feel lessened by life! Heaven would do me the favor; I would postpone the payment. Finally I got lost in my accounts.

"A thousand, a thousand," I repeated to myself.

Now, the substance of the benefit was immense, no less than the salvation or the shipwreck of my entire existence.

Thousand, thousand, thousand! I needed a sum that would
pay all the arrears. God might very well be irritated with my
forgetfulness and refuse to hear me without a promise of big
money. . . . Serious man, possibly these worries of a child
bore you, if you do not find them ridiculous. They were not
sublime. I cogitated deeply on how to wipe out my spiritual
debt. I found no other specie in which, with due consideration for my wish, the whole could be paid and the books of
my conscience closed without deficit. Have a hundred Masses
said, or climb the ascent to Nossa Senhora da Gloria on my
knees to hear one, go to the Holy Land, all that old slave
women had told me of famous promises came to mind without taking my fancy. It was hard to climb a hill on your
knees: you would bruise them, of necessity. The Holy Land
was very far. The Masses would be numerous; perhaps I
could once more mortgage my soul. . . .

21. Cousin Justina

ON THE veranda I found Cousin Justina pacing back and
forth. She came to the landing and asked me where I had
been.

"I was over there, talking to Dona Fortunata, and I didn't
notice the time. It's late, isn't it? Did Mamma ask for me?"

"She did, but I told her that you had already come in."

The lie took my breath away, no less than the frank admis-
sion of it. It was not that Cousin Justina spoke in riddles:
she said frankly to Peter the evil that she thought of Paul,
and to Paul what she thought of Peter; but to confess that
she had lied struck me as a novelty. She was a woman of

forty, thin, pale, with a haughty mouth and inquisitive eyes.
My mother had her live with us out of kindness and from
selfish motives too, for she liked to have a lady companion,
and rather a relative than an outsider.

We walked for some minutes on the veranda, in the light
of the great lantern. She wanted to know if I had forgotten
my mother's ecclesiastical projects, and when I said "no," she
inquired as to my liking for the life of a priest. I answered
evasively:

"The life of a padre is very fine."

"Yes, it's fine; but what I asked was if you would like to be
a padre," she explained with a laugh.

"I'd like whatever Mamma wants."

"Cousin Gloria is very anxious for you to take orders, but
even if she weren't, there's someone inside there who would
put the idea in her head."

"Who?"

"Who! Who would it be? It isn't Cousin Cosme: he doesn't
give a hang; nor is it I."

"José Dias?" I concluded.

"Naturally."

I wrinkled my forehead interrogatively, as if I knew nothing. Cousin Justina completed her piece of news by saying
that that very afternoon José Dias had reminded my mother
of her ancient promise.

"Cousin Gloria, as the days go by, might easily forget her
promise; but how can she with someone always at her elbow
yapping about the seminary. And the speeches he makes, the
eulogies of the Church, and the life of a padre is this and
that, all as only he knows how to say it, and that affected
air . . . Mind you, he only does it to make trouble, for he's
as religious as that lantern. Yes, it's true, even today. Don't

let on that you know . . . This very afternoon he spoke in a way such as you could never imagine . . ."

"But did he just bring it up out of a clear sky?" I asked, to see if she would tell of his informing on my making love to the neighbor girl.

She did not tell that; only made a vague gesture as if to indicate that there was something else which she could not tell. Once more she advised me not to let on that I knew, and summed up her bad opinion of José Dias, and it was very bad —a trouble maker, a self-seeking, prying toady, and, in spite of his veneer of politeness, a vulgar boor. After a few seconds I said:

"Cousin Justina, would you be willing to do something?"

"What?"

"Could you . . . Suppose that I didn't want to be a padre . . . could you ask Mamma . . ."

"Not that," she cut in quickly. "Cousin Gloria has this business fixed firm in her head, and there's nothing in the world that would make her change her resolution—only time. You were still a little boy, and she had already told it to the whole circle of our friends, and even to acquaintances. Remind her, never, for I don't work for the unhappiness of others; but ask her to do something else, I won't do that either. If she should ask my advice, all right! If she should say to me: 'Cousin Justina, what do *you* think?', my answer would be: 'Cousin Gloria, I think that if he wants to be a padre, let him go to the seminary; but if he doesn't, let him stay away.' That's what I'd say, and will say, if she ever asks my advice. But go speak to her without being asked—that I won't do."

22. Another's sensations

I DID not get any more out of her, and in the end I repented
having spoken. I should have followed the advice of Capitú.
Then, as I was about to go inside, Cousin Justina detained
me a few minutes longer, talking of the heat and the coming
Feast of the Conception, of my old oratories, and finally of
Capitú. She did not say anything bad about her; on the contrary, she insinuated that she might come to be a pretty girl.
I, who already considered her beautiful, would have shouted
that she was the fairest creature on earth, if fear had not
made me discreet. Even so, as Cousin Justina began to praise
her manners, her gravity, her habits, her devotion to her
parents, the affection she had for my mother—all this inflamed
me to the point of praising her too. When it was not with
words, it was with an approving gesture for each of Justina's
assertions, and certainly with the joy that must have lighted
up my face. I was not aware that I thus confirmed the information that she had heard from José Dias that afternoon in
the living room—if she had not actually suspected something
before. I did not think of this until I was in bed. Only then
did I realize that Cousin Justina's eyes had seemed to feel
me as I spoke, listen to me, smell me, taste me—do the offices
of all the senses. Jealousy it could not have been: between a
boy my age and a widow of forty there was no place for
jealousy. At any rate, after a while she modified her praise of
Capitú, and even made a few disparaging remarks about her.
She said that she was a little sly and had a way of looking at
you from under her eyelids. Still, I do not believe that it was
jealousy. I believe rather . . . yes . . . yes, I believe that it

was this. I believe that Cousin Justina found in the spectacle
of another's sensations, a vague resurrection of her own.
Pleasure may also be sipped from lips that narrate.

23. Notice served

"I MUST speak to you tomorrow, without fail. Choose the
place, and let me know later."

I am sure that José Dias found my manner of speaking un-
usual. The tone was not so imperative as I had feared, but
the words were. And my not asking questions, no polite
requesting, no hesitating, as was proper for a boy, and was
habitual with me—all that surely gave him the idea of a
changed person and a changed situation. It was in the hall,
as we were going in to tea that night—José Dias came march-
ing along full of the Walter Scott that he had been reading to
my mother and Cousin Justina. He read with measure and
cadence. The castles and parks came out of his mouth bigger,
and the lakes had more water, and the "celestial vault of
heaven" counted some thousands more scintillating stars. In
the dialogues he alternated the voices, so that they were
slightly heavy or thin according to the sex of the speaker. He
reproduced, with moderation, their tenderness and their
anger.

As he said goodnight to me, on the veranda, he murmured,
"Tomorrow in the street. I have some purchases to make, you
can go with me, I'll ask Mamma. Is it the day for a lesson?"

"I had my lesson today."

"Good. I won't ask you what it is; I am sure that it is something serious and proper."

"Yes, senhor."

"Till tomorrow."

Everything turned out perfectly. There was only one slight change: my mother thought the weather too warm and would not consent to my going on foot; we took the omnibus in front of our door.

"It makes no difference," José Dias told me, "we can get off at the gate of the Passeio Publico."

24. Mother and servant

JOSÉ DIAS treated me with the tender care of a mother and the attentions of a servant. The first thing he did when I was old enough to go out by myself was to get rid of my lackey: he became my lackey and accompanied me in the street. He took care of my things at home, of my books, my shoes, my hygiene, and my enunciation. At eight years of age, my plurals sometimes lacked precise terminations: he corrected them, half seriously, to give authority to the lesson and half laughingly to obtain pardon for the correction. In this way he aided the work of my primary teacher. Later, when Padre Cabral taught me Latin, religion and sacred history, he attended the lessons, made ecclesiastical reflections and finally asked the padre: "Is it not true that our young friend is coming along splendidly?" He called me "a prodigy"; told my mother that he had known children who were very intelligent but that I surpassed them all, without mentioning that, for my age, I already possessed a certain number of solid moral qualities. Though I did not appreciate the full value of this last bit of praise, I enjoyed the bit of praise: it was a bit of praise.

25. In the Passeio Publico

WE ENTERED the Passeio Publico. Old faces, others that were sick, or only aimless, here and there along the path which leads from the gate to the terrace. We went on toward the terrace. As we walked, in order to give myself courage, I talked of the garden:

"It's a long time since I've been here, perhaps a year."

"Pardon me," he cut in, "it's not more than three months since you were here with our neighbor Padua. Don't you remember?"

"That's true, but only walking through . . ."

"He asked your mother to let him take you with him, and she, because she is good, like the Mother of God, consented. But listen to me, now that we are on the subject, it's not proper for you to walk along the street with Padua."

"But I've gone with him a lot of times . . ."

"When you were younger. You were a child, it was all right, he could pass for a servant. But you are getting to be a young man, and he becomes more familiar all the time. In the end, Dona Gloria is not going to like it. The Paduas are not entirely bad. Capitú, in spite of those eyes that the devil gave her . . . Did you ever notice those eyes of hers? Gypsy's eyes—oblique and sly. Well, in spite of them she could pass, if it were not for her conceit and her smooth talk. Oh, what a smooth tongue she has! Dona Fortunata deserves respect, and I don't deny that *he* may be honest, he has a good job, owns the house he lives in, but honesty and respect are not enough, and the other qualities lose their worth, considering the bad company he keeps. Padua inclines toward rough people. If he gets wind of a coarse, ill-bred fellow, they become fast friends. I don't say this because I dislike him, nor because he talks about me and makes fun of me, the way he did the other day of my run-down heels . . ."

"Pardon," I interrupted. I paused in my walking, "I have never heard him say anything uncomplimentary about you, senhor. On the contrary, one day not long ago, he told someone in my presence, that you were 'a man of talent and could speak like a member of the Chamber of Deputies.' "

José Dias smiled delightedly, but he made a great effort and straightened his face, then went on:

"I owe him no thanks for it. Others, of better blood, have paid me the honor of their high opinion. And none of this keeps him from being what I say."

We had begun to walk again, we went up to the terrace and looked out to sea.

"I see that you have no other wish but for my happiness," I said after a few moments.

"What else, Bentinho?"

"In that case, I am going to ask you a favor."

"A favor? Command, order, what is it?"

"Mamma . . ."

For some time I could not say the rest, though it was not much, and I had it by heart. José Dias again asked what it was, shook me gently, raised my chin and fixed his eyes on me, anxiously, just as Cousin Justina had on the evening before.

"Mamma what? What about Mamma?"

"Mamma wants me to be a padre, but I cannot be a padre," I said finally.

José Dias stiffened, thunderstruck.

"I can't," I continued, no less thunderstruck than he, "I

have no talent for it, I have no liking for the life of a padre. I am ready to do anything that she wants; Mamma knows that I'd do anything she told me. I'm willing to be whatever she likes, even a driver of an omnibus. Padre—no; I cannot be a padre. The career is fine, but not for me."

This whole speech did not pour out of me thus, all together, in a natural flow, and peremptory, as it may appear on the printed page, but in pieces, mumbled, in a voice that was faint and timid. Notwithstanding, José Dias heard it aghast. He certainly had not reckoned with my resistance, however feeble it might be; but what dismayed him still more was this conclusion:

"I count on you, senhor, to save me."

The eyes of our dependent flew open, his eyebrows arched, and the pleasure that I had counted on giving him with my choice of a protector did not manifest itself in a single muscle. His whole face was inadequate to his stupefaction. No doubt the matter of my speech had revealed a new soul to him; I did not recognize myself. But it was the final words that bore a unique vigor. José Dias was stunned. When his eyes returned to their ordinary dimensions:

"But what can *I* do?" he asked.

"A lot. You know that at our house everyone values your opinion. Mamma often asks your advice, doesn't she? Uncle Cosme says that you are a person of talent . . ."

"Kindnesses," he retorted, flattered, "favors from worthy persons who deserve everything that . . . There you are! No one will ever hear me say the slightest thing against such persons. Why? Because they are noble and virtuous. Your mother is a saint, your uncle a most perfect gentleman. I have known distinguished families: none could compare with yours in nobility of sentiment. The talent that your uncle finds in me—I confess I have it, but it is only one—it is the talent of recognizing what is good, and worthy of admiration and esteem."

"Surely you also have the talent of protecting your friends —such as me."

"How can I help you, angel of heaven? I can't dissuade your mother from a project which has been, aside from a promise, her ambition and dream for many years. Even if I could have once, it's too late. Just yesterday she did me the honor of saying to me: 'José Dias, I must put Bentinho in the seminary.'"

Timidity is not such vile coin as it is represented. If I had been without fear, it is likely that with the indignation I felt, I would have burst out and called him a liar; but then it would have been necessary to admit that I had been eaves-dropping, and one action would have offset the other. I con-tented myself with replying that it was not too late.

"It is not too late; there is still time if you want."

"If I want! What else do I want, but to serve you? What do I desire except that you be happy, as you deserve?"

"Well then, there is still time. Look, it is not because of laziness. I am ready to do anything. If she would like me to study law, I'll go to São Paulo. . . ."

26. The law is beautiful

OVER THE face of José Dias passed something which resem-bled the reflection of an idea—an idea which cheered him extraordinarily. He was silent for a few moments. I had my eyes on him; he had turned his toward the harbor. And as I persisted:

"It's too late," he said, "but to prove that there's no lack of willingness on my part, I'll speak to your mother. I do not promise to win her over, but I will do my best; I will throw my whole soul into it. Really and truly, you don't want to be a padre? The law is beautiful, my dear boy . . . You could go to São Paulo, to Pernambuco, or even to more distant places. There are good universities in other lands. Go to the law, if that is your vocation. I'll speak to Dona Gloria, but don't count on me alone; speak to your uncle."

"I suppose I should."

"Ask the help of God too—of God and the Most Holy Virgin," he concluded, pointing to the sky.

The sky was half clouded over. In the air, near the shore, great black birds flew in circles, hovering, or, with a flapping of wings, they swooped down to dip their feet in the water, and rose again to descend once more. But neither the dark shadows of the sky nor the fantastic dances of the birds drew my thoughts from my advocate. After answering that I would, I added:

"God will do what you wish, senhor."

"Don't blaspheme. God is master of all things. He is, of and through Himself, earth and heaven, the past, the present and the future. Pray to Him for your happiness, as I do . . . Since you feel that you cannot be a padre and prefer the law . . . The law is beautiful, with no offense to theology, which is better than all else, as the ecclesiastical life is the most holy. Why shouldn't you go abroad to study law? The best thing is to go at once to some university, and at the same time that you study, travel. We can go together; see foreign lands, hear English, French, Italian, Spanish, Russian, and even Swedish. Dona Gloria probably couldn't go with you; even if she could, and does go, she won't want to take care of business matters, papers, details of matriculation, lodging, nor travel with you from place to place . . . Oh! the law is most beautiful!"

"Agreed, then you will ask Mamma not to put me in the seminary?"

"I will ask, but to ask is not to gain her consent. Angel of my heart, if the will to serve were the power to command, we would be there, we would be on board ship. Ah! You can't imagine what Europe is! Oh! Europe . . ."

He lifted his foot and did a pirouette. One of his ambitions was to return to Europe. He spoke of it many times but could never tempt my mother or Uncle Cosme, however much he praised its climates and its beauties . . . He had not counted on this possibility of going with me and remaining there during the eternity of my studies.

"We are already aboard, Bentinho, we are aboard!"

27. In the gateway

IN THE gateway of the Passeio, a beggar extended his hand toward us. José Dias went on, but I thought of Capitú and of the seminary. I took two pennies out of my pocket and gave them to the beggar. He kissed the coins. I asked him to pray for me, that I might satisfy all my desires.

"Yes, my devout one."

"My name is Bento," I added to enlighten him.

28. In the street

JOSÉ DIAS was so content that he changed from the man of graver moments, such as he was in public, to the springy, restless man. He waved his arms and legs, spoke of everything, made me stop before every shop display or theater bill. He told me the plot of several plays, recited monologues in verse, did all his errands, paid accounts, collected rents; for himself he bought a twentieth of a lottery ticket. Finally the tense man drove out the volatile, and he reverted to his slow, deliberate speech, with the superlatives. I did not see that the change was natural; I was afraid that he had changed his mind, and I tried to ingratiate myself by affectionate words and gestures, until we boarded the omnibus.

29. The emperor

ON THE way, we met the emperor, who was coming from the School of Medicine. The omnibus on which we were riding stopped, like all the other vehicles. The passengers got off and stood with heads uncovered in the street until the imperial coach passed. When I returned to my seat, I took with me a fantastic idea, the idea of going to see the emperor, of telling him everything and of asking him to intervene. I would not confide this idea to Capitú. "If His Majesty asks, Mamma will give in," I thought to myself.

I then saw the emperor listening to me, reflecting, and finally saying "yes," that he would go speak to my mother;

I would tearfully kiss his hand. And as soon as I reached
home, I would wait until I heard the beat of horses' hooves—
the imperial guard. It's the emperor! it's the emperor! Everyone would run to the window to see him pass but he would
not pass, the coach would stop at our door, the emperor
would alight and enter. Great excitement in the neighborhood: "The emperor went into Dona Gloria's house! What
can it be? What could it be?" Our household would go out
to receive him; my mother would be first and kiss his hand.
Then the emperor, all smiles, entering the front room, or
not entering—I don't remember very well, dreams are often
confused—would ask my mother not to make me a padre, and
she, flattered and obedient, would promise she would not.

"Medicine—why not have him taught medicine?"

"Since it is Your Majesty's pleasure . . ."

"Have him taught medicine: it is a fine career, and we
have fine professors here in the city. Have you never been to
our school? It is a beautiful school. We already have doctors
of the first rank, worthy to rub elbows with the best in the
world. Medicine is a great science; it is great to be able to
bring health to others, recognize diseases, combat them, conquer them. You yourself must have seen miracles, senhora.
Your husband died, but his illness was fatal, and he didn't
take care of himself . . . It is a fine career; send him to our
school. Do this for me, eh? Are you willing, Bentinho?"

"If Mamma is willing . . ."

"I am willing, son. His Majesty commands."

Then the emperor would again extend his hand to be
kissed, and go out accompanied by all of us, the street full of
people, faces crowding the windows, an awed silence. The
emperor would get into the coach, bow and make a gesture
of farewell, still saying: "Medicine, our school!" And the

coach would go off in the midst of the envy of the neighbors and the profuse thanks of our family.

All this I saw and heard. No, the imagination of Ariosto is not more fertile than that of children and lovers, nor did this vision of the impossible require more than a corner of the omnibus. I cheered myself for instants, let us say minutes, until the outlines dissolved and returned me to the dreamless faces of my fellow passengers.

30. The Blessed Sacrament

YOU WILL have understood that the advice of the emperor concerning medicine was no more than the suggestion of my small desire to leave Rio de Janeiro. Daydreams are like other dreams, they weave themselves on the pattern of our inclinations and memories. Let me go, if need be, to São Paulo, but to Europe . . . It was very far, with a wide sea and a long expanse of time. Viva medicine! I would tell these hopes to Capitú.

"They must be taking out the Blessed Sacrament," said someone on the omnibus. "I hear the bell; yes, I think it's in Santo Antonio dos Pobres. Stop, conductor!"

The conductor pulled the cord which was attached to the arm of the driver, the omnibus stopped, the man got off. José Dias gave two rapid jerks of the head, took hold of my arm and made me get off with him. We too would accompany the Blessed Sacrament. As it happened, the bell was calling the faithful to the service of extreme unction. There were already a number of people in the sacristy. It was the first time I had ever found myself in such solemn surroundings.

I obeyed the instructions, at first with constraint, but soon
with a feeling of satisfaction, not so much from the charity
of the service but because it conferred on me the office of a
man. When the sacristan commenced to distribute the vestments, someone ran in all out of breath; it was my neighbor
Padua. He too would accompany the Blessed Sacrament. He
caught sight of us, came over and spoke. José Dias made a
gesture of annoyance, scarcely acknowledged his greeting, and
kept on looking at the priest, who was washing his hands. Afterward, when Padua was talking to the sacristan in a low voice,
José Dias went up to them; I did the same. Padua was begging
the sacristan to let him carry one of the poles of the canopy.
José Dias asked for one too.

"There is only one not already taken," said the sacristan.

"Well, that one then," said José Dias.

"But I asked first," insisted Padua.

"You asked first, but you came in last," retorted José Dias.
"I was already here. You carry a candle."

Padua, in spite of his awe of José Dias, continued to demand the pole, in a low, muffled voice. The sacristan found
a way to settle the difficulty: he undertook to get one of the
other bearers of the canopy to give up his pole to Padua,
who was known in the parish, as was José Dias. This was
done, but José Dias spoiled even this arrangement. No, seeing
that there was another pole available, he requested it for me,
"the young seminarist," to whom this distinction would more
properly fall. Padua turned pale as the candles. It was putting
a father's heart to the test. The sacristan who recognized me
from seeing me there with my mother on Sundays, asked me
curiously if I was really a seminarist.

"Not yet, but he will be," answered José Dias, winking his
left eye at me. In spite of the wink, it made me angry.

"All right, I'll give it up to our Bentinho," sighed Capitú's father.

For my part, I wanted to let him keep it. I remembered that he was accustomed to accompany the Blessed Sacrament to the dying and he always carried a candle; but the last time he had succeeded in getting one of the poles of the canopy. The special honor attaching to the canopy was that it covered the vicar; for a candle, anyone would do. It was he himself who had told me all this, and he was filled with a pious and cheerful glory as he did so. This accounts for the excitement with which he had entered the church. It would be his second time at the canopy, and that was why he went straightway to ask for it. And nothing! He had to go back to the vulgar candle. Another case of a shattered interimity: the administrator had to return to his old post . . . I wanted to give him my pole but our dependent prevented me from this act of generosity by asking the sacristan to put us, him and me, at the two front poles that we might break the way for the canopy.

Vestments on, candles distributed and lighted, priest and ciborium ready, sacristan with the hyssop and bell in his hands, the procession went forth into the street. When I found myself holding one of the poles and passing through lines of the faithful, who knelt, I was moved. Padua gnawed his candle in bitterness. It is a metaphor; but I cannot think of a more vivid way to describe the pain and humiliation of my neighbor. I was not able to look at him for very long however, nor at the dependent, who, parallel to me, raised his head on high with an air of being himself the God of Hosts. In a short while I felt tired; my arms sagged; luckily the house was near by, in the Rua do Senado.

The sick woman was consumptive, a widowed lady. She

had a daughter of fifteen or sixteen who was crying at the
door of her room. The girl was not beautiful, perhaps there
was nothing charming about her: her hair hung uncombed,
tears had wrinkled her eyes. Still, the scene spoke and cap-
tured my heart. The vicar confessed the sick woman, gave
her communion and the holy oils. The weeping of the girl
increased so that I felt my own eyes moisten, and turned
away. I went to a window. Poor soul! Grief in itself is conta-
gious; mixed up with thoughts of my mother, it affected me
more, and when I came to think of Capitú I felt an impulse
to sob. I went out into the hall and I heard someone say to
me:

"Don't cry like that!"

The image of Capitú went with me, and my imagination,
as it had attributed tears to her a minute before, now filled
her mouth with laughter; I saw her write on the wall, speak
to me, turn with her arms in the air; I distinctly heard my
name in a tone so sweet it made me drunk. The lighted candles, so lugubrious under the circumstances, took on the air
of a nuptial lustre. What was a nuptial lustre? I do not know;
it was something the opposite of death, and, as far as I can
see, the opposite of death is a wedding. This new sensation
swayed me until José Dias came up and whispered in my ear:

"Don't grin like that!"

I quickly became serious. It was time for us to leave. I
picked up my pole. As I already knew the distance—and now
we were returning to the church, which made it seem less—
the weight of the pole was greatly diminished. Besides, the
sun out there, the animation in the street, the boys of my
own age who watched with envy, the devout who came to
their windows or knelt in doorways at our passage, all filled
my soul with a new gaiety.

Padua, on the contrary, appeared more and more humiliated. Even though I was taking his place, he could not console
himself for the candle, the miserable candle. And yet there
were others who carried candles, and it was with difficulty
that they maintained the proper sedateness: they did not
strut, but at the same time they were not sorrowful. One
could see that they marched with honor.

31. Capitú's curiosity

CAPITÚ PREFERRED anything to the seminary. Instead of
being downcast at the threat of a long separation, she declared herself satisfied if the idea of Europe should win out.
And when I related my imperial dream:

"No, Bentinho, let us leave the emperor in peace," she
said, "Let us stick for the present to the promise of José Dias.
When will he speak to your mother?"

"He didn't set the day; he promised that he would see, that
he would speak as soon as possible, and that I should ask the
help of God."

Capitú wanted me to repeat all the dependent's answers,
his changes of gesture, and even the pirouette, which I had
hardly mentioned. She asked about the tone in which he had
spoken. She was minute and attentive. And she seemed to
chew it all over within herself. Or one might say that she was
checking, labeling, and filing away in her memory everything
I had told her. This image is perhaps better than the other,
but better still is none. Capitú was Capitú, that is, a very
special creature, more woman than I was man. If I have not
said this before, there it is. If I have, there it is anyway. There

are concepts that must be impressed on the soul of the reader by force of repetition.

She was also most curious. The curiosity of Capitú is good for a chapter. It was of various sorts, explainable and inexplicable, useful as well as useless, on grave subjects and on frivolous; she liked to know everything. In the school where from the age of seven she had learned reading, writing and arithmetic, French, religion, and needlework, she did not learn, for example, to make lace; for this very reason she wanted Cousin Justina to teach it to her. If she did not study Latin with Padre Cabral, it was because the padre, after proposing it to her in fun, ended by saying that Latin was not a language for little girls. Capitú admitted to me one day that this reason fired her desire to know it. In compensation she decided to study English with an old professor who was a friend and whist crony of her father; but it fell through. Uncle Cosme taught her backgammon.

"Let me give you a little capot, Capitú," he would say to her.

Capitú would obey, and she played with facility, attention and, I do not know whether I should say, with love. One day I found her making a pencil sketch; she was giving it the final strokes, and asked me to wait and see if it was like. It was a portrait of my father, copied from the canvas my mother kept in the living room, the portrait I have now. It was not perfection: on the contrary, the eyes goggled, and the hair consisted of little circles one atop the other. But, considering that she did not know a single rudiment of the art and that she had done it from memory in a few seconds, I found it a work of much merit—you may discount my youth and my sympathetic feelings. Even so, I am of the opinion that she would easily have learned to paint, as she learned music much later. She was already in love with our piano, an old useless piece of junk, scarcely more than a keepsake. She used to read our novels, leaf through our books of engravings: she wanted to know about the ruins, the people, the campaigns, the name, the story, the place. José Dias gave her these bits of information with a certain air of erudite pride. His erudition was not much more imposing than his backwoods homeopathy.

One day Capitú wanted to know who the figures in the living room were. The dependent told her, briefly, though he lingered a little on Caesar, with exclamations and Latin:

"Caesar! Julius Caesar! Great man! *Tu quoque, Brute?*"

Capitú did not find the profile of Caesar handsome, but his actions, recited by José Dias, caused her gestures of admiration. She remained a long time with her face turned toward him. A man who could do everything! A man who would give a lady a pearl worth six million sesterces!

"And how much is a sesterce worth?"

José Dias, not having the value of a sesterce handy, answered with enthusiasm:

"He is the greatest man in history!"

Caesar's pearl lighted up Capitú's eyes. It was on this occasion that she asked my mother why she no longer wore the jewels of the portrait: she was referring to the one in the living room, beside that of my father; it showed a great necklace, tiara, and earrings.

"They are widowed jewels, like me, Capitú."

"When did you wear them last?"

"It was at the Coronation festivities."

"Oh, tell me about the Coronation!"

She already knew what her parents had told her, but she probably suspected that they knew little more than what had taken place in the street. She wanted to know what went on in the Imperial Chapel and in the ballrooms. She had been born long after these celebrated festivities. Since she had heard the Majority mentioned several times, she persisted one day in finding out what that event was. They told her, and she thought the emperor did right in wanting to ascend the throne at the age of fifteen. Everything was matter for Capitú's curiosity: antique furniture, old things around the house, customs, stories of Itaguahy, the childhood and youth of my mother, a saying from here, a recollection from there, an old saw from over yonder . . .

32. Eyes like the tide

EVERYTHING WAS matter for the curiosity of Capitú. There was a case, however, in which I am not sure whether she learned or taught, or did both—as I did. I will tell of it in the next chapter. In this one I will only say that a few days after the agreement with the dependent, I went to see my little friend. It was ten o'clock in the morning. Dona Fortunata, who was in the garden, did not even wait for me to ask for her daughter.

"She's in the living room combing her hair," she said to me. "Go quietly and scare her."

I went quietly, but either my foot or the mirror gave me away. It may be that it was not the latter, for it was a tiny mirror bought for a *pataca* (pardon the cheapness) from an Italian pedlar; it had a rough frame and hung by a little tin chain on the wall between the two windows. If it was not that, then it was my foot. One or the other, for scarcely had I

entered the room when comb, hair, all of her, flew up in the
air, and all I heard was this question:

"Anything happened?"

"No," I answered, "I just came to see you before Padre
Cabral comes to give me my lesson. How did you sleep?"

"Fine. José Dias hasn't spoken yet?"

"Apparently not."

"But when is he going to speak?"

"He said that today or tomorrow he intends to broach the
subject—but gradually—he'll do a lot of talking to feel out the
ground. Later he will come to the point. He wants to see first
if Mamma is really fixed in her resolve . . ."

"But she is, she is," interrupted Capitú. "And if it weren't
necessary for someone to talk her out of it now and forever,
we wouldn't have spoken to him. I don't know whether José
Dias has so much influence. I think that he will do all he can,
if he feels that you really don't want to be a padre, but will
he be able to succeed? . . . She listens to him; still, if . . .
Oh, it's hell! Be firm with him, Bentinho."

"I will. He's got to speak this very day."

"You swear it?"

"I swear it! Let me see your eyes, Capitú."

I had remembered the definition that José Dias had given
of them, "gypsy's eyes, oblique and sly." I did not know what
"oblique" was, but I knew "sly," and I wanted to see if they
could be called that. Capitú let me look at her, and examine
them. She only asked what it was, and if I had never seen
them before. I found nothing extraordinary in them; their
color and gentleness were my old friends. The length of my
contemplation, I think, gave Capitú another idea of my intent: she imagined that it was a pretext to look closer, with

my own long, unflickering eyes enmeshed in hers. And it is to
this that I attribute the fact that they began to grow larger,
larger and shadowy, and with an expression that . . .

Grammar of lovers, give me an exact and poetic comparison to describe those eyes of Capitú's. I can find no image—
without breaking the dignity of my style—to convey what
they were and what they did to me. Eyes like the tide? Yes,
like the tide. That's what they were. They had some mysterious and force-giving fluid that drew everything up into them,
like a wave that moves back from the shore when the undertow is heavy. In order not to be swept under, I grasped at
other, neighboring parts, her ears, her arms, at her hair that
was spread over her shoulders; but as soon as I sought the
pupils of her eyes again, the wave that came from them kept
growing, cavernous, dark, threatening to engulf me, to pull
me, drag me into itself. How many minutes did we pass in
that game? Only the clocks of heaven will have noted this
space of time which was infinite yet brief. Eternity has its
clocks: even though it is endless, it wants to know how long
joys and sufferings last. It must double the pleasure of the
blest in heaven to know the sum of torments that their enemies in hell suffer. And the amount of pleasure which their
hated adversaries in heaven enjoy increases the agony of the
damned in hell. This is a torment that escaped the divine
Dante; but I do not care to emend poets at the moment. I was
simply on the point of telling how at the end of an unmarked
time, I finally grasped Capitú's hair, but this time with my
hands, and I said to her—to be saying something—that I
would comb it for her if she liked.

"You?"

"I."

"You'll get it all tangled."

"If I tangle it, you can untangle it later."

"Let's see what you can do."

33. The combing of the braids

CAPITÚ TURNED her back to me and faced the mirror. I
took her hair, gathered it all together and began to smooth it
with the comb, from her forehead to the very ends, which
reached her waist. With Capitú standing it was awkward. Do
not forget that she was a shade taller than I, but even though
she had been the same height . . . I asked her to sit down.

"Sit here, that will be better."

"Let's see the great hairdresser," she said with a laugh. I
continued to smooth her hair with great care, and divided it
into two equal portions, to make the two braids. I did not
make them right off, nor so very fast, as regular hairdressers
may suppose, but slowly, very slowly, as I savored by my
touch those heavy threads that were a part of her. The work
kept getting bungled, at times through clumsiness, at times
on purpose, in order to undo what was done and do it over
again. My fingers brushed along her neck or over the calico-
covered shoulders, and the sensation was sweet. But finally I
came to the end of her hair, however much I wished it in-
terminable. I did not ask heaven that it might be as long as
Aurora's, because I did not yet know this divinity which the
old poets presented to me later; but I longed to comb it
through all the ages of ages, to weave two braids that might
enfold the infinite an unnameable number of times. If this
seems overemphatic, miserable reader, it is because you have

never combed a girl's hair, never placed your adolescent hands on the youthful head of a nymph . . . A nymph! I am all mythology. Even before, when I was speaking of her eyes like the tide, I wrote Thetis—then crossed it out. Let us also cross out nymph. Let us say only, loved creature, a word which embraces all the potencies, Christian and pagan. At last I finished the two braids. Where was the ribbon to fasten the ends together? On top of the table, a sad bit of crumpled stuff. I joined the ends of the braids, tied them with a bow, touched up the work—loosening here, smoothing there, until I exclaimed:

"There!"

"How is it?"

"Look in the mirror."

Instead of going to the mirror, what do you think Capitú did? Do not forget, she was seated with her back to me. Capitú bent back her head so far that I had to prop it up with my hands; the back of the chair was low. Then I leaned over her, face to face, but inversely, with the eyes of one in line with the mouth of the other. I begged her to raise her head, she might get dizzy, hurt her neck. I even told her she looked ugly; but *that* reason did not move her.

"Sit up, Capitú!"

She would not. She did not raise her head, and we remained like that, looking at each other, until she made a movement with her lips. I lowered mine, and . . .

The sensation of the kiss was immense and sudden: Capitú rose quickly from her chair; I recoiled clear to the wall, with a kind of dizziness, speechless, my eyes dark. When my vision cleared I saw that Capitú had her eyes on the ground. I did not venture to speak. If I had, I would not have known what to say. I was held, stunned, I could find no gesture, no im-

pulse that would pry me loose from the wall and send me to
her with a thousand warm and caressing words . . . Do not
scoff at my fifteen years, precocious reader. At seventeen, Des
Grieux (and what is more he was Des Grieux) had not yet begun to think on the difference in the sexes.

34. A man!

WE HEARD steps in the hall: it was Dona Fortunata. Capitú
hastily composed herself, so hastily that when her mother appeared in the doorway she was shaking her head and laughing
—no trace of paleness, not a quiver of embarrassment—a clear,
spontaneous laugh, which she explained in these merry
words:

"Mamma, see what this gentleman-hairdresser has done to
my hair; he asked to finish combing it, and he did this. Look
at the braids!"

"What's wrong with them?" replied her mother kindly.
"It looks all right, no one would guess that it had been done
by someone who had never combed hair before."

"What, Mamma? This?" protested Capitú as she undid
the braids. "Oh, Mamma!"

And with a charming air of crossness that she assumed at
times, she took the comb and smoothed her hair and began to
braid it over. Dona Fortunata called her silly and told me not
to mind, that it was only her daughter's foolishness. She
looked at us with gentleness, at me and then at her. Then, I
think, she had a doubt or two. When she saw me silent, dazed,
shrunk against the wall, she suspected that perhaps there had
been something more than combing hair between us, and she
smiled and pretended not to notice. . . .

I wanted to speak too, to disguise the state of my feelings, and I summoned some words from there inside, and they came promptly, but in a herd, and filled my mouth so that not one could get out. Capitú's kiss had closed my lips. Not one exclamation, not a simple article, no matter how bravely they attacked, succeeded in breaking through my teeth. And all the words, as they withdrew to my heart, murmured: "Here is one who will make no great mark in the world, if his slightest emotions rule him."

Thus, caught by her mother, we were two and contrary: she covered over with words what I published with my silence. Dona Fortunata took me out of my perplexity by saying that my mother had sent for me for my Latin lesson; Padre Cabral was waiting for me. It was an escape. I said goodbye and went into the hall. As I walked away, I heard the mother scolding the daughter; the daughter said nothing.

I ran to my room and picked up my books, but I did not go to the schoolroom; I sat down on the bed and recalled the combing of Capitú's hair and the rest. I had chills, I had moments in which I lost consciousness of myself and the things around me—I seemed to exist way off somewhere, somehow. I came back to myself again, saw the bed, the walls, the books, the floor, heard some sound outside, vague, near, far away, and then everything was gone, and I felt only Capitú's lips . . . Capitú's lips extending to mine, and mine reaching for hers, and I felt them uniting. Suddenly, without willing it, without thinking, I uttered these words of pride:

"I am a man!"

I imagined they had heard me because it slipped out in a loud voice. I ran to the door of my room. There was no one outside. I went back and, in a low tone, repeated that I was a man. Even now I have the echo of it in my ears. The satisfac-

tion I felt was tremendous. Columbus felt no greater when he
discovered America, and pardon the banality in consideration of the aptness: every adolescent has within him an undis-
covered world, an admiral and an October dawn. I made
other discoveries later; none so dazzled me. The denuncia-
tion of José Dias had roused me, and the lesson of the old
coco tree; the sight of our names cut in the garden wall made
me tremble, as you have seen; none of those things compared
with the sensation of the kiss. Those other things might have
been lies or illusion. Though true, they were but the bones
of Truth, they were not her flesh and blood. Even our hands,
touching, clasping, melting into one another, could not say
everything.

"I am a man!"

When I repeated this for the third time, I thought of the
seminary, but as one thinks of a danger that is past, of an
averted evil, a vanished nightmare. All my nerves told me
that men are not padres. My blood was of the same opinion.
Once more I felt Capitú's lips. Perhaps I dwell too much on
my oscular reminiscences; but longing is that very thing: it
is the passing and repassing in review of old memories. Of all
my memories of the time, I believe that this one is the sweetest, the most fresh, the most all-embracing—the one that entirely revealed me to myself. I have others, vast and numerous, sweet also, of various sorts, some intellectual, likewise
intense, when I had become a grown man too, but the mark
they left was less.

35. The protonotary apostolic

FINALLY I caught up my books and ran to my lesson. I did
not run, precisely; halfway I stopped, reflecting that it must
be very late and they might read something in my looks. I
had a notion to lie, allege that I had had a dizzy spell; but
the scare it would cause my mother made me reject the idea.
I thought of promising some dozens of paternosters; I had,
however, another promise hanging fire, another favor pend-
ing . . . No, let us wait and see. I walked on. I heard gay
voices chattering noisily. When I entered the living room, no
one scolded.

Padre Cabral had received a message the evening before
from the internuncio; had gone to see him and had learned
that by pontifical decree he had just been named protonotary
apostolic. This distinction from the Pope gave him great joy,
as it did all our household. Uncle Cosme and Cousin Justina
kept repeating the title admiringly. It was the first time that
it had fallen on our ears, which were accustomed to canons,
monsignori, bishops, nuncios, and internuncios; but what
was a protonotary apostolic? Padre Cabral explained that it
was not, properly speaking, an appointment to the Curia, but
the honors of it.

Uncle Cosme saw himself exalted in his old crony at cards,
and kept repeating, "protonotary apostolic." Turning to
me, he said, "Prepare yourself, Bentinho! *You* may come to
be a protonotary apostolic."

Cabral listened with pleasure to the repetition of the title.
He would stand, take a few steps, smile, beat a little tattoo on
the lid of his snuffbox. The size of the title, as it were, dou-

bled its magnificence, but made it too long to place before his name. This last reflection was Uncle Cosme's. Padre Cabral hastened to add that it was not necessary to use the whole of it: it was enough to call him Protonotary Cabral, the Apostolic being taken for granted.

"Protonotary Cabral."

"Yes, that's it, Protonotary Cabral."

"But, Senhor Protonotary," put in Cousin Justina, in order to become accustomed to the use of the title, "does this oblige you to go to Rome?"

"No, Dona Justina."

"No, it is only the honors," observed my mother.

"Still, that doesn't prevent," said Cabral, who had gone on reflecting, "that doesn't prevent one, in cases of greater formality, in public announcements, formal letters, etc., from using the entire title: protonotary apostolic. For ordinary use, protonotary is sufficient."

"Of course!" they all assented.

José Dias, who came in soon after me, applauded the distinction and recalled, apropos, the first political Acts of Pius IX, the great hopes of Italy . . . No one took up the subject. The thing of the hour was my old Latin teacher. Recovering from my apprehensiveness, I realized that I ought to compliment him too, and this applause of mine touched his heart no less than that of the others. He patted me on the cheek in a fatherly manner, and ended by giving me a holiday. It was a great deal of felicity for a single hour. A kiss and a holiday! I imagine that my face said as much, for Uncle Cosme, with his belly shaking, called me a gay dog.

José Dias checked our merriment: "One must not revel in truancy. Latin will still be necessary to him, *even if he never becomes a padre.*"

By this I knew my man. It was the first word, the seed cast into the earth, thus, in passing, as if to accustom the family's ears to it.

My mother smiled at me, a smile brimming with love and sadness, but answered promptly, "He will be a padre, a fine handsome padre."

"Don't forget, Sister Gloria, and protonotary too. Protonotary apostolic."

"Protonotary Santiago," repeated Cabral with emphasis.

Whether it was the intention of my Latin teacher to get accustomed to the use of his title with a name, I do not exactly know. What I do know is that when I heard my name linked to that title, it gave me a strong urge to say a bad word. But the urge in this case was rather an idea, an idea without tongue, which remained quiet and mute, just as other ideas, a few minutes later . . . But these demand a special chapter. Let us bring this one to a close by saying that the teacher of Latin spoke for some time of my ordination to sacred orders, though without great interest. He was trying to talk about something else in order to appear unmindful of his own glory; but *it* was the thing that dazzled him on the present occasion. He was a thin old man, endowed with good qualities. And he had a few defects. The most eminent of these was a fondness for good food, not that he was a glutton exactly. He ate little but he appreciated the fine and the rare, and our cuisine, if it was simple, was not quite as poor as his. Thus, when my mother told him that he should stay to dinner and celebrate, the look with which he accepted may have been that of a protonotary, but it was not apostolic. To be agreeable to my mother, he again fastened on me, describing my ecclesiastical future, wanting to know if I was to enter the

seminary now, in the coming year, and offering to speak to
"My Lord Bishop"—and the whole shot through with "Protonotary Santiagos."

36. Idea without legs and idea without arms

I LEFT them on a pretext of going to play, and went off to
muse over my adventure of the morning. It was the best thing
I could do, with no Latin, and even with Latin. At the end
of five minutes I decided to run over to the house next door,
grab Capitú, undo her braids, redo them and finish them in
that particular manner, mouth on mouth. That's it, come,
let's go . . . Idea! Nothing more! Idea without legs! The
other legs wished neither to run nor walk. It was much later
that they moved off in leisurely style and carried me to
Capitú's house. When I arrived, I found her in the living
room, the same living room, seated on the sofa, a pillow on
her lap, sewing tranquilly. She did not look me in the face,
but askance and fearfully, or if you prefer the phraseology
of the dependent, obliquely and slyly. Her hands lay still,
after running the needle into the cloth. I stood at the other
side of the table, and did not know what to do. Once more,
the words I had brought deserted me. In this way we wasted
several long minutes, until she left her sewing entirely, rose
and waited for me. I went to her, and asked if her mother had
said anything. She answered "no." Her lips as she replied
were such that, I believe, they provoked in me a gesture of
approximation. At any rate Capitú drew back a little.

Now was the time to grab her, pull her to me, kiss her . . .
Idea! Idea without arms! My own hung limp and dead. I

knew nothing of the Scriptures. If I had, it is probable that
the spirit of Satan would have prompted me to give the
mystic language of the Canticles a direct and natural signifi-
cation. Then I would have obeyed the first versicle: "Let him
place his lips on mine and kiss me with the kisses of his
mouth." And as regards the arms, which in my case were
inert, it would be enough to carry out vs. 6 of Ch. II: "His
left hand *is* already under my head and his right hand doth
now embrace me." Here, my brethren, you see the chronol-
ogy of the gestures. It was only a matter of putting it into
effect. Still, even though I had known the text, Capitú's attitude was now so shrinking that I do not know if I would not
have continued stock-still. It was she, meanwhile, who freed
me from that situation.

37. The soul is full of mysteries

"HAD PADRE CABRAL been waiting long?"

"I didn't have a lesson today. I got a holiday."

I explained the reason for the holiday. I told her too
how Padre Cabral had talked of my entering the seminary,
backed up my mother's resolve, and I said some nasty things
about him. Capitú reflected a while, then asked if she might
go and pay her compliments to the padre, that afternoon, at
my house.

"Sure, but what for?"

"Papa will naturally want to go too, but it is better for him
to go to the padre's house, it will be more proper. But not for
me, since I'm almost a young lady," she concluded with a
laugh.

The laugh cheered me. Her words seemed to be a joke on herself, seeing that, since morning, she had become a woman, as I a man. I found her witticism charming and, to tell the truth, determined to prove to her that she was a full-grown young lady. I lightly took hold of her right hand, then of her left, and stood there, amazed and trembling. It was an idea with hands. I wanted to pull Capitú's hands in order to oblige her to come after them, but the action still did not respond to my intention. Nonetheless, I felt strong and bold. I was not imitating anyone. I did not associate much with older boys who might have instructed me with tales of love. I had never heard of the rape of Lucretia. As far as the Romans were concerned, I scarcely knew more than that they spoke by the rules of Padre Pereira's Grammar and were countrymen of Pontius Pilate. I do not deny that the conclusion to the hair-combing that morning was a big step along the road of lover's progress, but the gesture then was exactly contrary to this one. In the morning she bent back her head; now, she shrank from me. It was not only in this respect that the hazards differed. On another point, though there seemed to be repetition, there was contrast.

I think I made a move to pull her to me. I won't swear to it. I was becoming so joyously excited that I was not quite conscious of all my acts. But I gather that this was the case, because she drew back and tried to pull her hands from mine. Then, perhaps because she could back away no further, she placed one foot in front to brace herself, and pulled back with her chest. It was this gesture that obliged me to hold on to her hands with force. Her chest finally grew weary and yielded but her head still refused to yield, and thrown back nullified all my efforts, for by this time, I was making efforts, dear reader. Since I was not familiar with the lesson of the

Canticles, it did not occur to me to extend my left hand and place it under her head. Besides, this gesture presupposes an accord of wills, and Capitú, who was now resisting me, would have taken advantage of the gesture to tear herself free from my other hand and escape me entirely. We stood fixed in this struggle, without a sound, for in spite of the attack and of the defense we did not abandon the caution necessary to keep from being heard in the house: the soul is full of mysteries. Now I know that I was pulling her. Her head continued to hold back until it too grew weary; but then it was the mouth's turn. Capitú's mouth initiated an inverse movement in relation to mine, going to one side when I sought it on the other. In this counterpoise we jerked back and forth without my daring a little more, and a little more would have been enough. . . .

Then we heard knocking and a shouting at the front door. It was Capitú's father. He had come home from the office a little early, as he did sometimes. "Open up, Nanata! Capitú, open the door." Apparently it was the same hazard as that morning, when her mother had come upon us, but only apparently. Actually it was quite different. Consider that in the morning everything had ended and Dona Fortunata's step was a signal for us to compose ourselves. Now we were struggling with locked hands, and nothing had even started.

We heard the bolt shot back: it was Capitú's mother opening the door. Seeing that I am making a complete confession, I will say right here that I did not have time to let go my ladylove's hands. I thought of it. I was on the point of doing it, but Capitú, before her father could come into the room, made an unhoped for gesture, she placed her mouth on mine, and gave willingly what she had refused to yield to force. I repeat: the soul is full of mysteries.

38. "My goodness, what a start!"

BY THE time Padua came through the hall and into the living room, Capitú was standing with her back to me, bending
over her sewing, as if to gather it up, and she was asking in a
natural tone:

"But, Bentinho, what is a protonotary apostolic?"

"Well, bless you!" exclaimed her father.

"My goodness, what a start you give a person!"

Now the hazard is the same. If I relate the two hazards of
forty years ago, just as they happened, it is to show that
Capitú was mistress of herself not only in the presence of her
mother; her father did not frighten her a bit more. In the
midst of a situation which left me tongue-tied, she talked
away with the greatest ingenuousness in the world. My belief
is that her heart beat neither faster nor slower. She claimed
to be startled, and put on a half-scared look; but I, who knew
the whole story, saw that it was false, and envied her. She
came right up to her father who was shaking my hand and
asking what his daughter meant with her talk of protono-
taries apostolic. Capitú repeated for him what she had heard
from me and expressed the opinion that he ought to go compliment the padre at his house, and that she would go to
mine. And, gathering up her sewing tackle, she went out into
the hall, calling childishly, "Mamma, dinner, Papa's home."

39. The call

PADRE CABRAL was in that first hour of glory in which the slightest congratulations are as good as odes. A time comes when the man of distinction receives praise as a wonted tribute, with blank face, without thanks. The rapture of the first hour is better; that state of soul which sees in the bending of a plant in the wind the homage of universal *flora,* brings more intimate, more delicate sensations than any other. Cabral heard Capitú's words with infinite pleasure.

"Thank you, Capitú, thank you very much. I am glad that you are pleased too. Papa well? And Mamma? There's no need to ask about you; those rosy cheeks speak for themselves. And how are we coming along with our prayers?"

To all the questions, Capitú answered promptly and correctly. She had on a nice little dress and her Sunday shoes. She did not come in with her usual familiarity, but delayed an instant at the door of the room before going to kiss my mother's hand, and that of the padre. As she gave the latter, twice within five minutes, the title of protonotary, José Dias, in order to get ahead in the competition made a little speech in honor of "the fatherly and most august heart of Pius IX."

"You are a great speechifier," said Uncle Cosme, when he finished.

José Dias smiled without taking offense. Padre Cabral confirmed the dependent's praises, but without his superlatives. To this José Dias added that Cardinal Mastai had quite evidently been cut out for the tiara from the very beginning. And, winking at me, he concluded:

"The call is everything. The ecclesiastical state is most perfect, provided that the priest comes to it dedicated from his cradle. If he does not feel the call, I mean a sincere and true call, a young man might better study the humanities, which are also useful and honorable."

Padre Cabral took him up quickly, "The call is a great deal, but the power of God is sovereign. A man may have no liking for the Church, and even persecute it, and one day the voice of God speaks to him and he ends up an apostle. Look at St. Paul!"

"I don't deny it, but what I say is something else. What I say is that it is quite possible to serve God, and serve him well, without being a padre, out in the world. Is that possible or isn't it?"

"It is."

"Well then!" exclaimed José Dias looking triumphantly about him. "Without the call, you cannot have a good padre; and, in any honorable profession one may serve God, as we all ought."

"Perfectly true, but the call does not necessarily originate in the cradle."

"Man, it is better so."

"A boy without any liking for the ecclesiastical life may end by being a very good padre. All is as God determines. I do not want to set myself up as an example, but here am I, who was born with the *call* to medicine. My godfather, who was coadjutor of Santa Rita, kept after my father to put me in the seminary; my father gave in. Well, sir, I acquired such a liking for the studies and for the company of the padres, that I ended by taking orders. But suppose that it had not turned out so, and my *call* had not changed, what would have happened? I would have studied subjects at the seminary that are good to know and are always better taught in those institutions.

Cousin Justina put in her oar: "What? is it possible to enter a seminary and not come out a padre?"

Padre Cabral answered "yes," that one could. Then, turning to me, he spoke of my *call*, which was manifest: my toys had always been church things, and I adored the divine service. The proofs proved nothing. All the children of my time were devout. Cabral added that the rector of São José, to whom he had recently told the story of my mother's promise, considered my birth a miracle, and *he* was of the same opinion. Capitú, hugging my mother's skirts, paid no heed to the anxious looks I sent her. Neither did she seem to give ear to the conversation about the seminary and its sequel, and yet she got most of it by heart, as I came to learn afterwards. Twice I went to the window, in the hope that she would come too, and we would stay there, snug and alone till the end of the world, if it should ever end, but Capitú did not come to me. She did not leave my mother except to go home. It was getting on toward dusk. She said goodbye.

"Go with her, Bentinho," said my mother.

"No, there's no need, Dona Gloria," she laughed, "I know the way. Goodbye, Senhor protonotary . . ."

"Goodbye, Capitú."

I made a step in the direction of crossing the room. Clearly, it was my duty, my desire, all the impulses of my youth and of the occasion were to cross that room, to follow my neighbor along the hall, go down through the grounds, enter her garden, give her a third kiss, and say good night. I took no notice of her refusal for I thought it simulated, and went out into the hall. But Capitú, who was walking rapidly, stopped and motioned me back. I did not obey. I came up to her.

"No, don't come! We'll talk tomorrow."

"But I want to tell you . . ."

"Tomorrow."

"Listen!"

"No, stay here!"

She spoke softly. She took hold of my hand and placed her finger on her lips. A Negress, who had come from inside to light the great hall lantern, seeing us in that attitude, almost hidden in the shadows, laughed sympathetically and murmured, in a tone loud enough for us to hear, something which I scarcely marked yet did not fail to understand. Capitú whispered to me that the slave suspected something and would perhaps tell the others. Once more she intimated to me that I should remain, and began to move away. I remained motionless, fixed, rooted to the ground.

40. A mare

LEFT ALONE, I reflected a while, and had a fantasy. You are already acquainted with my fantasies. I told you the one of the imperial visit. I have told you the one about this house in Engenho Novo reproducing the Matacavallos house . . . Imagination has been the companion of my whole existence —lively, swift, restless, at times timid and balky, most often ready to devour plain upon plain in its course. I believe I have read in Tacitus that Iberian mares conceived from the wind. If it was not he, it was some other ancient author who was careful enough to preserve this nonsensical belief. In this particular my imagination was a great Iberian mare: the slightest breeze gave her a foal which sprang forth at once a Bucephalus. But let us leave these metaphors which are bold and unsuited to my fifteen years. Let us state the case simply. The fantasy of that hour was to confess my amours to my mother in order to let her know that I did not feel the ecclesiastical call. The conversation on the call came back to me in its entirety, and while it filled me with terror it offered me a way out at the same time. "Yes, that's it," I thought, "I will tell Mamma that I do not feel the *call*. I will confess our love-making. If she doubts, I will tell her what happened the other day, of the hair-combing, and the rest . . ."

41. The private audience

"THE REST" made me remain a while longer in the hall, thinking. I saw Dr. João da Costa go in, and the table of ombre was made up as usual. My mother came out of the living room, and, catching sight of me, asked if I had seen Capitú home.

"No, senhora, she went alone." And almost throwing myself into her arms, "Mamma, I want to tell you something."

"What is it?" All alarmed, she wanted to know where the pain was, in my head? In my chest, in the stomach? She felt my forehead to see if I had a fever.

"I haven't any pain at all, senhora."

"Then what is it?"

"It's something, Mamma . . . But . . . look, it's better after tea, later . . . It's nothing bad. You get alarmed at everything, Mamma. It's nothing to worry about."

"You don't feel sick?"

"No, senhora."

"But you do, your cold has come back. You're pretending so that you won't have to take medicine but you have a cold; I know it by your voice."

I tried to laugh, to show that nothing was wrong with me. It was no good. She would not let me postpone my confidence. She took hold of me, led me to her bedroom, lighted a candle and ordered me to tell her everything. I asked her, in order to make a beginning, when it was that I entered the seminary.

"The first of the year, after the holidays."

"I'll go . . . to stay?"

"To stay?"

"I won't ever come home?"

"You'll come home on week ends and holidays. It's better so. After you are ordained, you will come live with me."

I wiped my eyes and my nose. She gently soothed me, then decided to reprimand me, but I believe that her voice trembled, and it seemed to me that her eyes were moist. I told her that I too felt our separation. She said it was not a separation, only a certain amount of absence for the sake of my studies; only the first few days. In a short time I would accustom myself to my schoolmates and teachers, and would come to love my life with them.

"I only love you, Mamma."

There was no calculation in this response, but I was glad to have said it, to make it appear that she was my only love; it would divert suspicion from Capitú. How many wicked intentions climb aboard a pure and innocent phrase, after it is already on its way! It is enough to make one suspect that lying is, many a time, as involuntary as breathing. On the other hand, gentle reader, note that I wished to divert suspicion from Capitú, when I had sought out my mother for the express purpose of confirming such suspicion; but contradictions are of this world. The truth is that my mother was candid as the first dawn, before the first sin. Not even by simple intuition could she deduce one thing from another: that is, she would never conclude from my sudden opposition that I had been getting into corners with Capitú, as José Dias had said. She was silent a few moments, then replied without any imposition or assertion of authority so that I was encouraged to resist, to speak to her of the *call* which had been discussed that afternoon, and to confess I did not feel it within me.

"But you used to *want* to be a padre," she said. "Don't you remember how you'd beg to go watch the seminarists come out of São José, with their cassocks? And when José Dias called you Your Reverence you used to laugh so delightedly. How can it be that now, you . . . ? No, Bentinho, I can't believe it. Then . . . The call? But the call comes with habit," she continued, repeating the observations she had heard from the lips of my Latin teacher.

As I sought to argue with her, she reproved me, not sharply but with some firmness, and I again became the submissive son. Then she spoke gravely and at length of the promise she had made. She did not tell me the circumstances, nor the occasion, nor her reasons—things which I did not come to know until much later. She reaffirmed the main point, that is, that it had to be fulfilled, in payment to God.

"Our Lord heard my prayer, and spared your life. I must not lie nor fail Him, Bentinho. There are things which cannot be done without sin, and God, who is great and powerful, would not let me off so. No, Bentinho, I know that I should be punished, well-punished. It is a good and holy thing to be a padre. You know many, like Padre Cabral, who lives so happily with his sister. An uncle of mine was a padre, just missed being made a bishop, they say . . . Give over these sly tricks, Bentinho."

I believe the eyes which I turned upon her were so reproachful that she quickly changed the word. Trick, no it could not be a trick. She knew well that I was fond of her and would not feign something that I did not feel. Softness—is what she wanted to say, that I should stop being soft, that I should be a man and bend to the task, for her sake and for the good of my soul. All these things, and others, were said a little stumblingly, and her voice was not clear but husky and choked. I saw that her emotion was again great though she did not retreat from her position, and I ventured to ask her:

"But if you should beg God to release you from your promise, Mamma?"

"No, I won't beg Him. Are you out of your head, Bentinho? And how should I know whether God released me?"

"Perhaps in a dream. I dream sometimes of angels and saints."

"So do I, my son; but it's no use . . . Come, it's late. Let us go down to the living room. Is it understood? In the first or second month of the coming year, you will enter the seminary. What I should like is for you to know the books you are studying, thoroughly. It will look well, not only for you, but also for Padre Cabral. At the seminary they are all eager to meet you because Padre Cabral speaks of you with enthusiasm."

She walked toward the door. We both went out. But before crossing the threshold she turned toward me, and I almost saw her throw her arms around my neck and tell me that I did not have to become a padre. This was her inmost desire, now that the time drew closer. She was seeking a way of paying the debt that she had contracted, other coin, which would be worth as much, or more, and she found none.

42. Capitú reflects

ON THE following day I went to the house next door, as soon as I could. Capitú was saying goodbye to two friends who had come to pay her a visit, Paula and Sancha, girls she had known at boarding school—the former fifteen years old, the latter seventeen; the first, a daughter of a physician, the second, of a dealer in American goods. She was in low spirits, and had a handkerchief tied around her head. Her mother told me that it was because of too much reading the night before, before and after tea, in the living room and in bed, until long after midnight, and with a night lamp . . .

"If I had lighted a candle, you would have been angry, Mamma. I'm all right now."

And as she untied the handkerchief, her mother suggested timidly that it would be better to keep it on, but Capitú answered that it wasn't necessary, that she felt better.

We remained alone in the living room. Capitú confirmed her mother's story, and added that she had passed a bad night because of what she had heard at my house. I told her what had happened to me, the talk with my mother, my pleas, her tears, and then her final, decisive replies: within two or three months I would enter the seminary. What would we do then? Capitú heard me with greedy attention, then somberly. When I finished she breathed heavily, as if about to burst with anger, but she contained herself.

It is so long ago that this happened, that I cannot say for sure whether she actually cried, or whether she only wiped her eyes. I guess she only wiped her eyes. When I saw the gesture, I caught hold of her hand to cheer her, but I too needed to be cheered. We sank down on the sofa and sat staring into the air. No, I'm wrong, she was staring at the floor. I did the same, as soon as I noticed her. . . . But I believe that Capitú was looking inward, within herself, while I was really and truly looking at the floor, the worn cracks, two flies out walking, a splintered chair leg. It was not much, but it took my mind off my troubles. When I looked back at Capitú, I saw that she sat rigid and still, and I was so frightened that I shook her gently. Capitú came back to the world, and asked me to tell her once more what had taken place between me and my mother. I complied, only I watered the text this time so as not to vex her. Don't call me deceitful, call me compassionate. It is true that I was afraid of losing Capitú if all her hopes faded, but it pained me to see her suffer. Now, the final truth, the truth of truths, is that I already repented having spoken to my mother before there had been any effective work on the part of José Dias. On thinking it over, I would rather not have received the disillusionment even though I knew that it was certain, sooner or later. Capitú reflected, reflected, reflected. . . .

43. Are you afraid?

SUDDENLY SHE stopped reflecting, fixed me with her eyes that were like the tide, and asked me if I was afraid.

"Afraid?"

"Yes, I want to know if you are afraid."

"Afraid of what?"

"Of getting a beating, of being put in jail, of fighting, of going ahead, of working . . ."

I did not understand. If she had said simply, "Let's run away!" perhaps I would have obeyed and perhaps not. In any case I would have understood. But a vague question like that, out of a clear sky—I could not imagine what it meant.

"But . . . I don't understand. Get a beating?"

"Yes."

"From whom? Who would beat me?"

Capitú made a gesture of impatience. Her eyes like the tide did not move and seemed to grow larger. I could not figure it out by myself, and did not want to ask her again. I wracked my brains: How would I get a beating? and why? and why would I be put in jail? and who would put me there? God help me! in my mind's eye, I saw the *Aljube,* a dark, evil-smelling hole. And I saw the prison ship, and the Barbonos barracks, and the House of Correction. All these fair social institutions enveloped me in their mystery, and still Capitú's tide-like eyes went on growing larger and larger until they drove these other things completely out of my mind. It was Capitú's mistake not to let them go on growing infinitely instead of diminishing them to their normal dimensions and giving them their customary movement.

Capitú became her old self, told me that she was only joking, for me not to worry, and with a gesture that was full of grace, tapped me on the cheek, and smiling said,

"Coward!"

"Who me? . . . But . . ."

"It's nothing, Bentinho. For who would beat you or put you in prison? Forgive me, I'm half crazy today. I meant it as a joke."

"No, Capitú. You were not joking. At a time like this neither one of us feels like joking."

"You are right. It was only my craziness. See you later."

"What do you mean, 'see me later'?"

"My headache is coming back. I'm going to put a slice of
lemon on my temples."

She did as she had said, and tied the handkerchief back on
her forehead. Then she went out into the yard with me to
say goodbye. But there we tarried a few minutes more,
seated on the edge of the well. A wind had come up, the sky
was clouded over. Capitú spoke once more of our separation,
as of a certain and definite fact. In my fear of that very thing
I cast about for reasons to cheer her. When she was not speaking she sketched on the ground with a stick of bamboo, noses
and profiles. Since she had begun to draw, it was one of her
diversions; anything served as paper and pencil. I remembered our names that she had cut in the wall and wanted to
do the same on the ground. I asked her for the bamboo. She
did not hear me, or paid no attention.

44. The first child

"GIVE IT here. Let me write something."

Capitú looked at me, but in a way that made me think of
José Dias' definition, "oblique and sly." She raised her gaze
without raising her eyes. And in a small voice, she asked:

"Tell me something, but speak the truth. Don't hold back.
You must speak frankly."

"What is it? Go ahead."

"If you had to choose between me and your mother, which would you choose?"

"Choose?"

She nodded.

"I would choose . . . but why choose? Mamma would never ask me such a thing."

"Maybe not, but I am asking you. Suppose that you are in the seminary and receive word that I am going to die . . ."

"Don't say such a thing!"

". . . or that I will kill myself for love if you don't come right away, and your mother doesn't want you to come, tell me, would you come?"

"I would."

"Against the order of your mother?"

"Against Mamma's order."

"You would leave the seminary, leave your mother, leave everything to see me die?"

"Don't talk about dying, Capitú!"

Capitú gave a colorless little laugh of disbelief, and with her stick of bamboo, wrote a word on the ground. I leaned over and read: *liar*.

This was all so strange that I could find nothing to say. I could not fathom the reason for the written word, as I had not fathomed the spoken ones. If I had thought of an insult, big or little, perhaps I would have written too, with the same piece of bamboo, but I could think of nothing. My head was a vacuum. At the same time, I was overpowered by a fear that some one might hear or read. Who, if we were alone? Dona Fortunata had come to the door once, but went right back inside. The solitude was complete. I remember that some swallows passed over the garden and went off in the direction of the Morro de Santa Theresa. Nothing else. In the distance,

vague, confused voices; in the street a clatter of hooves; from
the direction of the house, the shrill twittering of Padua's
little birds. Nothing more, or only this curious phenomenon:
the name written by Capitú not only leered up at me from
the ground but even seemed to tremble in the air. Then I
had an abominable idea: I told her that, after all, the life of a
padre was not so bad, and that I could accept it without great
sorrow. It was a childish way of lashing back at her; but I
nursed a secret hope that she would fling herself into my
arms, bathed in tears. Capitú limited herself to opening her
eyes very wide, and finally she said:

"Padre is good, there is no doubt. Better still would be
canon, because of the purple stockings. Purple is a very
pretty color. Come to think of it, canon would be better."

"But it is not possible to be canon without first being a
padre," I said, biting my lips.

"All right, begin with the black stockings. Later will come
the purple ones. What I want to be sure of is not to miss your
first Mass. Let me know in time to make a dress in the latest
style, with a hoop skirt and a big flounce— But perhaps the
style will be different then. You must have a big church,
Carmo or São Francisco . . ."

"Or Candelária."

"Or Candelária. Anyone of them will do, provided that I
hear your first Mass. I'll cut a handsome figure. People will
ask, 'Who is that charming young lady, over there, in the
beautiful dress?'

" 'Oh, that's Dona Capitolina, a young lady who used to
live in Rua de Matacavallos . . .' "

"Who used to live? Are you going to move?"

"Who knows where one will live tomorrow?" she said in a
tone of faint melancholy. Then, returning to her sarcasm:

"And you at the altar, in your alb, with a gold cape over it, chanting . . . *Pater noster* . . ."

Ah! how I regret not being a romantic poet to tell this duel of ironies! of my thrusts and hers, the grace of one and the agility of the other, and the blood flowing, and rage in the soul, until my final thrust home, which was this:

"Of course, Capitú, you shall hear my first Mass, but upon one condition."

She answered, "Your Reverence may speak."

"Will you promise one thing?"

"What is it?"

"Say whether you promise."

"I won't promise without knowing what it is."

"To tell the truth there are two things," I went on, for another idea had come to me.

"Two? Tell me what they are."

"The first is that you confess only to me, I alone shall give you penance and absolution. The second is . . ."

"The first is promised," said Capitú as she saw me hesitate, and she added that she was waiting to hear the second.

What it cost me to get it out, and would that it had never passed my lips! I would not have heard what I heard, and I would not have to write here something that one may find hard to believe.

"The second . . . yes . . . is this. . . . Promise me that I shall be the padre who marries you."

"Who marries me?" she echoed a little shaken.

Then she drooped the corners of her mouth and shook her head. "No, Bentinho," she said. "It would mean waiting a long time. You are not going to become a padre over night. It takes many years . . . Look, I'll promise something else: I promise that you shall baptize my first child."

45. Shake your head, reader

SHAKE YOUR head, reader. Make all the gestures of incredulity there are. Even throw away this book, if its tediousness has not already driven you to this long since; anything is possible. But if you have done so only now, rather than before, I trust you will pick it up again and open to the same page, without necessarily believing in the veracity of the author. And yet there is nothing more exact. It was just so that Capitú spoke, and in those very words. She spoke of her first child as if it were her first doll.

As for my amazement, though it was great, it was mixed with an odd sensation. I felt a fluid course through me. That threat of a first child, Capitú's first child, her marriage with another then, absolute separation, loss, annihilation, all this so wrought on me that I found neither word nor gesture, but sat stupefied. Capitú smiled; I saw her first-born playing on the ground. . . .

46. Peace

PEACE IS made like war, quickly. If I aimed at glory in this book, I would say that the negotiations were begun by me; but no, it was she who initiated them. A few moments later, as I sat with my head hanging, she too lowered *her* head but with her eyes turned upward, looking into mine. I let her beg me. Then I decided to get up and go away, but I did not get up, nor do I know whether I would have gone. Capitú looked at me with eyes that were so tender, and their position made them so beseeching, that I stayed. I slipped my arm around her waist; she caught hold of my finger tips, and . . .

Once more Dona Fortunata appeared in the doorway. I do not know why, for she did not even give me time to pull away my arm; she disappeared at once. Perhaps it was only to relieve her conscience, a ceremony, like routine prayers said without devotion and mumbled through in a bunch, unless it was to prove to her own eyes the reality which her heart whispered to her. . . .

Be that as it may, my arm continued to encircle her daughter's waist, and it was thus that we made our peace. The best of it was that we each wanted to take the blame, and begged each other's forgiveness. Capitú alleged in excuse, her sleeplessness, her headache, dejection of spirits, and finally her "nasty temper." I, who was easily moved to tears in those days, felt my eyes grow moist. . . . It was pure love, it was the effect of my darling's sufferings, it was the tenderness of reconciliation.

47. "Madam has gone out"

"ALL RIGHT, it is ended," I said finally, "but explain one thing to me. Why did you ask me if I was afraid of getting a beating?"

"It was not for nothing," answered Capitú. Then, after some hesitation, "But why bother about that?"

"Go on, tell me. Was it because of the seminary?"

"Yes, it was. I've heard that they give beatings there . . . No? I don't believe it either."

The explanation was agreeable to me; I received no other.

If, as I suspect, Capitú was not telling the truth, one is forced
to recognize that it was because she could not tell it, and the
lie was one of those servants who are quick to reply to visitors
that "madam has gone out," when madam does not wish to
talk to anyone. This complicity has a certain relish. The sin
shared in common makes the condition of the persons in-
volved, for the time being, equal, not to mention the pleasure
afforded by the expression on the face of the deceived visitor,
and of his back and shoulders as he walks away. . . . Truth
had not gone out, she was still at home, in Capitú's heart, nodding over her repentance. And I did not go away sad or
angry. I found the maid genteel, captivating, better than the
mistress.

The swallows now came from the opposite direction, or
perhaps they were not the same ones. It was we who were the
same: we sat there reckoning the sum of our illusions, our
fears, and already commencing to count our memories.

48. Oath at the well

"NO!" I exclaimed suddenly.

"No what?"

I had reflected a few minutes in silence and come up with
an idea; my exclamation was so loud that it startled my little
neighbor.

"No, it shan't be so!" I went on. "They say we are not old
enough to marry, that we are children, babes—that's what
they called us. All right, but two or three years pass quickly.
Will you swear to something? Will you swear to marry no one
but me?"

Capitú did not hesitate to swear, and I even saw her cheeks redden with pleasure. She swore twice and a third time.

"Even if you marry someone else, I'll keep my oath and never marry—ever."

"If I marry someone else?"

"Anything can happen, Bentinho. You may find another girl that likes you, fall in love, and marry her. Who am I for you to remember me at such a time?"

"But I too swear! I *swear,* Capitú, I swear by Almighty God that I will marry no one but you. Is that enough?"

"It should be," she replied. "I dare not ask more. Yes, you have sworn . . . But let us swear in another manner. Let us swear that we will marry each other, come what may."

You see the difference. It was more than the election of a mate; it was an affirmation of matrimony. My darling's head could think clearly and fast. Truly the previous formula was limited, merely exclusive. We could end up bachelor and old maid, like the sun and the moon, without breaking our oath. This formula was better, and had the advantage of strengthening my heart against the ecclesiastical investiture. We swore by the second formula, and we became so happy that all fear of danger disappeared. We were religious; we had heaven as witness. I no longer dreaded even the seminary.

"If they insist I will go, but I will look upon it as an ordinary college. I will not take orders."

Capitú dreaded our separation but finally accepted this plan as the best. We would not distress my mother, and the time would come when we could marry. Any resistance, however, would confirm José Dias' information. This reflection was not mine, but hers.

49. A candle on Saturdays

THAT IS how, after so many toils, we touched the port in which we should have taken refuge without delay. Do not censure us, accursed pilot, hearts are not navigated like the other seas of this world. We were content; we began to speak of the future. I promised my bride a tranquil and beautiful life, in the country or just outside the city. We would return here once a year. If it should be on the outskirts of the city, it would be far away where no one would bother us. The house, in my opinion, ought not be large or small, but a happy medium. I planted flowers round it, chose furniture, a chaise, and an oratory. Yes, we would have a pretty oratory, high, of jacaranda, with an image of Our Lady of the Conception. I lingered more over this than over the rest, in part because we were religious, in part to compensate for the frock that I was going to toss in the bushes; but there was still another part which I attribute to a secret and unconscious intent to snare the protection of heaven. We would light a candle on Saturdays. . . .

50. A middle term

SOME MONTHS later I went off to the seminary of São José. If I could count the tears that I wept on the eve and the morning of my departure, they would add up to more than all those shed since Adam and Eve. There is some exaggeration in this, but it is good to be overemphatic now and again, to pay off this devil of exactitude that torments me. And yet, if I rely only on my memory of the sensation, I am not far from the truth: at the age of fifteen, everything is infinite. Prepared though I was, my suffering was great. My mother suffered too, but deep within. Besides, Padre Cabral had found a middle term: to make trial of my *call*. If, at the end of two years, I had not revealed a call to the Church, I would pursue another career.

"Promises must be fulfilled, but according as God wills. Suppose that Our Lord has denied your son the disposition, and that the life in the seminary does not give him the liking for it that it yielded me, then it means the Divine Will is opposed. You, senhora, could not put into your son, even before birth, a call that Our Lord had refused him. . . ."

It was a concession from the padre. He was giving my mother an anticipatory pardon by making the renunciation of the debt come from the creditor. Her eyes shone, but her lips said "no." José Dias, since he had not attained his goal of going to Europe with me, seized on the next best thing, and seconded "the proposal of Senhor protonotary"; only it seemed to him that one year would be sufficient.

"I am certain," said he, giving me a wink, "that within a year our Bentinho's call to the Church will manifest itself clearly and definitely. He is sure to make a magnificent padre. And, if it doesn't happen in a year . . ."

Later he told me privately, "Go for a year. A year passes quickly. If you don't feel any liking for it whatsoever, it means that God is unwilling, as the padre says, and in that case, my young friend, the best remedy is Europe."

Capitú gave me similar advice when my mother announced my definite departure for the seminary.

"My daughter, you are going to lose your childhood companion. . . ."

This name of *daughter* made her feel so good (It was the first time my mother had called her by it.) that she had no room for sadness. She kissed my mother's hand, and told her that she already knew about it from me. In private she encouraged me to endure everything with patience. 'At the end of a year things would be changed, and a year would soon go by.' It was not yet the moment of our farewell; that took place on the night before I left, in a way that demands a special chapter. All I say here is that the fonder we grew of each other, the more Capitú set about to captivate my mother: she became more solicitous, more tender, hung constantly about her, with eyes for nobody else. My mother was by nature sympathetic and sensitive, easily moved to sorrow or to joy. She began to find a great many new graces in Capitú, fine and rare gifts. She gave her a ring of hers, and some other trifles. She would not consent to have her picture taken as Capitú begged, so that she could give her a photograph; but she had a miniature, made when she was twenty-five, and after some hesitation, decided to give it to her. Capitú's eyes, as she received the token, cannot be described. They were not oblique, nor like the tide: they were direct, clear, and shining. She kissed the portrait with fervor; my mother did the same to her. All this reminds me of our farewell.

51. Between dusk and dark

BETWEEN DUSK and dark, all must be brief as that instant. Our farewell did not last long, and yet it lasted as long as it possibly could. It took place at her house, in the living room, before the candles were lit. We swore again that we would marry each other. And it was not a handclasp that sealed the contract, as it had been in the garden: it was the uniting of our loving mouths. . . . Perhaps I'll scratch this out when it goes to press, unless I decide otherwise. If I decide otherwise, it stands. And until then let it stand, for after all it is our defense. What the divine commandment enjoins is that we shall not swear *in vain* by the holy name of God. I was not being false to the seminary seeing that I had a duly executed contract on file in the archives of heaven itself. As for the seal, as God made clean hands, so He made clean lips, and the evil is rather in your own perverse head than in that of those two adolescents. . . . O sweet companion of my childish days, I was pure, pure I remained and pure I entered the halls of São José to seek, in appearance, the sacerdotal investiture; and before it, the *call*. But the call was you, the investiture, you.

52. Old Padua

NOW I will tell of old Padua's goodbyes. Bright and early he came to our house. My mother told him to go up and speak to me in my room.

"May I?" he asked putting his head in the door.

I went to shake hands with him. He tenderly put his arms around me.

"May you be happy!" he said to me. "You will be missed, believe me, by me and mine. We all regard you highly, senhor, as you deserve. If they tell you anything else, don't believe it. It's malicious gossip. I too was the victim of malicious gossip, at the time of my marriage. It accomplished nothing. God is great and uncovers the truth. If you should one day lose your mother and your uncle—a thing which I hope, by this light that shines upon me, may never come to pass, for they are good people, excellent people, and I am grateful for the kindnesses they have shown me . . . No, I am not like some others, certain parasites, outsiders who work to break up families, low flatterers; no, I am of another sort. I don't live by sponging meals off others, living in another man's house . . . Well, they are the lucky ones!"

"Why does he talk like that?" I mused. "He probably knows that José Dias says things about him."

"But, as I was saying, if you should one day lose your relatives, you can count on our friendship. It is as nothing in importance, but our affection is immense, believe me. Padre though you be, our house is always yours to command. All I ask is that you do not forget me: don't forget old Padua . . ."

He sighed and went on, "Don't forget your old Padua, and, if you have some little old thing that you could leave me for remembrance, an old Latin notebook, no matter what, a vest button, something no longer of any use to you . . . The value is in the remembrance."

I gave a start. I had a lock of my hair wrapped in a paper, a long, beautiful lock I had cut the night before. My intention was to take it to Capitú when I left; but I decided to give it to her father. The daughter would know enough to take it and keep it. I picked up the packet and gave it to him.

"Here, take this."

"A lock of your hair!" exclaimed Padua, opening and closing the wrapping. "Oh! Thank you! I thank you for myself and my family! I'll give it to my old wife to keep safe, or to the youngster. She is more careful than her mother. How beautiful it is! How could you cut off such a handsome swatch? Give me a hug! Another! One more! Goodbye!"

His eyes were moist in earnest. His face wore a disenchanted look, like a man who has spent his whole hoard of hopes on a single lottery ticket and sees the cursed number come out a blank—such a sweet number!

53. We're off!

I LEFT for the seminary. Spare me the other farewells! My mother hugged me to her breast. Cousin Justina sighed. Perhaps she wept very little or not at all. There are people whose tears do not flow immediately, nor ever. It is said that they suffer more than the others. Probably Cousin Justina concealed her inner sufferings in seeing to things that my mother had overlooked, in offering me good advice, in giving orders. Uncle Cosme, when I kissed his hand in farewell, said to me with a laugh, "Get along, lad; come back to me a Pope!"

José Dias, composed and grave, said nothing at first. We had talked the night before, in his room, where I had gone to see if it was still possible to avoid the seminary. It no longer was, but he gave me hope and, what was most important, courage. Before the year was out, we would be on board ship. As I found this rather brief, he explained himself:

"They say that it is not a good time to cross the Atlantic. I will inquire; if it isn't, we will go in March or April."

"I could study medicine right here."

José Dias ran his fingers along his suspenders in a gesture of impatience, pursed his lips, went so far as to formally reject the proposal.

"I would not hesitate to approve the idea," said he, "if it weren't that in our School of Medicine they teach the allopath filth exclusively. Allopathy is the error of the ages and it will die out; it is murder, falsehood and illusion. If they tell you that you can learn, in the School of Medicine, that part of the science common to all systems, it is true. Allopathy is in error when it comes to therapeutics. Physiology, anatomy, pathology, are neither allopathic nor homeopathic, but it is better to learn everything straight off, once and for all, from the books and from the lips of men dedicated to the truth. . . ."

That is the way he had spoken on the night before, in his own room. Now he said nothing, or proferred some aphorism on religion and the family. I remember this one: "To share him with God is still to possess him." And when my mother gave me her final kiss, he sighed, "A *most* loving picture!"

It was the morning of a beautiful day. The little colored boys chattered in soft whispers. The Negresses asked for my blessing: "Blessing, *nhô* Bentinho! Don't forget your Joanna! Your Miquelina will be praying for you, master!"

In the street, José Dias urged his hopes: "Stick it out for a year. By then everything will be arranged."

54. Panegyric of Saint Monica

AT THE seminary . . . Ah! I am not going to tell the story of the seminary; one chapter would not be enough. No, my dear sir. Some day, yes, it is possible that I will compose a brief account of what I saw there and the life I led, of those I lived with, of the customs and all the rest. This itch to write, when you catch it at fifty, never leaves you. In youth it is possible for a man to cure himself of it; and, without going further, right here in the seminary I had a comrade who composed verses in the manner of Junqueira Freire, whose book of the poet friar had just come out. He took orders. Some years afterward I ran across him in the choir of São Pedro, and asked him to show me his latest verses.

"What verses?" he asked half startled.

"Yours. Don't you remember, at the seminary . . ."

"Ah!" he smiled.

He smiled, and went on looking, in the book open before him, for the hour at which he had to say Mass on the following day. He confessed he had not written any verses since he was ordained. It had been a tickling of youth; he scratched, it went away, he was well. And he spoke in prose of an infinity of things of the day: the high cost of living, a sermon of Padre X's . . . a vicarship in Minas. . . .

The contrary of this was a seminarist who did not go on with the career. His name was . . . But it is not necessary to give his name: the case will speak for itself. He had composed a *Panegyric of Saint Monica,* which was praised by several people and then read among the seminarists. He obtained permission to print it, and dedicated it to Saint Augustine. All this is ancient history. What is more recent is, that one day in 1882 I went to see about a certain matter in the Navy Department. There I bumped into this classmate of mine who had become head of an administrative division. He had abandoned the seminary, abandoned letters, got married and forgotten everything except the *Panegyric of Saint Monica,* some twenty-nine pages, which he went distributing down through life. As I needed some information, I went and asked it of him. It would be impossible to find greater promptness and willingness: he gave me everything—clearly, exactly, copiously. Naturally we talked of the past, personal recollections, tales of the classroom, trifling incidents, a book, a word, a saying, all the old chaff was dragged out, and we laughed together, and sighed congenially. We relived some of our days at the old seminary. And the memories, either because they were of the seminary or because we were then young, bore such a power of happiness that if there was any darkening shadow then, it did not appear now. He confessed that he had lost sight of all our classmates.

"I too, almost all. Once ordained, they naturally returned to their provinces, and those from here received parishes elsewhere."

"A happy time!" he sighed.

And after some reflection, he peered into my face with faded, insistent eyes, and asked, "Did you keep my *Panegyric*?"

I could not think of a thing to say. I tried to move my lips, but no words came. Finally I asked, "*Panegyric?* What panegyric?"

"My *Panegyric of Saint Monica.*"

I still did not remember, but the explanation had to do. After several instants of mental search, I answered that I had kept it for a long time, but what with moving, traveling . . .

"I'll bring you a copy."

Before twenty-four hours had passed he was at my house with the little book, a little old book, twenty-six years old, soiled, mottled with age, but with nothing missing, and a respectful dedication written in his hand.

"It is the next to the last copy," he told me. "I have only one left now, and I cannot give that to anyone."

And, as he watched me leaf through the opusculum, "See if you recall some bit of it," he said to me.

An interval of twenty-six years kills off closer and more constant friendships, but it was common courtesy, it was simple charity to recall some page or other. I read one of them aloud, stressing certain phrases to give the impression that they found an echo in my memory. He agreed they were beautiful, but preferred others, and pointed them out.

"Remember them?"

"Perfectly. *Panegyric of Saint Monica!* How it takes me back over the years to my youth! I have never forgotten the seminary, believe me. The years pass, events come crowding one upon the other, new sensations, and there come new friendships, which disappear in their turn: such is the law of life. . . . In short, my dear classmate, nothing has dimmed the memory of those days of fellowship, the padres, the lessons, the games . . . our games, do you remember them? Padre Lopes, oh! Padre Lopes . . ."

With his eyes in the air, he seemed to be listening, and probably he was, though he made only one remark and that after some silence, as he withdrew his eyes and sighed, "People have liked it, this *panegyric* of mine!"

55. A sonnet

THIS SAID, he shook my hands with all the force of a tremendous gratitude, said goodbye and went off. I was left alone with the *Panegyric,* and the things that its leaves recalled to me deserve a chapter or more. Before, however—because I too had my *Panegyric*—I will tell the story of a sonnet that I never wrote. It was during the time of the seminary, and the first verse is as follows:

O flower of heaven! O flower bright and pure!

How and why this verse sprang from my brain, I do not know. It sprang forth like that, as I lay in bed—an abrupt exclamation. And when I noted that it had the measure of verse, I thought of composing something to go with it, a sonnet. Insomnia, the muse with staring eyes, did not let me sleep for a long hour or two. The tickling asked for fingernails. I scratched with my whole soul. I did not choose the sonnet right away. At first I considered other forms, rhymed as well as blank verse, but finally I settled on the sonnet: a poem that was brief and adaptable. As for the idea, the first verse was not yet an idea, it was an exclamation; the idea would come later. Thus, lying in bed, wrapped up in the sheet, I essayed to poetize. I had the startled sensation of a mother who feels within her the stirrings of her first child. I was going to be a poet. I was going to compete with that monk of Bahia who had been discovered a short time before and was then the rage. I, a seminarist, would tell my woes in verse as he had told his from the cloister. I got the verse well by heart, and repeated it in a soft voice, to the sheets. Frankly, I found it handsome, and even now it does not seem bad to me.

O flower of heaven! O flower bright and pure!

What was the flower? Capitú, probably; but it could be virtue, poetry, religion, whatever other concept the metaphor of *flower* and *flower of heaven* fits. I waited for the rest, reciting the verse over and over, first on my right side, then on the

left; finally I lay on my back, with my eyes on the ceiling.
Even in this position, nothing more came to me.

Then I remarked that the most highly extolled sonnets
were those that closed with a golden key, that is, with one of
those verses which are a triumph of thought and form. I
decided to forge such a key, for, I reflected, if the final verse
came forth in chronological order after the preceding thirteen, one could scarcely expect it to have the approved perfection. I imagined that such keys were poured before the
lock itself. Thus it was that I determined to compose the
final verse of the sonnet, and after much sweating, this
emerged:

> *Life is lost, the battle still is won!*

Without vanity, and looking at it as if it were by someone
else, it was a magnificent verse. Sonorous, beyond question.
And it had a thought—victory is gained at the cost of life itself—an exalted and noble thought. It may not have been
exactly novel but neither was it commonplace. And even now
I cannot explain in what mysterious way it came into such
a youthful head. At the time, I found it sublime. I recited
the golden key again and again. Then I repeated the two
verses in sequence, and made ready to connect them by the
twelve center ones. As for the idea, it seemed to me now, in
view of the final verse, that it would be better if it were not
Capitú; it would be *justice.* It was more appropriate to say
that in the struggle for justice life is lost perchance but the
battle still is won. It also occurred to me to accept *battle* in
its ordinary sense and make it the fight for one's country, for
example. In that case, the *flower of heaven* would be *liberty.*
This acceptance of the term, however, since the poet was a
seminarist, might not fit so well; and I spent several minutes

in choosing one or the other. I found *justice* the better, but in the end I accepted a new idea—*charity*. I recited the two verses, each in its own style, the one languidly:

> *O flower of heaven! O flower bright and pure!*

and the other with spirit:

> *Life is lost, the battle still is won!*

The feeling I had was that a perfect sonnet was about to be born. To begin well and end well was no small thing. In order to give myself a bath of inspiration, I called to mind several celebrated sonnets, and I noted that most of them were quite facile. The verses, with the idea already in them, flowed so naturally one out of the other one could not decide whether it was the idea that had fashioned the verses, or they that had summoned the idea. Then I turned back to my sonnet, and once more repeated the first verse and waited for the second. The second was not forthcoming, nor the third, nor the fourth, nor any of them. I had several fits of rage, and more than once considered getting out of bed and going to try ink and paper. Perhaps in writing, the verses would flock to me, but . . .

Worn out with waiting, I decided to alter the meaning of the final verse by the simple transposition of two words, thus:

> *Life is won, the battle still is lost!*

The meaning turns out to be exactly the opposite, but perhaps this in itself would coax inspiration. In this case, it would be irony: by not practicing charity one may win life but lose the battle of heaven. I took heart and waited. I did not have a window. If I had had, it is possible I would have gone to beg an idea of the night. And who knows if the fireflies flashing here below would not have seemed to me like rhyming bits of stars and this living metaphor given me the elusive verses with their proper consonances and meanings.

I toiled in vain, I searched, I hunted, I waited. No verses came. Since then I have written more than one page of prose, and now I am composing this narrative, though I still find nothing in this world more difficult than writing, well or ill. Well, sirs, nothing consoles me for that sonnet I did not write. But, as I believe that sonnets spring ready made, as do odes and dramas and the other works of art, by a law of metaphysical order, I offer these two verses to the first idle soul who wants them. On a Sunday, or if it's raining, or in the country, or in any other moments of leisure, he can try to see if the sonnet will come. All he has to do is give it an idea and fill in the missing middle.

56. A seminarist

ALL THIS the devil of a little book kept telling me, with its old style type and Latin quotations. I saw rise from those leaves many a seminarist profile: the Albuquerque brothers for example, one of whom is a canon in Bahia, while the other went into medicine and, they say, has discovered a specific against yellow fever. I saw Bastos and his skinny legs— now a parish vicar in Meia-Ponte, if he is not already dead. Luiz Borges, though a priest, went into politics and ended up a senator of the empire. . . . How many other faces stared up at me from the cold pages of the *Panegyric*! No, they were not cold. They bore the warmth of budding youth, the warmth of the past, my own warmth. I wanted to reread them; here and there I caught the meaning of the text: it seemed as fresh to me as on the first day, though more brief. The little book cast a spell: at times, unconsciously, I turned the page as if I were actually reading. And then . . . I believe that it was when my eyes fell on the last word on the page, and my hand, accustomed to assist them, did its office . . .

Here was another seminarist. His name was Ezekiel de Souza Escobar. He was a slender boy, with clear, bright eyes that shifted constantly about, like his hands, like his feet, like his speech, like everything about him. Anyone who was not accustomed to him might feel ill at ease, not knowing where to have him. He did not look you in the eye, he did not speak plainly nor in logical sequence. His hands did not take hold of yours nor allow yours to take hold of them because his fingers were thin and short, and when you thought you had them between your own, you no longer had anything. The same was true of his feet, which were no sooner here than they were there. This difficulty in lighting was his greatest obstacle when he tried to take on the ways of the seminary. His smile was instantaneous, but he also had a great, merry laugh. One thing about him was not so fleeting and inconstant—his reflectiveness. Many times we would come upon him, withdrawn within himself, thinking. He always explained that he was meditating upon some spiritual point, or that he was thinking over the lesson of the day before. After he entered into my confidence, he frequently asked me for minute explanations and repetitions, and he had the memory to retain them all, even to the words. Perhaps this faculty robbed some other.

He was three years older than I, the son of a Curitiba lawyer; they had a relative in business in Rio de Janeiro, who acted as agent for his father. The father was a man of strong Catholic sentiments. Escobar had a sister, who was an angel, he said.

"It is not only in her beauty that she is an angel, but also in her kindness. You can't imagine what a kind soul she is. She writes to me often. I must show you her letters."

Indeed they were simple and affectionate, filled with endearments and advice. Escobar told me stories about her, which were interesting, and all pointed to the kindness and understanding of that devoted creature. They were such that they would have made me willing to marry her, if it had not been for Capitú. She died a little while afterward.

Seduced by his words, I was almost on the point of telling him my own story then and there. At first I had been timid, but he found his way into my confidence. Those shifty ways ceased when he wished, and time and the surroundings made them more reposeful. Escobar went on opening up his whole soul, from the street door to the back fence. A person's soul, as you know, is arranged like a house, not uncommonly with windows on all sides, with much light and pure air. There are also ones that are close and dark, without windows, or with few, and these with bars on them after the manner of convents and prisons. Others are like chapels and bazaars, simple sheds or sumptuous palaces.

I do not know what mine was. I was not yet *casmurro* nor *dom casmurro*. It was fear that barricaded my frankness, but as the doors did not have keys nor locks it was only necessary to push them, and Escobar pushed and came in. I found him here inside, here he remained until . . .

57. By way of preparation

AH! Not only the seminarists rose out of those old leaves of
the *Panegyric*. The book also brought me vanished sensations,
so many and so varied I cannot tell them all without stealing
space from the rest of the story. One of them, one of the first,
I would like to set down in Latin—not that the subject cannot
be expressed with propriety in our language, which is chaste
for the chaste, as it may be lewd for the lewd. Yes, *most chaste*
lady, as my late-lamented José Dias would say, you may read
the chapter clear to the end without alarm or fear of offense.

   I will save the story for another chapter. No matter how
modest and discreet it proves in the telling, still there is something less austere about it, demanding a few lines of repose
and preparation. Let this chapter serve as preparation—and
preparation is important, dear reader. For when the heart
examines the possibility of what is to come—the proportion
of the events and their abundance—it will be stout and ready,
and the evil will be lessened. If it is not lessened by this, then
it never will be. And now you will see a trick or two of mine,
for in reading what you are about to read, it is probable you
will find it less raw than you had anticipated.

58. The treaty

ONE MONDAY, as I was returning to the seminary, I saw
a lady fall in the street. My first gesture should have been
one of pity or laughter. It was neither for (and this is what

I would like to have told in Latin), the lady had on very clean hose and did not soil them, and she was wearing silk garters and did not lose them. Several persons ran to assist her but they were not in time to help her up. She jumped to her feet greatly vexed, dusted her skirts, thanked them, and turned down the next street.

"This craze for imitating the French girls of the Rua do Ouvidor," said José Dias as he walked along and commented on the accident, "is palpably silly. Our young ladies should walk as they have always walked, in their gentle, leisurely way, and not with this frenchified ticki-ticki. . . ."

I scarcely heard him. The lady's hose and garters gleamed white and spiraled before me, walked and fell, got up and marched off. When we reached the corner, I looked down the side street and in the distance saw our unfortunate lady going along at the same pace, ticki-ticki, ticki-ticki . . .

"Apparently she didn't hurt herself," I said.

"So much the better for her, but she must have scraped her knees. This racing about is an affectation."

I believe it was "affectation" that he said. I was still with the "scraped knees." From there on, clear to the seminary, I did not see a woman on the street but what I wished her a fall. Some, I surmised, had on smooth-fitting hose and snug garters. . . . There may even have been some who did not have on stockings at all. But I saw them with them on . . . Or . . . That too is possible.

I am unraveling this with ellipses so as to give a notion of my ideas, which were thus diffuse and confused. But I am probably not giving any idea at all. My head was hot and my step unsteady. The first hour at the seminary was unbearable. The cassocks had the air of skirts and reminded me of the lady's fall. It was no longer one that I saw fall. All that

I had met on the street now showed me, at a glance, their
blue garters. Yes, they were blue. At night I dreamt of them.
A multitude of abominable creatures walked about me ticki-
ticki . . . They were fair, some slender, others stout, all
agile as the devil. I awoke, I sought to rout them with con-
jurations and other methods, but no sooner did I go back
to sleep than they returned, and taking hands they wheeled
about me in a vast circle of skirts or mounting the air they
rained down feet and legs upon my head. This went on till
dawn. I slept no more. I recited paternosters, Ave Marias and
credos. And since this book is the absolute truth, I am forced
to confess I had to interrupt more than one prayer to go off
in the darkness after a shadowy figure, ticki-ticki, ticki-ticki
. . . then quickly took up the prayer again, right in the middle, to knit it well, as if there had been no interruption; but
I am sure that the new phrase did not take up where the old
one left off.

When the evil returned later in the morning, I tried to
conquer it, but in a way that would not wholly destroy it.
Ye who are learned in the Scriptures may divine what it was.
Even so. Since I could not cast out these pictures from me,
I resorted to a treaty between my conscience and my imagination. These female visions would henceforth be looked upon
as simple incarnations of the vices, and as such to be contem-
plated—as the best method of tempering the character and
strengthening it for the rude combats of life. I did not formu-
late this in words, nor was it necessary. The pact was made
tacitly, with some repugnance, but it was made. And for
several days it was I who summoned the visions, to fortify
myself, and I did not cast them from me except when they
themselves grew weary and went away.

59. Guests with good memories

THERE ARE remembrances that do not rest until the pen or the tongue publishes them. One of the ancients has said he loathed a guest with a good memory. Life is filled with such guests, and I perhaps am one of them, though proof of having a weak memory be the very fact that the name of that ancient does not occur to me at the moment, but he was one of the ancients and that's enough.

No, no, my memory is not good. On the contrary, it is comparable to a man who has lived in boarding-houses without retaining either faces or names, but only scattered details. If a man passes his life in the same family house with its eternal furnishings and customs, persons and affections, everything is chiseled into him by continuity and repetition. How I envy those who have not forgotten the color of their first trousers! *I* am not sure of the color of those I put on yesterday. I can only swear they were not yellow, because I detest that color —but even this may be forgetfulness and confusion. And rather forgetfulness than confusion! I will explain myself. There is no way of emending a confused book, but everything may be supplied in the case of books with omissions. For my part, when I read one of the latter type I am not bothered a bit. What I do, on arriving at the end, is to shut my eyes and evoke all the things which I did not find in it. How many fine ideas come to me then! What profound reflections! The rivers, mountains, churches, which I did not find on the written page, all now appear to me with their waters, their trees, their altars; and the generals draw swords that never

left their scabbards, and the clarion releases notes that slept
in the metal, and everything marches with sudden soul.

The fact is, everything is to be found outside a book that
has gaps, gentle reader. This is the way I fill in other men's
lacunae; in the same way you may fill in mine.

60. Beloved opusculum

THIS IS what I did for the *Panegyric of Saint Monica*, and I
did more: I put into it not only what it lacked of the saint,
but also things which had nothing to do with her. You have
seen the sonnet, the hose, the garters, the seminarist Escobar
and various others. You will now see the rest of what came
out of the yellowed pages of the opusculum that day.

Beloved opusculum, you were worth nothing, but how
much more is an old pair of slippers worth? And yet there is
often in a pair of slippers a kind of aroma and as it were
warmth of two feet. Broken and worn, they still remind us
that someone put them on in the morning getting out of
bed, or took them off at night getting into it. And if the comparison does not fit since slippers are really part of a person
and have felt the contact of his feet, there are other remembrances, such as the stone from a street, the door of a
house, a special whistle, a pedlar's cry, for instance that of
the *cocadas* which I mentioned in Chapter 18. When I told
about the *cocadas* song, I was so torn with longing that I had it
transposed by a friend who is a music teacher and glued it to
the end of the chapter. If I cut it out later, it was because another musician to whom I showed it confessed that, frankly,
he found nothing in the passage to awaken any longings. That

the same thing may not happen with other professionals who
chance to read me, it is better to spare the publisher of the
book the trouble and expense of the engraving. You see that I
have not appended anything, nor will I. I am convinced that
it is not enough that street-cries, like seminary opusculums,
hold within them incidents, persons and sensations: it is necessary to have known them and suffered them at the time—
without that all is mute and colorless.

But let us get on to the rest of what came forth from the
yellowed pages.

61. The Homeric heifer

THE REST was a great deal. I saw the first days of separation
come forth, hard, somber days, notwithstanding the words of
comfort I received from the padres and the seminarists, and
those of my mother and Uncle Cosme as brought to the seminary by José Dias.

"Everybody longs for you," he told me, "but the greatest
longing is naturally in the greatest heart. And which is that?"
he asked, giving away the answer with his eyes.

"Mamma."

José Dias grasped my hands with emotion and launched
into a portrait of my mother's sadness, how she spoke of me
every day, almost every hour. As he always agreed with her
and added some word or other relative to the talents God
had given me, my mother's dejection of spirit on these occasions was indescribable. And he told me all this, bubbling
over with a tearful admiration. Uncle Cosme had also grown
very tender.

"Just yesterday there was an interesting case. When I happened to tell Her Excellency that God had given her not a son but an angel from heaven, the doctor was so moved he could not hold back his tears except by making one of those mocking eulogies of me as only he knows how. Needless to say, Dona Gloria wiped away a furtive tear. Or she wouldn't be a mother! What a heart full of love! *Most* full!"

"But, Senhor José Dias, what of my getting out of here?"

"I am taking care of that. The trip to Europe is what is called for, but it can be made a year or two from now, in 1859 or 1860. . . ."

"Not till then!"

"It would be better to make it this year, but let us bide our time. Have patience, go on studying, nothing is lost in picking up some learning here; and, besides, even though you don't become a padre, the training of the seminary is useful, it is not a bad thing to go forth into the world, anointed with the holy oils of theology. . . ."

At this point—I remember it as if it were yesterday—José Dias' eyes flashed with such intensity I was filled with wonder. Then the lids closed over them and remained so for several instants, until they were raised once more and his eyes fastened on the patio wall as if drunk with something, if it was not with themselves. Finally they detached themselves from the wall and began to wander over the whole patio. I might compare him to the heifer in Homer: he encircled and moaned softly over the calf he had just borne. I did not ask him what had got into him. I held back, first from shyness and then because of two professors, one of theology, who were walking in our direction. As they were about to pass us, the dependent, who knew them, spoke to them with the deference that was their due, and asked about my progress.

"It is too early to make any promises," said one of them, "but it looks as if he will come through all right."

"That is what I was just telling him," José Dias put in quickly. "I am counting on hearing his first Mass. But even if he does not take holy orders, he couldn't have better instruction than that which he is getting here. And he will go forth on the voyage of life," he concluded, lingering on the words, "anointed with the holy oils of theology. . . ."

This time the flashing in his eyes was less and the lids did not fall nor the pupils go through the motions they had before. On the contrary, he was all attention and interrogation. At most, a bright and friendly smile fluttered about his lips. The professor of theology found the metaphor to his liking and told him so. José Dias thanked him, and explained they were ideas that slipped out in the course of conversation. He was not a writer or an orator.

I was the one who did not find it at all to my liking. And as soon as the professors had gone away, I shook my head:

"I don't want to hear anything about the holy oils of theology. I want to get out of here as soon as possible, or right away. . . ."

"Right away, my angel, is impossible; but it may be much sooner than we imagine. Who knows? Perhaps this very year of 58. I have a plan ready and am already thinking over the words to use in laying it before Dona Gloria. I am sure she will give in and go with us."

"I doubt if Mamma will go abroad."

"We shall see. A mother is capable of anything; but, with her or without her, I consider our departure a certainty, and I will spare no effort; just wait. Patience is all that is required. And don't do anything here that will give rise to criticism or complaint—great docility and every appearance of satisfac-

tion! Didn't you hear the professor's words of praise? You
have conducted yourself well. Well then, continue to do so."

"But 1859 or 1860 is very far off."

"It will be this year," replied José Dias.

"Three months from now?"

"Or six."

"No, three."

"All right, three. I have a new plan, which seems better to
me than any other. It is to combine the absence of the ecclesiastical call with the necessity for a change of air. Why
don't you cough?"

"Why don't I cough?"

"Oh, not right away. I will warn you to cough when there
is need of it, beginning gradually, a little dry cough and some
loss of appetite. I will be preparing Her Excellency. . . .
Oh, all this is for her own good. Seeing that her son cannot
serve the Church as it ought to be served, the best way of
accomplishing God's will is to dedicate him to something else.
The world is also a church for the good in heart. . . ."

Once more he seemed to me like the Homeric heifer: as if
his "the world is also a church for the good in heart" were
another bull calf, brother of the "holy oils of theology." But I
allowed him no time to express his maternal tenderness, and
cut in with, "Ah! I understand! let her see I'm not well in
order to get abroad, isn't that it?"

José Dias hesitated a little, then explained himself: "Let
her see the truth, because, frankly, Bentinho, I sometimes
have doubts about your chest. You're not strong in the chest.
As a little boy you had fevers and a hoarseness. . . . It all
went away, but there are days when your color isn't good. I
don't say you are ill now, but illness might come suddenly.
The house can collapse all at once. And so if that sainted lady

is unwilling to go with us—or to get her to go more quickly, I think that a good cough . . . If the cough is to come anyway, it is better to hasten it . . . Well . . . Leave it to me, I'll give you the word. . . ."

"All right, but I don't go climbing aboard ship as soon as I get out of here. First I get out, then we'll think about sailing. It's the trip that can wait till next year. Don't they say the best time to go is April or May? Well then let it be May. First I leave the seminary, in two months from now . . ."

And because the word was sticking in my throat, I turned quickly and asked point blank, "And Capitú—how is she?"

62. A touch of Iago

THE QUESTION was imprudent at a time when I was trying to postpone the sailing date. It was the same as admitting that the principal or sole reason for my aversion to the seminary was Capitú, and would make him think the voyage improbable. I realized this as soon as I had spoken. I wanted to correct myself but I did not know how nor did he give me time.

"She's gay and happy as ever. What a giddy creature! Just waiting to hook some young buck of the neighborhood and marry him. . . ."

I am sure I turned pale. At least I felt a chill run through my whole body. The news that she was gay and happy while I wept every night produced that effect, and it was accompanied by such a violent beating of my heart that even now I seem to hear it. There is some exaggeration in this, but human discourse is like that, compounded of exceeding great and exceeding small which compensate and offset each other.

On the other hand if we understand that the hearing in this case was not that of the ears but of the memory, we will arrive at the exact truth. My memory still hears the pounding of my heart at that instant. Do not forget it was the emotion of first love. I was just about to ask José Dias to explain Capitú's gayety, what she did, if she was always laughing, singing or jumping, but I checked myself in time, and then another idea . . .

Other idea, no, a cruel and unknown feeling, pure jealousy, reader of my heart. That is what gnawed into me as I repeated over to myself José Dias' words: "Some young buck of the neighborhood." Truly this was a disaster I had never considered. I lived so much in her, of her and for her that the intervention of a young buck was, as it were, a notion without reality. It had never occurred to me that there were young bucks in the neighborhood, various ages and types, great promenaders of an afternoon. Now I remembered that some of them used to stare at Capitú—and I had felt myself so lord of her that it was as if they had stared at me, a simple tribute of admiration and envy. Separated one from the other by space and destiny, the evil now appeared to me not only possible, but certain. And Capitú's gayety confirmed the suspicion. If she was gay, it meant she was already in love with another, following him with her eyes as he passed along the street, speaking to him at the window at nightfall, exchanging flowers and . . .

And . . . what else? You know what else they would exchange. If you can't figure it out for yourself there is no use in your reading the rest of the chapter, nor the rest of the book; you will be unable to figure out anything, even though I give you the etymology of each word. But if you have figured it out you will understand that after trembling, I had

an impulse to dash headlong through the great gate, race
down the steps, run, get to Padua's house, seize Capitú and
command her, force her to confess how many, how many, how
many he had given her—this young buck from the neighborhood. I did nothing. The same dreams which I am now telling
did not have, during those three or four minutes, this logic
of movement and thought. They were disconnected and
patched, badly patched, like a botched and crooked design,
a confusion, a whirlwind which blinded me and made me
deaf. When I came to myself José Dias was concluding a sentence of which I had not heard the beginning, and even the
end was vague: "the account that she gives of herself." What
account and who? I supposed naturally he was still talking
about Capitú, and wanted to ask him, but the wish died at
birth like so many other generations of them. I limited myself to asking the dependent when I would go home and see
my mother.

"I have a longing to see Mamma. May I go this week?"

"You will go Saturday."

"Saturday? Oh, yes, yes! Ask Mamma to send for me Saturday! Saturday! This Saturday, won't you? Have her send for
me without fail."

63. Halves of a dream

I was anxious for Saturday to come. Till then I was perse-
cuted by dreams, even when awake. I shall not tell them here,
in order to avoid prolonging this part of the book. I'll set
down only one, and in the least possible number of words, or
rather, it will be two because one grew out of the other—if

indeed they do not form two halves of a single dream. All this is obscure, lady my reader, but the fault is with your sex, which thus perturbed the adolescence of a poor seminarist. If it were not for it, this book would perhaps be a simple parish sermon if I had become a padre, or a pastoral if I had become a bishop, or an encyclical if Pope, as Uncle Cosme had charged me: "Get along, lad, and come back to me a Pope!" Ah! why did I not accomplish that wish? After Napoleon, lieutenant and emperor, all destinies are possible in this century.

As for the dream, it was this. As I was busy spying on the young bucks of the neighborhood, I saw one of them conversing with my love below her window. I ran to the place; he ran away. I went up to Capitú, but she was not alone; her father was beside her, wiping his eyes and staring at a sorry lottery ticket. Since this was not at all clear to me, I was about to ask for an explanation when he gave it to me of his own accord: the young buck had just brought him a list of the prize-winning numbers, and the ticket had come out a blank. He had the number 4004. He told me that this symmetry of figures was mysterious and beautiful, and probably the wheel had broken down; it was impossible that it should not have won the grand prize. While he was speaking, Capitú, with her eyes, was giving me all the prizes, great and small. The greatest of these ought to be given with the mouth. And here enters the second part of the dream. Padua disappeared, along with his hopes for the lottery ticket. Capitú leaned out the window, I glanced up and down the street, it was deserted. I took her hands, mumbled something or other, and woke up alone in the dormitory.

The interest of what you have just read is not in the matter of the dream, but in the efforts which I made to go back to sleep and get hold of the dream again. Never in this world can you imagine the energy and persistence I expended in closing my eyes and keeping them tight shut, in putting everything out of my mind in order to fall asleep. But I did not fall asleep. This very work made me lose my sleep until dawn. Toward dawn I succeeded in coaxing it to me, but then neither young bucks, nor lottery tickets, nor grand prizes or little prizes—nothing at all came to bother me. I dreamed no more that night and I recited my lessons badly the next day.

64. An idea and a scruple

AS I reread the last chapter, there came to me an idea and a scruple. The scruple is just this, whether to put the idea on paper, for there is nothing more banal on earth, though it be the banality of the sun and the moon which the heavens give us every day and every month. I turned away from the manuscript and looked at the walls. You know that this house in Engenho Novo, in its dimensions, arrangement and decoration, is the reproduction of my old Matacavallos house. And, as I told you in Chapter 2, my purpose in recreating the other house was to link together the two ends of my life, which, by the way, I have not accomplished. Well, the same thing happened to that dream at the seminary, no matter how much I tried to sleep and did sleep. From this I conclude that one of the offices of man is to close his eyes and hold them tight shut to see if the dream that was interrupted when the night was young will continue through the dead hours. This is the banal and novel idea I hesitated to write here, and it is only provisionally that I do it now.

Before concluding this chapter, I went to the window to ask of Night the reason why dreams must be so tenuous that they break and shred at the slightest opening of the eyes or turning of the body, and do not endure. Night did not answer me straightway. She was deliciously beautiful; low hills were pale with moonlight and the space died into silence. As I insisted, she made known to me that dreams were no longer under her jurisdiction. When they dwelt on the island that Lucian had given them, where she had her palace, and from whence she sent them forth with their faces of divers aspect, she might have given me possible explanations. The times had changed everything. The ancient dreams had been pensioned off, and the modern ones dwelt in a person's brain. And these, though they tried to imitate the former, could not do it: the isle of dreams, like the isle of love, and all the islands of all the seas, are now the object of the ambition and rivalry of Europe and the United States.

It was an allusion to the Philippines. Since I don't like politics, and still less international politics, I shut the window and returned to finish this chapter before going to bed. I no longer ask for Lucian's dreams, nor for the others, children of the memory and the digestion. I'm satisfied with a quiet, peaceful sleep. In the morning, when it is cool, I will go on with the rest of my story and its characters.

65. The deceit

SATURDAY ARRIVED, other Saturdays arrived, and I began to grow fond of the new life, alternating home and the seminary. The padres liked me, the boys too, Escobar more than the

other boys or the padres. At the end of five weeks I was ready
to tell him my troubles and hopes. Capitú held me back.

"Escobar is my very good friend, Capitú!"

"But he's not my friend."

"He may come to be; he has already told me that he wants
to come over and meet Mamma."

"It doesn't matter, you have no right to tell a secret that is
not only yours but mine too, and I do not give you permission to say anything to anyone."

She was right. I kept still and obeyed. Another instance in
which I obeyed her instructions was on the first Saturday,
when I went to her house. After a few minutes of conversation she advised me to go: "Don't stay here any longer today.
Go home, and I'll come over later. It's natural that Dona
Gloria should want to be with you most of the time, or the
whole time if possible."

In all this, my little friend gave proof of such lucidity that
I could well dispense with citing a third example, but what
are examples for except to be cited, and this one is so good
its omission would be a crime. It was on my third or fourth
return home. My mother—when I had answered the thousand
questions she asked about the way they treated me, my
studies, friendships, training, and if anything hurt me anywhere, and if I slept well, all the things that mother love
invents to weary the patience of a son—concluded by turning
to José Dias:

"Senhor José Dias, do you still doubt that a good padre will
come out of this boy?"

"Your Excellency . . ."

"And you, Capitú," interrupted my mother turning to
Padua's daughter, who happened to be in the room with her,
"Don't you think that our Bentinho will make a good padre?"

"I *do,* senhora," replied Capitú with conviction.

I did not like the conviction. I told her so the next morning, in her garden, as I recalled her words of the evening before. And I threw up to her, for the first time, the gayety she had displayed ever since my entering the seminary, while I ate my heart out with longing. Capitú became serious and asked me how I would have her act, seeing they already suspected us. She too had passed unhappy nights, and her days, in her own house, were as sad as mine; I could ask her father and mother. Her mother had even told her, in veiled language, that she should not think of me anymore.

"With Dona Gloria and Dona Justina, naturally, I act gay and happy so that José Dias' information may not seem true. If it should seem true, they would try to separate us even more, and perhaps would end by not receiving me. . . . For my part, it is enough that we have sworn to marry each other."

It was true: we had to dissemble in order to kill all suspicion, and at the same time, enjoy our former liberty, and calmly build our future. But the example is completed by what I heard the next day at breakfast. When Uncle Cosme remarked that he still wanted to see what kind of figure I would cut blessing the people at Mass, my mother told how a few days before when they were talking of girls marrying young, Capitú had said to her, "Well, as for me, the person who must marry *me* is Padre Bentinho. I'm waiting until he is ordained!"

Uncle Cosme laughed at the story. José Dias did not refuse a smile. Only Cousin Justina wrinkled her forehead and eyed me interrogatively. I, who had looked around at all of them, could not brave my cousin's look and busied myself with eating. But I ate little. I was so happy over Capitú's masterpiece of deceit I could think of nothing else. As soon as I finished breakfast I ran over and reported the conversation to her, and praised her astuteness. Capitú smiled gratefully.

"You are right, Capitú," I concluded, "we will fool the whole bunch of them."

"Won't we just?" she replied ingenuously.

66. Intimacy

CAPITÚ WAS making her way into my mother's heart. They were together most of the time, talking about me apropos of the sun and the rain or nothing. Capitú used to go there and sew in the mornings; sometimes she stayed for dinner.

Cousin Justina did not go along with her relative in these courtesies, but she did not treat my darling as badly as she might have. She was sincere enough to say the bad things she thought of a person, and she did not think well of anyone— perhaps of her husband, but her husband was dead. In any case, the man did not exist who could compete with him in affection, in industry and uprightness, in manners and in keenness of mind. This opinion, according to Uncle Cosme, was posthumous, for in life they had always been at each other's throats, and the last six months had lived apart. All the more honor to her sense of justice; praise of the dead is one way of praying for them. She was fond of my mother too, or if she thought anything bad about her, it was between herself and her pillow. It is understandable that she should outwardly pay her the proper respect. I do not think she aspired to any sort of legacy. Persons who are so disposed go beyond the ordinary services, they make themselves more agreeable, are more assiduous, multiply their attentions, outdo the servants. All this was contrary to Cousin Justina's nature, which was made up of sourness and obstinacy. Since she lived by favor in the house, it goes without saying, she would not show disregard for its mistress, and she would keep her resentments to herself, or only speak ill of her to God and the Devil.

Suppose she did harbor resentments against my mother— that was no reason for her to detest Capitú, nor did she need supplementary reasons. Capitú's intimacy, nonetheless, made her even more odious to my relative. If she did not treat her badly at first, with time she changed her manners and ended by avoiding her. The attentive Capitú, when she did not see her, would ask after her and look for her. Cousin Justina tolerated these attentions. Life is filled with obligations that people meet however great a desire they have to shirk them. Besides, Capitú was mistress of a certain magic which enslaved; in the end Cousin Justina would have to smile, even though it was a sour smile, but alone with my mother she would find something mean to say about the girl.

When my mother fell ill of a fever that brought her to death's door, she asked to have Capitú as her nurse. Though this relieved Cousin Justina of tiresome chores, she did not pardon my little friend the intrusion. One day she asked her if she did not have something to do at home. On another day, with a laugh, she let fly this epigram: "There is no need for you to run after it, whatever is to be yours will come to you of itself."

67. A sin

I WILL not raise the sick woman from her bed without telling what happened to me. After five days, my mother awoke one morning so troubled and confused that she ordered them to fetch me home from the seminary. To no avail Uncle Cosme's "Sister Gloria, you are alarming yourself over nothing; the fever will pass. . . ."

"No! No! Send for him! I may die, and my soul will not be saved if Bentinho is not here with me."

"We will alarm him."

"Well, don't tell him anything, but get him, now, now, don't wait."

They thought it was delirium; but since it cost nothing to send for me, José Dias was entrusted with the task. He came in so bewildered he frightened me. He told the rector in private what it was and I received permission to go home. In the street, we walked along without saying anything. He did not alter his customary step—the major premise before the minor, the minor premise before the conclusion—but kept his eyes on the ground and sighed from time to time so that I was afraid to look into his face for fear of what I might read there. He had spoken of the illness as a simple affair; but the call to her bedside, the silence, the sighs, might mean something more. My heart was pounding, my legs wobbled, more than once I thought I would fall. . . .

My desire to hear the truth was complicated with the fear of knowing it. It was the first time that death had come close to me, enveloping me, peering into my face with its dim sunken eyes. The further we walked along the Rua dos Barbonos, the more terrified I was at the idea of reaching the house, going in, hearing the weeping, seeing a dead body. . . . Oh, I could never describe here all I felt in those terrible minutes. The street, no matter how superlatively slow José Dias walked, seemed to vanish away beneath our feet, the houses flew past on one side and the other, and the notes of a bugle coming from the barracks of the Municipal Guard resounded in my ears like the trumpet of doom.

I went on, arrived at the Arches, turned into Rua de Matacavallos. The house was not right there, but a long way beyond the Casa dos Invalidos, near the Senate. Three or four times I had wanted to question my companion, without daring to open my mouth; but now I no longer had any such desire. I just kept walking, accepting the worst as a stroke of destiny, as a human necessity, and it was then that Hope, in order to combat Terror, whispered to my heart—not these words, for nothing was articulated in words, but an idea which could be translated by them—"With Mamma dead, that would be the end of the seminary."

Reader, it was a lightning flash; no sooner had it illumined the night than it fled away, leaving the dark more intense from the remorse that it left behind with me. It was the prompting of lust and selfishness. Filial devotion swooned for an instant at the prospect of certain liberty through the disappearance of the debt and the debtor. It was an instant, less than an instant, the hundredth part of an instant, but even so, sufficient to complicate my misery with remorse.

José Dias was sighing. Once he looked at me with such a sorrowful expression that he seemed to have guessed my thoughts, and I almost asked him not to say anything to anybody, that I would punish myself, etc. But his sorrow had so much love about it that it could not have been concern over

my sin; but then there was still the death of my mother. . . .
I felt a great anguish, a lump in my throat, I could stand it no
longer and burst into tears.

"What is it, Bentinho?"

"Mamma?"

"No, no! What an idea! Her condition is *very* serious but
it's not a fatal illness, and God is great. Wipe your eyes, it's
indecent for a boy your age to go crying down the street. It
won't amount to anything, a fever . . . Fevers hit one with
sudden force and leave in the same way . . . No, not with
your fingers, where is your handkerchief?"

I wiped my eyes, though of all José Dias' words only two
stuck in my heart: they were his VERY *serious*. I realized later
that he only meant *serious,* but habitual use of the superlative makes the mouth prolix, and for the sake of his period
José Dias multiplied my unhappiness. If you ever find a case
of the kind in this book advise me of it, reader, in order that
I may emend it in the second edition: nothing is more unseemly than to give *very* long legs to *very* brief ideas. I wiped
my eyes, I repeat, and walked on, now anxious to reach home
and ask forgiveness of my mother for the wicked thought I'd
had. Finally we got there, went in; with trembling feet I
climbed the six steps to the hall, and in a few moments I was
leaning over the bed and listening to my mother's words of
tenderness as she pressed my hands in hers and called me her
son. She was on fire, her eyes burned into mine, her whole
being seemed consumed by the volcano within her. I knelt
beside the bed, but, as it was high, I was too far from her
caresses:

"No, my son, get up, get up!"

Capitú, who was in the bedroom too, enjoyed seeing my
entrance, my gestures, words and tears, as she informed me

afterwards; but naturally she did not suspect all the reasons for my anguish.

After I had gone to my room I thought of telling my mother everything, as soon as she was well. But this idea did not get a real hold on me. It was a vague, indolent wish that I would never put into action, however much my sin pained me. Led by remorse, I once more made use of my old expedient of spiritual promises. I asked God to pardon me and save my mother's life and I would say two thousand paternosters. May the padre who reads me pardon this dodge of mine; it was the last time I made use of it. The crisis in which I found myself, no less than habit and faith, explains everything. They were two thousand more. Where were the old ones? I did not pay—neither these nor the others; but such promises, which issue from sincere, ingenuous souls, are like fiduciary money—though the debtor does not redeem them, they are worth the sum written on them.

68. Let us postpone virtue

FEW MEN would have the courage to confess that thought of mine in the Rua de Matacavallos. I shall confess everything that bears on my story. Montaigne wrote of himself: *ce ne sont pas mes gestes que j'écris; c'est mon essence.* Well, there is only one way of describing one's essence: it is to tell it all, the good and the bad. That is what I do whenever I recollect suitable bits for the construction or reconstruction of myself. For example, now that I have related a sin, I would be very happy to tell of some handsome act of mine from the same period if I remembered one; but I do not remember any. It shall be postponed till a more suitable opportunity arises.

Nor will you lose by waiting, my friend. On the contrary, it occurs to me that . . . Not only are handsome actions handsome on any occasion but they are also possible and probable—according to the theory I have of sins and virtues, which is no less simple than clear. It reduces itself to this: each person is born with a certain number of sins and virtues allied by matrimony to compensate each other in life. When one of these consorts is stronger than the other it alone guides the individual—without his being able to say however—not having practiced this virtue or committed that sin—that he is without the one or the other. But the rule is to give oneself up to the simultaneous practice of the two, with advantage to their carrier, and sometimes with great glory on earth and in heaven. It is a pity that I cannot give a basis to this with one or more cases from outside myself; but I lack time.

As far as I am concerned, it is certain I was born with several of these married couples, and naturally I still possess them. It recently happened here in Engenho Novo that one night when I had a bad headache I wished one of the trains of the Central would be blown up, far from my hearing, and the line interrupted for many hours, even though someone should die; and on the following day I missed a train of the same road because I offered my cane to a blind man who had no staff. *Voilà mes gestes, voilà mon essence.*

69. Mass

ONE OF the gestures which best expresses my essence was the devoutness with which I ran the next Sunday to hear Mass at Santo Antonio dos Pobres. The dependent wanted to go with me and began to dress, but he was so slow with his suspenders and trouser straps I could not wait for him. Besides, I wanted to be alone. I felt the necessity of avoiding any conversation that might divert my thoughts from the purpose for which I was going, and *this* was to reconcile myself with God after what had taken place in Chapter 67. It was not only to ask pardon for the sin, but also to thank Him for my mother's recovery, and—seeing that I am telling everything—to get him to forego collection on my promise. Jehovah, though divine—or for this very reason—is a Rothschild, only much more human: he does not make moratoriums, he pardons the debt in full, provided the debtor truly wishes to mend his ways and cut down his expenses. Well, I asked for nothing else; henceforth I would not make any more promises I could not pay, and those I did make I would pay as soon as I made them.

I heard Mass. At the elevation of the Host I thanked Him for the life and health of my mother. Then I begged forgiveness for the sin and cancellation of the debt, and I received the final blessing of the officiant as a solemn act of reconciliation. Afterward it occurred to me that the Church has established in the confessional the most authoritative of legal services, and in confession the most trustworthy of instruments for the adjustment of moral accounts between man and God. But my incorrigible timidity closed this sure door to me: I was afraid that I could not find words in which to tell the confessor my secret. How a man changes! Today I go so far as to publish it.

70. After Mass

I WENT on praying, I crossed myself, closed the prayer book, and walked toward the door. There were not many people, but the church was not large either, and I could only get out

slowly. There were men and women, old and young, silks
and calicos, and probably handsome eyes and ugly ones; but
I saw neither the one nor the other. I kept going in the direction of the door, with the wave, and heard the greetings and
the soft whispers. On the porch, where it was light, I looked
at them all. I saw a young girl and a man come out of the
church and stop. The girl looked at me and spoke to the man,
and the man looked at me as he listened to the girl. These
words reached my ears:

"But what is it you want?"

"I want to know about *her*. You must ask, Papa."

It was Sinhàzinha Sancha, Capitú's schoolmate, and she
wanted to know about my mother. Her father came over to
me. I told him my mother had recovered. Then we went out.
He pointed to his house, and as I was going in the same direction, we went together. Gurgel was a man of forty or a little
more, with a tendency toward a big stomach. He was very
obsequious. When we arrived at his door, he insisted that I
have breakfast with them.

"Thank you, Mamma is expecting me."

"We'll send a colored boy to say that you are staying to
breakfast and will come later."

"I will come another day."

Sinhàzinha Sancha, turned toward her father, listened and
waited. She was not bad-looking. The only resemblance to
her father was her nose, which was also thick at the end; but
there are features that take beauty from one face and give it
to another. She was simply dressed. Gurgel was a widower
and lived for his daughter. As I had refused breakfast, he
begged me to stop and rest a few minutes. I could not refuse
and went in. He wanted to know my age, my studies and my
faith, and gave me advice in case I should become a padre.

He told me the number of his store in Rua da Quitanda. Finally I said goodbye. He came to the landing of the stairs; the daughter sent her regards to Capitú and to my mother. When I looked up from the street, the father was in the window and made a grand gesture of farewell.

71. Visit from Escobar

AT THE house, they had already lied, telling my mother I had returned and was changing my clothes.

"The eight o'clock Mass must be over. . . . Bentinho ought to be back. . . . Do you think something could have happened, Brother Cosme? Send someone to see. . . ." Thus she talked on from minute to minute; but I walked in and with me tranquillity.

It was a day of pleasant surprises. Escobar came to visit me and inquire after my mother's health. He had never paid a visit before, nor were our relations then as close as they came to be later, but since he knew the reason for my leaving school three days before, he took advantage of Sunday to call on me and ask if there was still danger. When I told him that there was not, he sighed.

"I was frightened," said he.

"Do the others know?"

"Apparently; some do."

Uncle Cosme and José Dias liked the boy. The dependent told him that he had seen his father once in Rio de Janeiro. Escobar was very polite; and, although he talked more than was his habit later, even so it was not as much as boys of our age. On that day I found him a bit more expansive than

usual. Uncle Cosme invited him to dine with us. Escobar reflected an instant and then said that his father's agent was
expecting him. I remembered Gurgel's words and repeated
them:

"We'll send a colored boy to say you are dining with us
and will come later."

"So much trouble!"

"No trouble at all," interposed Uncle Cosme.

Escobar accepted and stayed for dinner. I noticed that the
quick movements which he kept under control in the classroom, he controlled now too, in the living room as well as at
table. The hour he spent with me was one of unreserved
friendship. I showed him the few books that I possessed. He
took a great fancy to the portrait of my father; after several
moments of contemplation he turned to me and said:

"It is obvious that this was a pure heart!"

Escobar's eyes, which were clear, as I have said, were also
very sweet. That is the way José Dias defined them after he
left, and I maintain the word in spite of the forty years that
have passed over it. In this case there was none of the dependent's exaggeration. Escobar's shaven face showed a fair,
smooth skin. His forehead perhaps was a trifle low (the part
in his hair came just above his left eyebrow) but it was still
high enough not to swallow up the rest of his features and
lessen their grace. Actually it was an interesting face: a fine
mouth with a salty lift to it, a curved, slender nose. He had a
trick of wriggling his right shoulder from time to time—he
lost it after one of us pointed it out to him one day at the
seminary—best example I have ever seen of a man curing
himself of a minor defect.

I could never help feeling a kind of dizzy pride when
my friends pleased everybody. My whole family took a great

liking to Escobar. Even Cousin Justina found him a very
estimable young man, in spite of . . .

"In spite of what?" asked José Dias when he saw that she
was not going to finish the phrase.

He got no answer, nor was he likely to come. Cousin
Justina probably did not find any obvious or important defect in our guest. The *in spite of* was a kind of safeguard
against some fault she might one day discover in him, either
that or it was the result of long habit which led her to make
a qualification where she found nothing to qualify.

Escobar left immediately after dinner. I took him to the
door, where we waited for the omnibus. He told me that
the agent's warehouse was in the Rua dos Pescadores, and
that it remained open until nine o'clock but that he did not
like to stay out late. We separated with great affection: inside
the omnibus, he still waved goodbye. I stayed at the door to
see if he would look back from the distance, but he did not.

"What great friend is this?" asked someone from a nearby
window.

There is no need to tell you that it was Capitú. There are
things which can be divined in life, as in books, whether they
be novels or true stories. It was Capitú, who had been peek-
ing out at us for some time from behind the Venetian blind,
and now opened the window wide and appeared. She had
seen our unabashed and affectionate goodbyes and wanted to
know who it was that meant so much to me.

"It was Escobar," said I. I went and stood beneath the
window and looked up.

72. A dramatic reform

NEITHER I, nor you, nor she, nor any other person in this story would have been able to answer more, so certain is it that destiny, like all dramatists, does not announce its sudden reversals of fortune, nor the final catastrophe. They each arrive at their appointed time, until the curtain falls, the lights go out and the spectators go home to bed. In this method there is perchance something to be desired in the way of reform, and I propose, by way of trial, that the drama begin with the end. Othello would kill himself and Desdemona in the first act; the next three acts would be given over to the slow decrescent action of jealousy; and the last would be left with the initial scenes of the threat of the Turks, the explanations of Othello and Desdemona, and the good advice of the shrewd Iago, "Put money in thy purse." In this manner, the spectator, on the one hand, would find in the theater his regular newspaper charade, for the last acts would explain the catastrophe of the first, which would be "the key" as it were; and, on the other hand, he would go to bed with a good impression of tenderness and love:

> "She lov'd me for the dangers I had pass'd,
> And I lov'd her that she did pity them."

73. The stage manager

DESTINY IS not only a dramatist, it is also its own stage manager. That is, it sets the entrances of the characters on scene, gives them letters and other objects, and produces the off-stage noises to go with the dialogue: thunder, a carriage, a shot. When I was young, they performed here, in some theater or other, a drama that ended with the Last Judgment. The principal character was Ahasuerus, who, in the last scene, concluded a monologue with this exclamation, "I hear the trumpet of the archangel!" No trumpet was heard at all. Ahasuerus, covered with shame, repeated the line, this time louder, to cue the stage manager, but still nothing. Then he walked toward the back, under a pretense of tragic gesture, but actually for the purpose of whispering into the wings, "The cornet! the cornet! the cornet!" The audience caught this word and burst into laughter, so that when the trumpet sounded in earnest and Ahasuerus shouted for the third time that it was that of the archangel, a little urchin in the pit corrected him from here below, "No, senhor, it is the archangel's cornet!"

In the same way may be explained my being under Capitú's window and the passage of a man on horseback, a *dandy,* as we used to say in those days. He sat astride a beautiful bay horse, firm in the saddle, rein in the left hand, the right at his belt, patent leather boots, elegant figure and posture; the face was not unknown to me. Others had passed by, and still others would come after; all were on their way to see their sweethearts. It was the custom of the time to make love from horseback. Reread Alencar: "Because a student (says one of his dramatic characters of 1858) cannot be without these two things, a horse and a sweetheart." Reread Alvares de Azevedo. One of his poems tells (1851) how he lived in Catumby and in order to see his sweetheart in Cattete, rented a horse for three milreis . . . Three milreis! All is swallowed up in the night of time!

Well, the *dandy* on the bay horse did not pass by like the others: he was the trumpet of doom, and sounded on time. That is the way with Destiny, which is its own stage manager. The rider was not content to pass on, but turned his head in our direction, the direction of Capitú, and looked at Capitú, and Capitú looked at him. The horse went on but the man's head continued to stare back.

This was the second fang jealousy sank into me. To tell the truth, it is natural to admire handsome figures; but that fellow used to pass by every afternoon. He lived in the old Campo da Acclamacão, and then . . . and then . . . Just try to reason with a heart of blazing coals. Not a word to Capitú! I left the street quickly, went into the hall and the next thing I knew I was in the living room.

74. The trouser strap

IN THE living room Uncle Cosme and José Dias were talking, the one seated, the other alternately walking about and stopping. At sight of José Dias I remembered what he had said in the seminary: "Just waiting to hook some young buck of the neighborhood and marry him. . . ." It was certainly an allusion to the man on horseback. This recollection aggravated the impression that I brought in from the street; but it may have been this phrase, guarded in my unconscious, that had disposed me to believe in the malice of their glances. What I wanted to do was grab José Dias by the collar, drag him into the hall, and ask him if he had spoken from actual truth or from hypothesis; but José Dias, who had stopped on seeing

me come in, went on walking back and forth and talking. I
was impatient to go to the house next door; I imagined that
Capitú had left the window in alarm and would not be slow
to appear, ask questions, and explain. . . . And those two
continued talking until Uncle Cosme rose to go and see the
sick woman, and José Dias came over to me in the recess of
the other window.

An instant before, I had had a desire to ask him what there
was between Capitú and the young bucks of the neighborhood. Now, when I imagined that he came to me for the
express purpose of informing me, I was afraid to hear. I
wanted to stop his mouth. José Dias saw something in my
face, different from its usual expression, and asked solic-
itously, "What's the matter, Bentinho?"

In order not to look at him, I let my eyes fall. As they fell, I
saw that one of the dependent's trouser straps—straps that
fastened under the shoe—was unbuttoned; and as he insisted
on learning what was wrong with me, I answered by pointing
my finger: "Look at the strap, button the strap."

José Dias bent over; I ran from the room.

75. Despair

I ESCAPED the dependent, I escaped my mother—I did not
go to her room—but I did not escape myself. I ran to my
room and entered behind myself. I talked to myself, perse-
cuted myself, threw myself on the bed, and rolled over and
over with myself. I wept, and stifled my sobs with the end
of the sheet. I swore I would not visit Capitú that afternoon,
nor ever again, and that I would become a padre straight off.

I saw myself already ordained, standing before her. She wept repentantly and begged my forgiveness, but I, cold and serene, had nothing but scorn, scorn and contempt. I turned my back on her. I called her perverse.

Twice I found myself gnashing my teeth, as if she were between them.

As I lay on the bed, I heard her voice. She had come to spend the rest of the afternoon with my mother, and probably with me, as she had other times; but no matter how much her coming moved me, it did not make me leave my room. Capitú was laughing loudly, talking loudly, as if to let me know she was there. I continued deaf, alone with myself and my scorn. And I was filled with a desire to drive my nails into her throat, bury them deep, and watch the life drain out of her with her blood. . . .

76. Explanation

SOME TIME later I felt quieted but weary and downcast. I found myself outstretched on the bed, eyes on the ceiling, and suddenly remembered that my mother had told me never to lie down after dinner, in order to avoid congestion. I started to my feet, but I did not leave my room. Capitú was laughing less now and spoke in a lower tone; probably she was hurt at my shutting myself away, but not even this moved me.

I ate no supper and slept badly. The next morning I did not feel better, I felt different. My anguish was now complicated by the fear of having gone beyond what was proper without looking into the matter. Though my head ached a

little, I pretended I felt worse, in order to stay home from
the seminary; go to and talk to Capitú. She might be angry
with me, might even no longer love me, and prefer the man
on horseback. I decided to settle everything, to hear and judge
her. Perhaps she had a defense and an explanation.

She had both. When she learned my reason for shutting
myself away the day before, she told me I had done her a
great injustice. She could not believe that after our exchange
of oaths, I could judge her to be so fickle, that I could believe . . . And here she burst into tears, and made a gesture
of separation; but I was at her side immediately. I seized her
hands and kissed them with so much soul and fervor that
I felt them tremble. She wiped her eyes with her fingers;
I kissed them again, for themselves and for the tears. Then
she sighed, and shook her head. She confessed to me that she
did not know the young man—no more than others who
passed by in the afternoons, on horseback or on foot. If she
had looked at him, that in itself was proof there was nothing
between them; if there had been, it would be natural to dissemble.

"And what could there be since he is about to be married?" she concluded.

"Married?"

He was about to be married; she told me to whom—a girl
in Rua dos Barbonos. This reason pleased me more than any
of the others, and she perceived it in my gesture. Even so, it
did not keep her from saying that to avoid further misunder-
standing, she would not look out of the window any more.

"No! No! No! I don't ask that of you!"

She consented to withdraw the promise, but made another;
it was that at the first suspicion on my part all would be

dissolved between us. I accepted the threat, and swore she would never have to carry it out; it was my first suspicion and my last.

77. Pleasure in old sufferings

IN TELLING of that crisis in my adolescent love, I feel something I do not know how to explain: Somehow the sufferings of that period have become so spiritualized with time that they have melted into pleasure. This is not clear—but not everything is clear in life or in books. The truth is I feel a particular pleasure in retelling this ordeal, while it is certain that it reminds me of others which I would not be reminded of for anything.

78. Secret for secret

EVEN AT the time I felt a certain necessity to tell someone what was going on between Capitú and me. I did not tell the whole story, but only part, and it was Escobar who received my confidence.

When I returned to the seminary on Wednesday, I found him anxious: he said he had made up his mind to go and see me if I stayed away another day. He asked with concern what I had had and if I was entirely well.

"I am."

As I answered, his eyes bored into mine. Three days later he told me that people were beginning to notice my absent-mindedness, and that it was best to conceal it as much as possible. He, for his part, had reasons to be absent-minded also, but he tried to be attentive.

"Then it is apparent? . . ."

"Yes, at times you don't seem to hear anything, with your thoughts way off somewhere. Pretend, Santiago."

"I have reasons . . ."

"I believe you; no one's mind wanders for nothing."

"Escobar . . ." I hesitated; he waited.

"What?"

"Escobar, you are my friend; I am your friend too. Here, in the seminary, you are the person who has made his way into my heart; and outside, except for the members of my family, I do not, properly speaking, have a friend."

"If I say the same thing," he retorted with a smile, "it will lose its charm; it will appear that I am repeating you. But the truth is, you are my only close friend here. And I believe it is noticed, but that makes no difference to me."

I was greatly moved, and I felt my voice rushing from my throat, "Escobar, can you keep a secret?"

"You ask? Then you must have doubts, and in that case . . ."

"Forgive me, it was a manner of speaking. I know that you are a serious fellow, and I consider it the same as confessing to a padre."

"If you need absolution, you are absolved."

"Escobar, I cannot be a padre. I am here, my people believe and expect me to be one; but I cannot be a padre."

"Nor I, Santiago."

"You also?"

"Secret for secret. I don't intend to finish the course either. My love is commerce, but don't say anything—absolutely

nothing, it is just between us. And it isn't that I'm not religious. I *am* religious, but commerce is my passion."

"Only that?"

"What else should there be?"

I walked about for a moment and then whispered the first
words of my confidence—so faint, so indistinct I did not hear
them myself. I know, however, that I said "a person . . ."
with reticence. A person? . . . Nothing more was needed for
him to understand. A person must be a girl. And do not
imagine he was amazed to discover that I was in love. He
found it quite natural, and once more his eyes bored into
mine. Then I told him as much as I could without going into
details, but so drawing it out as to have the pleasure of mull-
ing over my subject matter. Escobar listened with interest. At
the end of our conversation he assured me that it was a secret
buried in a cemetery. He advised me not to become a padre.
I could not bring into the Church a heart belonging to earth
rather than to heaven. I would make a bad padre, would not
even be a padre at all. On the other hand, God protected the
sincere. Since I could serve Him only in the world, it be-
hooved me to remain there.

You cannot conceive the pleasure it gave me to confide this
to him. For me it was just one more bit of felicity. That
youthful heart, listening to me, sympathizing with me, gave
to this world an extraordinary aspect. It was a great beautiful
world, life an excellent enterprise, and I nothing more nor
less than heaven's darling: those were my feelings. Note that
I did not tell him all, nor even the best part. I did not relate
the chapter on combing the braids, for example, nor others
of the sort; but what I told was a great deal.

That we returned to the subject, is needless to say. We
returned time and again. I praised Capitú's moral qualities

as matter suitable for the admiration of a seminarist: her sweet simplicity, her modesty, industry, and religious habits. I did not touch on the physical graces, nor did he ask about them; I barely hinted at the advantage of knowing her personally.

"Right now it is not possible," I told him, the first Monday after returning from home, "Capitú is going to spend a few days with a friend in Rua dos Invalidos. When she gets back you will go home with me; but you can come before that, you may come anytime. Why didn't you have dinner with me yesterday?"

"You didn't invite me."

"Do you have to be invited? They have all taken a great liking to you at my house."

"And I have taken a great liking to all of them; but if I may express a preference, I must confess that your mother is an angel."

"Isn't she though?" I replied eagerly.

79. Let us proceed to the chapter

YES, I enjoyed hearing him say it. You know what I thought of my mother. Even now, as I interrupt this sentence to gaze at her portrait on the wall, I find that quality imprinted on her face. And in no other way can one explain Escobar's opinion, for he had exchanged scarcely four words with her. A single word was enough to penetrate her inmost essence. Yes, yes, my mother was angelic. Even though she was then forcing me into a career I did not want, I could not help feeling that she was angelic, a saint.

And was it certain she was forcing me into an ecclesiastical career? Here I come to a point I had hoped to bring up later —I was even considering where to place the chapter. Actually, I ought not tell now what I suppose I did not discover until much later; but since I have touched on the point, it is best to have done with it. It is a weighty and complex point, delicate and subtle, in which the author must heed his child, and the child listen to the author, so that both may speak the truth—nothing but the truth, yet the whole truth. It is also suitable to note here that the point in question is just what makes the saint more saintly, without prejudice (quite the contrary!) to her human and terrestrial part. Enough of preface to the chapter. Let us proceed to the chapter.

80. Let us enter the chapter

LET US enter the chapter. My mother was God-fearing. You know of this, and of her religious practices, and the pure faith inspiring them. And you are not unaware that my ecclesiastical career was the object of a promise she made when I was conceived. Everything has been told in its proper place. You also know that, intending to tighten the moral bond of the obligation, she confided her projects and motives to her relatives and family friends. The promise, made with fervor, and accepted with mercy, was joyfully kept by her in the inmost depths of her heart. I think that I learned the taste of her felicity in the milk with which she gave me suck. My father, if he had lived, would possibly have altered her plans. As his calling was politics, he probably would have started me on that road, although the two careers have not been, and

still are not, incompatible—more than one padre has entered
party strife and the government of men. But my father died
without knowing anything about it, and she was left with the
contract, as sole debtor.

One of the aphorisms of Franklin states that for him who
must pay at Easter, Lent is short. Our Lent was no longer than
the others, and my mother, while she had me taught Latin
and Religion, began to defer the day of my entering the
seminary. It is what is called, commercially speaking, "extending a note." The Creditor was a multimillionaire; He
was not dependent upon payment in order to eat, and consented to postponements without even increasing the rate of
interest. One day, however, one of the friends who had en-
dorsed the note spoke of the necessity of paying the promised
sum: it is in one of the first chapters. My mother agreed and
I withdrew into São José.

Now, in that same chapter, she shed some tears which she
wiped away without explanation, and which none of those
present, neither Uncle Cosme, nor Cousin Justina, nor the
dependent José Dias, understood at all. I, who was behind
the door, understood no more than they. On re-examination
(despite the years), the tears seem to have indicated an anticipatory feeling of loneliness, the pain of separation—and it may
be too (now we come to the point), she repented her promise.
Catholic and devout, she knew very well that promises are to
be kept; the question was "is it right and proper to make all
of them?" and naturally she inclined to the negative. Why
would God punish her by denying her a second son? The Divine might have willed my being without any necessity of
dedicating it to Him *ab ovo*. It was a tardy bit of reasoning; it
should have been made the day I was conceived. In any case
it was a first conclusion, but not sufficiently conclusive to

make her break her promise: everything remained as it was, and I left for the seminary.

A nodding on the part of Faith would have resolved the question in my favor, but Faith kept vigil with great, ingenuous eyes. My mother would have made, if she could, an exchange of promises, giving part of her own years to keep me with her, outside the clergy, married and father of a family. That is what I presume, just as I suppose that she rejected the idea because it seemed dishonest to her. So I always found her in the course of everyday life.

However, my absence was soon tempered by the attentions of Capitú, who had begun to make herself indispensable. Little by little my mother was persuaded that this girl would make me happy. Then, finally hope that our love, rendering me absolutely intolerant of the seminary, would make me refuse to stay there either for God or the Devil: this intimate and secret hope began to invade my mother's heart. In this case, I would break the contract; she would receive no blame. She would keep me, without any act, strictly speaking, of her own. It was like entrusting the full amount of a debt to someone for delivery to the creditor, and then having the bearer keep the money for himself and deliver nothing. In ordinary life, the act of a third person does not release the contracting party from his obligation; but the advantage of making a contract with heaven is that intention has the same value as money.

You must have had similar conflicts yourself, and if you are religious, must have sought at times to reconcile heaven and earth in identically the same way, or something like it. In the end, heaven and earth are reconciled: they are almost twins—heaven having been made on the second day and earth on the third. Like Abraham, my mother took her son

to the mountain of the Vision; what is more, she brought the
wood for the burnt offering, the fire and the knife. And she
bound Isaac and placed him upon the bundle of wood, took
the knife and raised it high. Just as she was about to strike,
she heard the voice of the angel proclaim in the name of the
Lord: "Lay not thy hand upon thy son, neither do thou anything to him, for now I know that thou fearest God." This
must have been the secret hope of my mother.

Capitú was naturally the angel of the Scriptures. The truth
is that my mother could no longer bear to have her out of
sight. The increasing affection was manifested in extraordinary ways. Capitú came to be the flower of the house,
the sun of its mornings, the cool of its evenings, the moon
of its nights: there she lived hours and hours, listening, talking and singing. My mother sounded her heart, read her eyes,
and my name was between the two women like the watch-
word of the life to come.

81. Something my mother said

NOW THAT I have related what I afterward discovered, I
can tell here something my mother said. Now you will understand her saying on that Saturday when I arrived home and
learned that Capitú was in Rua dos Invalidos with Sinhàzinha
Gurgel:

"Why don't you go and see her? Didn't you tell me that
Sancha's father offered you his house?"

"He did."

"Well then? That is, if you like. Capitú was to have come
back today to finish a piece of work with me; her friend must
have asked her to stay overnight."

"Perhaps they have been flirting with some young men," insinuated Cousin Justina.

I did not kill her because I did not have handy either steel or rope, pistol or dagger; but the eyes I turned on her, if they could have killed, would have done the work of all. One of the mistakes of Providence was to leave man only his arms and teeth as weapons of attack, and his legs as weapons of flight or defense. The eyes might have answered the former purpose. One glance would halt or fell an enemy or rival, would execute prompt vengeance, and in addition, to throw justice off the track these same murderous eyes would be pitiful eyes, and weep for the victim. Cousin Justina escaped mine; I was the one who did not escape the effect of her insinuation. On Sunday, at eleven o'clock, I ran to the Rua dos Invalidos.

Sancha's father received me, unkempt and sad. His daughter was ill: the day before, she had come down with a fever, which had been getting worse. Since he was very fond of his daughter, he thought he saw her already dead and announced to me that he would kill himself also. Here is a chapter funereal as a cemetery—deaths, suicides and assassinations. I longed for a ray of sunshine and blue sky. It was Capitú who brought them to the door of the room by coming to tell Sancha's father that his daughter had asked for him.

"Is she worse?" asked Gurgel in alarm.

"No, senhor, but she wants to speak to you."

"Wait here a moment," he said to her, and turning to me, "She is Sancha's nurse—she'll have no other. I'll be right back."

Capitú showed signs of fatigue and worry, but as soon as she saw me she changed completely into her old charming self, fresh and gay, and not a little amazed. She could hardly believe it was I. She talked to me, made me talk to her, and in fact we conversed for several minutes, but so low and muffled that not even the walls heard, and they have ears. Moreover, if they heard anything, they understood nothing, neither they nor the pieces of furniture, which were as sad as their master.

82. The settee

OF THESE, only the settee appeared to have understood our spiritual situation, for it offered us the services of its cane bottom with such insistence that we accepted and sat down. The rather special opinion I hold of the settee dates from this time: intimacy and decorum are united in it, and it defines a whole house without one's ever leaving the front room. Two men seated on it can debate the destiny of an empire, and two women the style of a dress; but a man and a woman —only by an aberration of natural law will they talk of anything but themselves. That is what we did, Capitú and I. I vaguely remember that I asked her if she would stay there long. . . .

"I don't know. The fever seems to be disappearing but . . ."

And I also remember, vaguely, that I explained my visit to Rua dos Invalidos with absolute truth, that is, as having been my mother's suggestion.

"Her suggestion?" murmured Capitú. And her eyes added, shining with extraordinary brilliance, "We shall be happy!"

I repeated the words, simply with my fingers, by squeezing hers. The settee, whether or not it saw, continued to lend its services to our clasped hands and to our heads leaning close together, almost touching.

83. The portrait

GURGEL CAME back to the living room and told Capitú that
his daughter was asking for her. I rose quickly. I lost my composure and kept my eyes on the furniture. Capitú, on the
contrary, got up in a natural manner and asked if the fever
was worse.

"No," he replied.

No starting up, no air of mystery, on the part of Capitú.
She turned to me and told me to remember her to my mother
and to Cousin Justina, and goodbye for then. She extended
her hand to me, then went out into the hall, and I could not
help but envy her. How was it possible for Capitú to control
herself so easily, and I not?

"Quite a young lady!" observed Gurgel, also looking after
her.

I murmured "yes." Truly, Capitú was growing up by
leaps and bounds, her figure was taking on new curves, a new
firmness; and so also her spirit. She was a woman within and
without, a woman to the right and to the left, woman on
every side and from head to foot. This blossoming was faster
now that I saw her at intervals of a few days; each time I
came home I found her taller and more womanly. Her eyes
had a new reflectiveness; her mouth a new imperiousness.

Gurgel turned toward the wall of the room where a portrait of a young lady was hanging, and asked me if Capitú
was not like the portrait.

One of my life customs has been to always agree with the
probable opinion of the person with whom I am talking, so
long as the matter does not aggravate, disgust or obligate me.

Before looking to see whether Capitú was really like the portrait, I went ahead and answered "yes." Then he told me it was a portrait of his wife, and that people who had known her said the same thing. He too thought the features similar, especially the forehead and the eyes. As for their natures, they were one. You would think they were sisters.

"Add to this the friendship that she has for Sanchinha; her mother was no greater friend to her. . . . Sometimes, in life, there are these strange resemblances."

84. Hailed

IN THE vestibule and in the street, I continued to ask myself if he had really suspected anything, but decided he had not and started to walk off. I was satisfied with the visit, with Capitú's joy, with Gurgel's praises—so much so that I did not immediately heed a voice that was calling to me.

"Senhor Bentinho! Senhor Bentinho!"

It was only after the voice grew louder and its owner appeared in the door that I stopped and saw who it was and where I was standing. I was already in Rua de Matacavallos. The place was a china shop, meagre and poor; its doors were partly closed, and the person who was calling me was a poor man with iron-gray hair and wearing old clothes.

"Senhor Bentinho," he said to me, and he was crying, "did you know that my son Manduca is dead?"

"Dead?"

"He died a half hour ago; he will be buried tomorrow. I just sent word to your mother and she did me the kindness of sending some flowers to put on the coffin. My poor son! He

had to die, and it was best that he die, poor thing, but even
so it hurts. The life that he had! . . . Only a day or so ago
he mentioned you, senhor, and asked if you were in the
seminary. . . . Would you like to see him? Come in and see
him. . . ."

It is painful for me to admit this, but it is better to tell
too much than too little. I wanted to say "no" that I did not
want to see Manduca, and I even made a move to run away.
It was not fear; on another occasion I might even have entered with eager curiosity, but at that moment I was so content! To see a dead boy on the way home from a love tryst
. . . There are things which do not fit together nor har-
monize. The news in itself upset me. My golden thoughts
lost their lustre and their metal turned to ashes, dark, ugly
ashes, and I could no longer make out anything. I think I
succeeded in saying that I was in a hurry, but I probably
did not speak in clear words, nor even human ones, because
he, as he leaned in the doorway, opened the way for me with
a gesture, and I, without courage either to go in or to run
away, let my body do what it would and my body went in.

I do not blame the man: for him the most important thing
at the moment was his son. Do not blame me either: for
me the most important thing was Capitú. The trouble was
that the two things came together on the same afternoon,
and that the death of one came and stuck its nose into the
life of the other. There is the whole trouble. If I had come
by before or later, or if Manduca had waited a few hours
to die, no unpleasant note would have come to interrupt
the melodies of my soul. Why die exactly a half hour before?
Any hour is appropriate for departing this life; one can die
very nicely at say six or seven in the evening.

85. The dead boy

THIS WAS the confused feeling with which I entered the
china shop. The shop was dim and the inside of the house
had less light now that the windows on the court were darkened. I saw the mother crying in a corner of the dining room.
At the bedroom door, two children stared inside in frightened wonder, finger in mouth. The corpse lay on the bed.
The bed . . .

Let us put down our pen and go to the window to give
our memory a breath of air. Truly, the picture was ugly,
with death and with the dead boy, who was horrible. . . .
Now this, over here, is quite another thing . . . All that I
see here breathes life, a goat munching by the cart, a chicken
pecking in the dirt of the road, a train of the Brazil Central
puffs, whistles, smokes, and passes, a palm tosses against the
sky—finally there is the church spire, though it has neither
muscles nor leafy branch. The boy in the alley, sending up
his paper kite, is not dead, is not dying, though he too is
named Manduca.

It is true, the other Manduca was older—a little older. The
other Manduca must have been eighteen or nineteen, but
you would as easily have thought him fifteen or twenty-two:
his face did not disclose his age, rather it hid it in the folds
of . . . Come, let it all be told! He is dead, his relatives are
dead, if one of them still lives he is not prominent enough
to be embarrassed or hurt. Let it all be told: Manduca suffered from a cruel disease, nothing less than leprosy. In life
he was ugly; in death he seemed horrible. When I saw him
stretched out on the bed, the pitiful body of him who had

been my neighbor, I was horrified, and turned away my eyes.
I do not know what unseen hand compelled me to look a
second time, even fleetingly; I yielded, I looked, kept looking,
until I backed away completely and left the room.

"He suffered!" sighed the father.

"Poor little Manduca!" sobbed the mother.

My one thought was to get away: I told them that I was
expected at home, and said goodbye. The father asked me
if I would do them the favor of going to the funeral. I
answered truthfully that I did not know, that I would do as
my mother decided. And I left him quickly, went through
the shop, and leapt into the street.

86. Love, lads!

IT WAS so close by that in less than three minutes I found
myself inside our house. I stopped in the hall to catch my
breath. I was trying to forget the dead boy, the pallor and
the deformity, and the rest that I have not told so as not to
give a hideous aspect to these pages, but you can imagine it.
I wiped it from my sight in a few seconds: all I needed was
to think of that other house, and better still of the life and
the fresh, lovely face of Capitú . . . Love, lads! and, above
all, love beautiful, spirited girls. They have a remedy for ills,
fragrance to sweeten a stench; for death they give you life. . . .
Love, lads, love!

87. The chaise

WHEN I arrived at the top step, an idea entered my brain, as if it had been waiting for me behind the grillwork of the gate. I heard from memory the words of Manduca's father asking me to go to the funeral on the following day. I stood still on the step. I reflected an instant. Yes, I could go to the funeral; I would ask my mother to rent me a carriage . . .

Do not imagine that it was the desire to ride in a carriage, however much pleasure I might take in a ride. As a little boy, I remember that I used to go thus many times, with my mother to pay friendly or formal calls, and to Mass if it was raining. It was an old chaise of my father's which she kept as long as she could. The postillion, who was a slave of ours, and as old as the chaise, would see me at the door, dressed up, waiting for my mother, and would say with a laugh:

"Old João's going to drive the young master!"

And it was seldom that I did not give him this recommendation: "João, remember to hold back the mules, go slowly. . . ."

"Nhá Gloria doesn't like me to."

"Slow them down anyway!"

You understand, it was in order to savor the pleasure of riding in the chaise, not for the sake of vanity, because one could not be seen by those outside. It was an old, obsolete two-wheeled chaise, short and narrow, with two leather curtains in front which could be pulled to the sides when one got in or out. Each curtain had a glass eye-hole through which I liked to peek.

"Sit back, Bentinho!"

"Let me peek out, Mamma!"

And when I was smaller, I used to stand with my face against the glass and see the postillion with his great boots, straddling the mule on the left and clutching the reins of the one on the right; in his hand the long, heavy whip. Everything cumbersome—boots, whip, and mules—but he enjoyed it and so did I. On either side, I saw the houses go past, some with shops, open or closed, with people or without them, and, in the street, folk came and went or crossed in front of the chaise, with long strides or mincing steps. When people or animals got in the way, the chaise stopped, and then the spectacle was particularly interesting: persons standing on the sidewalk or in doorways stared at the chaise and talked among themselves, naturally about who was inside. As I grew older I imagined that they knew and said, "It's that lady from Rua de Matacavallos, who has a son, Bentinho. . . ."

The chaise went so well with my mother's secluded way of life that when there was no longer another of its kind, we continued to ride in it, and it was known along our street and in the neighborhood as the "old chaise." Finally my mother consented to give it up. She did not sell it at once though, and only parted with it at last because the expenses of the stable obliged her to do so. The reason for keeping it (though useless) was exclusively sentimental: it was a remembrance of her husband. Everything that had belonged to my father was kept as a piece of him, a scrap of his person, of his very soul integral and pure. But the practice was also daughter of the conservatism which she admitted to her friends. My mother was a good example of fidelity to old habits, old customs, old ideas, old-fashioned ways. She had her museum of relics: toothless combs, a bit of a shawl, some

copper coins dated 1824 and 1825, and, that everything might
be ancient, she tried to make herself old, but I have already
mentioned that on this point she did not entirely attain her
wish.

88. An honorable pretext

NO, THE idea of going to the funeral did not come from the
memory of the carriage and its charms. The origin was something else: it was because, if I went to the funeral the next
day, I would not go to the seminary and could pay another
visit to Capitú, a more extended visit. There you have it.
The memory of the carriage may have come as an accessory,
afterward, but the principal, the immediate cause was the
other. I would return to Rua dos Invalidos on the pretext of
inquiring after Sinhàzinha Gurgel. I was counting on everything turning out for me as it had on that day: Gurgel full
of anxiety, Capitú with me on the settee, our hands clasped,
the combing of the braids . . .

"I am going to ask Mamma."

I opened the gate. Before passing through, just as I had
heard from memory the words of the dead boy's father, now
I heard his mother's, and I repeated softly:

"Poor little Manduca!"

89. The refusal

MY MOTHER was puzzled when I asked to go to the funeral.

"Lose a day at the seminary . . ."

I called her attention to the friendship Manduca had felt

for me, and then they were poor people . . . I gave all the reasons I could think of. Cousin Justina expressed an opinion for the negative.

"You don't think he should go?" asked my mother.

"No, I don't. What friendship is this, that I never heard of?"

Cousin Justina won out. When I related the case to the dependent, he smiled and said that my cousin's hidden motive was probably to deprive the funeral of "the lustre of my presence." Be that as it may, I remained sullen. The next day, as I thought over her motive, it did not displease me; later, I took a certain relish in it.

90. The argument

THE NEXT day, I passed by the house of the dead boy without going in, or even stopping—or if I did stop it was only an instant still more brief than the one it takes to tell you of it. If I am not mistaken, I walked even more quickly, fearing that they would call to me as on the day before. Now that I was not going to the funeral, better keep as far away as possible. I kept on walking and thinking of the poor devil.

We were not friends, nor had we known each other very long. Intimacy—what intimacy could there be between his sickness and my health? We enjoyed brief and distant relations. I thought of them as I went along, and began to recall some of them. They all reduced themselves to one argument between us, two years before, apropos of . . . You will hardly believe what it was apropos of. It was the Crimean War.

Manduca lived in the dingy quarters behind the shop, stretched out in bed, reading to pass the time. On Sunday, toward afternoon his father got him into a dark nightshirt and brought him to the back of the shop. From there he could peek out at a hand's breadth of the street and see the people passing. It was his only recreation. It was there that I saw him one time, and was not a little startled. The disease had begun to eat away part of his flesh; his fingers were shriveled. His appearance was not attractive, certainly. I was thirteen or fourteen years old. The second time I saw him there, we spoke of the Crimean War, which was then at its height and in all the papers. Manduca said that the Allies were bound to win, and I said "no."

"Well, we shall see," he replied. "Only if justice does not triumph in this world—which is impossible—for justice is on the side of the Allies."

"No, senhor, right is on the side of the Russians."

Naturally, we went by what was said in the city newspapers, which in turn copied the foreign ones, but it is possible too that each of us held the opinion of his own temperament. I was always a bit Muscovite in my ideas. I defended the position of Russia. Manduca did the same for the Allies. And the third Sunday that I entered the shop we once more touched on the subject. Then Manduca proposed that we exchange arguments in writing; and on Tuesday or Wednesday I received two sheets of paper containing the exposition and defense of the Allies' position and of the integrity of Turkey, and concluding with this prophetic phrase: "The Russians will not enter Constantinople!"

I read it and set about refuting it. I do not recall a single one of the arguments I employed, and perhaps it would be of no interest to know them now that the century is about to expire; but my recollection of them is that they were un-answerable. I took my paper to him in person. They showed me into the bedroom, where he lay stretched out on the bed, half covered with a patchwork quilt. Either my taste for polemics or something else which I cannot put my finger on, kept me from feeling all the loathsomeness that came from the bed and from the sick boy; the pleasure with which I gave him the paper was sincere. And yet, repulsive as was Manduca's face, the smile that illumined it glossed over the physical ugliness. The assurance with which he took the paper from me and said that he would read it and answer it, is something which no words in our language, nor in any language, can describe in its full truth. It was not elated, not boisterous, it was without gestures (nor would the sickness have permitted them); it was simple, grand, profound, an infinite savoring of victory, before knowing my arguments. He already had paper, pen and ink beside his bed. A few days later I received his reply. I do not remember if it con-tained anything new or not; what had increased was the heat; and the end was the same: "The Russians will not enter Constantinople!"

I answered, and from then on there continued for some time a fiery polemic in which neither of us yielded, each de-fending his clients with force and spirit. Manduca was more lengthy and prompt than I. Naturally, I had a thousand other things to distract me—school, diversions, family, and my own robust health, which called me to other exercises. Manduca, except for the hand's breadth of street on Sunday afternoons, had only this war, talk of the city and of the world—but which no one came to discuss with him. Chance had given him an adversary in me. He had a flair for writing and threw himself into the debate as if it were a new and radical remedy. The long, sad hours were now short and happy, his eyes forgot how to cry if indeed they had cried before. I perceived this change in him from the behavior of his father and mother.

"You can't imagine how he is since you have been writing him those papers, senhor," said the owner of the shop one day, at the street door. "He's always talking and laughing. As soon as I send off the clerk to take you his papers, he begins to ask about the reply and whether it will be long in coming and if I will ask your slave boy when he goes by. While he is waiting, he rereads the newspapers and takes notes. But then, the minute he receives your papers, he pounces on them, reads them, and begins straight off to write a reply. There are times when he doesn't eat, or very little. In fact, I would like to ask one thing of you, that is, not to send them at breakfast or dinnertime. . . ."

I was the first to tire of it. I began to slow down with my replies until finally I made none at all. He still persisted two or three times after my silence, but when he received no contestation whatever, he too, either through weariness, or not to bother me, put an end to his apologies. The last one, like the first, like all of them, affirmed the same eternal prediction:

"The Russians will not enter Constantinople!"

Indeed, they did not enter, neither then, nor later, nor up to now. But will the prediction be eternal? Will they not succeed in entering some day? A difficult problem. Manduca himself, in order to enter the tomb, spent three years in dissolution, so certain is it that Nature, like History, does not proceed carelessly. Like Turkey his life resisted. If it finally yielded, it was because he lacked an alliance like the Anglo-French—for one cannot consider as such, the simple accord between medicine and pharmacy. He died at last, as states die. In our particular case the question is not whether Turkey will die, because death spares none, but if the Russians will one day enter Constantinople: that was the question for my leprous neighbor beneath his sad, torn, and filthy patchwork quilt. . . .

91. A consoling discovery

IT IS clear that the reflections which I have just set down were not made then, on my way to the seminary, but now, in my study in Engenho Novo. Then, I really did not make any, unless it was this: that I brought solace one day to my neighbor Manduca. Today, on thinking it over, I find I not only brought him solace, but even happiness. And the discovery consoles me; henceforth I will never forget that I gave two or three months of happiness to a poor devil, making him forget his pain and all the rest. It will mean something in the liquidation of my life. If there is, in the other world, some reward or other for the unintentional virtues, this one will pay for one or two of my many sins. As for Manduca, I do not believe that it was a sin to express an opinion against Russia, but, if it was, he has been expiating for forty years in purgatory, the happiness he enjoyed for two or three months. From this he will conclude (too late) that it might have been better to have just groaned away, without expressing any opinion whatsoever.

92. The devil is not so black as he is painted

MANDUCA got buried without me. This has happened to many others without my feeling it much one way or the other, but this case grieved me particularly for the reason already mentioned. I also felt a certain melancholy at the recollection of the first argument of my life, the pleasure with which he would receive my papers and propose to answer them—not counting the pleasure of the carriage. . . . But Time quickly blotted out all those sad longings and resurrections. Nor was it only he; two persons came to aid him: Capitú, whose image slept with me that night, and another whom I will tell of in the next chapter. The rest of this chapter is only to beg that if anyone has to read my book with somewhat more attention than the price of the copy calls for, he will not fail to conclude that the devil is not so black as he is painted. I mean . . .

I mean that my neighbor of Rua de Matacavallos, by tempering his illness with anti-Russian opinion, gave his rotting flesh a spiritual reflection which consoled it. There are greater consolations, surely, and one of the most excellent is not to suffer this or any other ill, but Nature is so divine that she amuses herself with such contrasts, and beckons to the most loathsome and wretched with a flower. And perhaps thus the flower takes on beauty. My gardener claims that violets, in order to have a superior fragrance, require hog manure. I have not investigated, but it must be true.

93. A friend for a dead boy

AS FOR the other person with obliterative force, it was my schoolmate Escobar, who came to Matacavallos in the forenoon of that Sunday. A friend thus made up for a dead boy, and so much a friend that he stood for almost five minutes with my hand in his, as if he had not seen me for months.

"Will you have dinner with me, Escobar?"

"That's what I came for."

My mother thanked him for his friendship toward me, and he answered with great politeness, though somewhat hesitantly, as if he lacked a ready tongue. You have already seen that this was not so; his tongue obeyed him—but a man is not always the same at all moments. What he said, in brief, was that he valued me for my good qualities and genteel upbringing; they were all fond of me at the seminary, and it could not help but be so, he added. He stressed the upbringing, the good examples, "the sweet and precious mother" that heaven had given me. . . . All this in a husky, tremulous voice.

They were all delighted with him. I was as pleased as if Escobar had been my own invention. José Dias fired a salute of two superlatives, Uncle Cosme two capots, and Cousin Justina found nothing to find fault with—later, yes, on the second or third Sunday, she pointed out that my friend Escobar was a bit meddlesome and had policeman's eyes that missed nothing.

"Those are *his* eyes," I explained.

"I don't say that they are anyone else's."

"They are reflective eyes," was Uncle Cosme's opinion.

"No doubt about it," put in José Dias, "though Senhora

Dona Justina may be partly right. The truth is that the one does not interfere with the other, and reflection often accompanies natural curiosity. He seems to be curious, yes, he seems so, but . . ."

"He seems to *me* to be a very serious boy," said my mother.

"Exactly!" declared José Dias, in order not to differ from her.

When I told Escobar my mother's opinion of him (without mentioning the opinion of the others, naturally), I saw that his delight knew no bounds. He thanked me, saying that she was very kind, and in turn praised my mother—a grave, distinguished and youthful lady, so very youthful . . . What might her age be?

"Oh, past forty," I answered vaguely, out of vanity.

"It's not possible!" exclaimed Escobar. "Forty! She doesn't look thirty, so youthful and pretty. And no wonder! You had to take after some one with those eyes God gave you; they are exactly like hers. Did she become a widow many years ago?"

I told him what I knew of her life and my father's. Escobar listened attentively, asked more questions about the parts I skipped over or left obscure. When I said that I did not remember anything about the country because I had left it when I was so little, he related two or three incidents from his third year that were still fresh in his memory. And didn't we plan to return to the country?

"No, we'll never go back now. Look, that colored man over yonder is from there. Thomas!"

"Senhor!"

We were in the kitchen garden, and the Negro was going about his task. He came up to us and waited.

"He's married," I said to Escobar. "Where is Maria?"

"She's pounding corn, yes, Senhor."

"You still remember the plantation, Thomas?"

"I 'member, yes, Senhor."

"All right, you may go."

I pointed out another and another and still another: "This is Pedro, that's José, that other Damião . . ."

"All the letters of the alphabet," interrupted Escobar.

In fact, they were different letters, and it was only then that I noticed it. I pointed to still other slaves, some with the same names but distinguished by a nickname either from their looks like Yellow João, Fat Maria, or from their country like Pedro Benguela, Antonio Mozambique. . . .

"And are they all here at home?" he asked.

"No, some are out earning money in the streets, others are hired out for wages. It wouldn't be possible to keep them all at home. And these are not all that were on the plantation. Most of them stayed there."

"What surprises me is that Dona Gloria could get used to living in a city house, where everything is so small and cramped; the house out there is probably very large."

"I don't know, but I imagine so. Mamma has other houses bigger than this. She says, however, that she will die here. The others are rented. Some are very large, like the one on Rua da Quitanda. . . ."

"I know that one; it's very pretty."

"She also has one in Rio Comprido, in Cidade-Nova, one in Cattete. . . ."

"She won't want for roofs over her head," he concluded with a friendly smile.

We walked toward the back. As we came to the washing-place, he stopped an instant and gazed at the stone on which clothes were beaten, and made some remarks apropos of cleanliness; then we went on. What the remarks were, I don't remember now. I remember only that I found them ingenious and laughed; he laughed too. My joy awakened his, and the sky was so blue, and the air so clear, that Nature herself seemed to be laughing with us. That is the way it is with the happy hours of this world. Escobar noted this accord of inner harmony with the external in such fine, exalted words that I was moved; then, apropos of the moral beauty which blends with the physical, he again spoke of my mother, "a double angel," he called her.

94. Arithmetical ideas

I WILL not tell everything, for it would be too much. He not only knew how to eulogize and think, he also knew how to calculate fast and well. He was one of Holmes' arithmetical heads $(2 + 2 = 4)$.

You cannot imagine the facility with which he would add or multiply in his head. Division, which was always one of the most difficult operations for me, was like nothing for him. He would half-close his eyes, roll them upward, mumble the denominations of the figures—and he had it! This with seven, thirteen, twenty numbers. His talent was such that it made him love the very symbols of the sums themselves; and he held the opinion that the digits, being few, were much more ingenious than the twenty-six letters of the alphabet.

"There are useless letters and letters which could be dispensed with," he would say. "What separate function do d and t perform? They have almost the same sound. The same goes for b and p, the same for s, c, and z, the same for k and g, etc. They are calligraphic folderol. Look at the digits: there are no two which perform the same function: 4 is 4, and 7 is 7. And consider the beauty with which a 4 and a 7 form this thing which is represented by 11. Now double 11 and you have 22. Multiply it by itself, it makes 484, and so on. But where the perfection is greatest is in the use of *zero*. The value of *zero* is, in itself, nothing; but what is the function of this negative symbol?—to augment! A 5 alone is a 5; place oo with it, it is 500. Thus, that which has no value makes great value, something which doubled letters don't do, for I *approve* as much with one *p* as with two *p's*."

Brought up in the spelling of my fathers, it pained me to hear such blasphemies, but I did not venture to refute him. Still, one day, I proffered a few words of defense, to which he replied that it was prejudice, and added that arithmetical ideas could go to the infinite, with the advantage that they were easier to handle. Thus I was not able to resolve, then and there, a philosophic or linguistic problem, whereas he could add up, in three minutes, *any* amounts.

"For example . . . give me a case, give me a bunch of numbers that I do not know and could not know before-hand . . . Look, give me a list of your mother's houses and the rent of each, and if I do not tell you the total sum in two, in one minute, hang me!"

I accepted the wager, and the following week, I brought him a paper with a list of the rents on it. Escobar took the paper, ran his eyes down the figures in order to memorize them, and while I looked at my watch he rolled up the pupils of his eyes, lowered the lids, and muttered . . . Oh! the wind is not more swift! It was said and done; in half a minute he shouted to me:

"The total is 1,070 milreis per month."

I was dumbfounded. Consider that there were no less than nine houses and that the rents varied from one to the other going from 70 milreis to 180. And all that which would have taken me three or four minutes—with pencil and paper— Escobar did casually, in his head.

He looked at me triumphantly and asked if it was not correct. Just to prove that it was, I drew out of my pocket a scrap of paper with the total sum on it, and showed it to him; it was exactly the same, not one error: 1,070.

"That proves that arithmetical ideas are more simple and so, more natural. Nature is simple. Art is cumbersome."

I was so enthusiastic over the mental ability of my friend that I could not help giving him a hug. It was in the patio; other seminarists noticed our effusiveness; a padre who was with them did not like it.

"Modesty," he said to us, "does not countenance these excessive gestures. You may show regard for each other, but with moderation."

Escobar remarked to me that the others and the padre spoke out of envy and suggested that we keep apart. I interrupted him and said "no," if it was envy, so much the worse for them.

"We'll fix them!"

"But . . ."

"Let us be greater friends than ever."

Escobar furtively gripped my hand so hard that my fingers still tingle. This tingling is an illusion, surely, if it is not the effect of the long hours that I have been writing without pause. Let us lay aside the pen for a few instants. . . .

95. The Pope

THE FRIENDSHIP of Escobar became great and fruitful; that of José Dias refused to lag behind. At the end of that week, he said to me, at home:

"It is now certain that you will leave the seminary soon."

"What?"

"Wait till tomorrow. I must play cards; they have sent for me. Tomorrow, in your room, in the garden, or in the street on the way to Mass, I'll tell you about it. The idea is so sacred that it wouldn't be out of place in the sanctuary itself. Tomorrow, Bentinho."

"But is it really certain?"

"Absolutely certain!"

The next day he revealed the mystery. At first sight, I confess, I was dazzled by it. It bore a note of grandeur and spirituality that spoke to my seminarist's eyes. It was nothing less than this: My mother, as it seemed to him, repented what she had done and wished to see me out in the world, but she realized that the moral bond of her promise held her fast. It would be necessary to break it: for this there were the Scriptures which conferred the power of unbinding on the apostles. And so he and I would go to Rome to ask the absolution of the Pope. . . . How did it strike me?

"It strikes me as all right," I answered after a few seconds of reflection. "It might be a good way out."

"It is the only one, Bentinho, the only one! I'll go right away, today, and have a talk with Dona Gloria, explain it all to her, and we can leave in two months, or before. . . ."

"Better speak to her *next* Sunday. Let me think it over first . . ."

"Oh! Bentinho!" interrupted the dependent. "Think over what? What you want . . . Shall I tell you? You won't be angry with your old Dias? What you want is to consult a certain person."

Strictly speaking, it was two persons, Capitú and Escobar, but I flatly denied that I wanted to consult anyone. And what person, the rector? It was not likely that I would confide such a matter to *him*. No, not the rector, nor a teacher, nor anyone —only time to reflect, a week, on Sunday I would give my answer, and I could tell him right off that it didn't seem like a bad idea.

"No?"

"No."

"Then let's settle it today."

"One doesn't go skipping off to Rome carelessly."

"He who has a tongue goes to Rome, the tongue in our case is cash. Well, you can afford to spend something on yourself . . . Not on me: a pair of trousers, a couple of shirts and my daily bread, that's all I need. I will be like Saint Paul, who lived by his trade while he went about preaching the divine word. Well, I go not to preach it but to seek it. We will take letters from the internuncio and the bishop, letters to our minister, letters from Capuchins. . . . I know well the objection that can be made to this idea: they will say that we can ask for dispensation from here. But aside from all else that I might say, it is enough to reflect that it is much more solemn and fitting for that one who is himself the object of the favor, the promised Levite who comes to beg the dispensation of God for his most tender and most gentle mother, to enter the Vatican and prostrate himself at the feet of the Pope. Consider the picture: you kissing the foot of the Prince of the Apostles; His Holiness, with an evangelic smile, inclines, interrogates, hears, absolves and blesses. The angels look on, the Virgin recommends to her Most Holy Son that all your desires, Bentinho, be satisfied, and that all that you love on earth be likewise loved in heaven . . ."

I will not tell any more because I have to end my chapter, and he did not end his speech. He spoke to all my feelings as a Catholic and as a lover. I saw the soul of my mother comforted, Capitú's heart joyful, and both of them at our house, and I with them, and he with us, all in consideration of a little trip to Rome. Rome . . . I knew only geographically where it was; spiritually also; but the distance that it might be from Capitú's desire—that I did not know. There is the essential point. If Capitú should find it far, I would not go; but it was necessary to hear her opinion, and likewise Escobar's, who would be sure to give me good advice.

96. A substitute

I TOLD Capitú José Dias' idea. She listened attentively, and then became sad.

"You will go away," she said, "and forget me entirely."

"Never!"

"You will forget. Europe, they say, is so beautiful, and particularly Italy. Isn't that where the sopranos come from? You will forget me, Bentinho. And is there no other way? Dona Gloria is dying to have you leave the seminary."

"Yes, but she considers that she's held by her promise."

Capitú could think of no other plan and could not bring herself to adopt this one. Meanwhile, she begged me, if I did

go to Rome, to swear that I would be back at the end of six
months.

"I swear it."

"By God?"

"By God, by everything. I swear that within six months I
will be back."

"But if the Pope has not yet released you?"

"I will send word to that effect."

"And if you lie?"

This word cut me deeply, and I could not think of a
reply for the moment. Capitú made a joke of it, laughed
and called me a sly dog. Then she professed to believe that I
would keep my oath; but even so she did not give her consent:
she would see if there was not some other way, and I too
should try to think of something else.

When I went back to the seminary, I told the whole thing
to my friend Escobar, who heard me with similar attention
and finally with the same sadness as Capitú. His eyes, usually
so restless, almost devoured me with their intensity. Suddenly, I saw his face illumined with a great light, the reflection of an idea, and I heard him say in a torrent of words:

"No, Bentinho, it's not necessary. There is a better—I
won't say better, because the Holy Father is always greater
than anything else—but there is something which will pro-
duce the same effect."

"What is it?"

"Your mother made a promise to God to give him a priest,
isn't that right? Well then, let her give him a priest, as long
as it's not you. She can easily take some orphan boy, have him
ordained at her expense; a padre is given, without your . . ."

"I get it, I get it, that's the very thing!"

"Don't you think so?" he continued. "Ask the protonotary

about it. He will tell you whether it's not the same thing, or I myself will consult him if you like; and if he hesitates, we can speak to the Lord Bishop."

I was reflecting: "Yes, this seems to be the answer. For really, the promise is kept, if a padre is produced."

Escobar observed that, from the economic side, the question was simple: my mother would spend the same for him as for me, and an orphan would not require great comforts. He cited the sum of the rents from the houses, 1,070 milreis, not to mention the slaves. . . .

"It's the only thing," said I.

"And we will leave together."

"You too?"

"I too. I am going to improve my Latin and then I leave. I won't bother with theology. Even Latin is not necessary. What for, in business?"

"In hoc signo vinces," I laughed.

I felt gay and witty. Oh! How hope gladdens everything! Escobar smiled as if he enjoyed my remark. Then we each fell into our own reverie, our eyes gazing off. His were still thus when I returned to reality, and again thanked him for the plan he had devised; it could not have been better. Escobar listened contentedly.

"Once more," he said gravely, "religion and liberty become boon companions."

97. The sallying-forth

EVERYTHING was done along these lines. My mother hesitated a little, but finally yielded after Padre Cabral consulted the bishop and brought back word that "yes," it could be done. I left the seminary at the end of the year.

I was then a little more than seventeen. . . . Right here should be the middle point of my book, but inexperience has made me lag behind my pen, and I arrive almost at the end of my supply of paper, with the best of the story yet to tell. Now there is nothing for it but to pull it along with great strides, chapter on chapter, with little correction, little reflection, everything cut short. Already, this page must do for months, others will do for years, and so we will reach the end. One of the sacrifices that I make to this hard necessity is the analysis of my seventeen-year-old emotions. I do not know if you were once seventeen. If you were, you must know that it is an age in which a half man and a half child form a curious whole. I was a *most* curious whole, as my dependent José Dias would say, and he would not be far wrong. What this superlative quality made me, I could never tell here without falling into the error that I condemned above; and yet the analysis of my emotions of that period did enter my plan. Though a son of the seminary and of my mother, I had already begun to feel beneath my chaste restraint, twitches of immodesty and boldness. They came from the blood but also from the girls, who, whether in the street or at their windows, would not leave me alone. They found me handsome, and told me so. Some wanted to admire my good looks at closer range, and vanity is a beginning of corruption.

98. Five years

REASON WON; I went off to school. I passed my eighteenth birthday, my nineteenth, twentieth, twenty-first; at twenty-two I was a Bachelor of Laws.

Everything around me had changed. My mother had made up her mind to grow old; even so, the white hairs came grudgingly, few and far between; the cap, the dress, the plain noiseless shoes were the same as in the old days. She no longer walked back and forth so much. Uncle Cosme suffered from his heart, and had to rest. Cousin Justina was only older. José Dias too, but not so old that he did not pay me the courtesy of attending my graduation, and coming back down the mountain with me—as gay and exuberant as if *he* were the Bachelor. Capitú's mother had died; her father had retired from the same post he had occupied at the time he wished to take leave of life.

Escobar was beginning to trade in coffee, after working four years for one of the finest firms of Rio de Janeiro. It was Cousin Justina's opinion that he had toyed with the idea of inviting my mother to a second marriage. But whether or not he had had such an idea, one must not forget the great difference in age. Perhaps he was only thinking of associating her with his first commercial ventures; and, as a matter of fact, at my request, my mother advanced him certain moneys, which he repaid as soon as he could, not without this gibe: "Dona Gloria is a timorous mouse and has no ambition."

Separation did not cool our friendship. He was intermediary in the exchange of letters between Capitú and me. From the moment he saw her, he encouraged me in our love. The business relations he entered with Sancha's father tightened those he already had with Capitú, and made him serve us both as a friend. At first, it was difficult for her to accept him, she would have preferred José Dias, but José Dias was unacceptable to me because of a remnant of childish awe. Escobar won out; though vexed, Capitú handed him her first letter, which was the mother and grandmother of the others.

Not even after he was married did he suspend this kindly service. . . . Yes, he married—guess whom? He married gentle Sancha, Capitú's friend and almost a sister to her, so much so that once in writing to me he called her his "little sister-in-law." Thus are formed affections and family relationships, adventures and books.

99. The son is the image of his father

MY MOTHER almost burst with happiness when I came home a Bachelor of Laws. I still hear the voice of José Dias recalling the Gospel of St. John, and saying as he saw us embrace, "Woman, behold thy son! Son, behold thy mother!"

And my mother, between her tears: "Brother Cosme, he's the image of his father, isn't he?"

"Yes, there is something, the eyes, the shape of the face. He's his father, only a little more modern," he concluded, as a joke. "And tell me now, Sister, wasn't it better for him not to go through with being a padre? Can you imagine this young buck making a good padre?"

"How is my substitute?"

"He's coming along. He takes orders next year," answered Uncle Cosme. "You must go and see him ordained. I too, if 'Senhor Heart' consents. It will be good for you to feel yourself in the soul of the other, as if you yourself were receiving the consecration."

"Quite so!" exclaimed my mother. "But take a good look, Brother Cosme, see if he isn't the picture of my dear departed. Look this way, Bentinho, look at me. I always thought I saw

a resemblance; now it is much greater. The moustache spoils
it a little. . . ."

"Yes, Sister Gloria, the moustache, for a fact . . . but he is
very like."

My mother kissed me with a tenderness that I do not know
how to put into words. Uncle Cosme, to cheer her up, called
me "doctor," José Dias also, and everyone around the house,
the cousin, the slaves, the visitors, Padua, his daughter, and
she herself, kept repeating the title.

100. "You will be happy, Bentinho!"

As I unpacked my trunk, in my own room, and took the
Bachelor's diploma out of its case, my thoughts ran on happiness and glory. I saw my marriage and an illustrious career,
while José Dias helped me, zealously and in silence. An invisi-
ble fairy floated down into that room and said to me in a
voice at once gentle and wise, "You will be happy, Bentinho;
you are going to be happy."

"And why wouldn't you be happy?" asked José Dias
straightening up and staring at me.

"You heard?" I asked, also rising in my astonishment.

"Heard what?"

"Heard a voice which said I would be happy?"

"That's a good one! It was you yourself who said . . ."

Even now I could swear the voice was that of the fairy. It
is probable that the fairies, driven out of tales and verses,
have taken up their abode in people's hearts and speak out
from there inside. This one, for example—I have heard her
many times, clearly and distinctly. She must be a cousin of

the Scottish witches: "Thou shalt be king, Macbeth!"—
"Thou shalt be happy, Bentinho!" After all, it is the same
prediction, to the selfsame tune, which is universal and eternal. When I recovered from my astonishment, I heard the
remainder of José Dias' speech . . .

". . . You will be happy, as you deserve, just as you de-
served that diploma over there, which is not a favor from
anyone. The distinction which you attained in all your subjects is proof of it. I have already told you that I personally
heard the highest praise from the lips of your professors.
Besides, happiness is not glory alone, it is also something else.
Ah, you didn't confide everything to your old José Dias! Poor
old José Dias is tossed aside like a sucked orange, he's not
good for anything; now it's the new ones, the Escobars. . . .
I don't deny that he is a very distinguished young man, and
hardworking, and a model husband; but after all an old man
knows how to love also. . . ."

"What's this?"

"What should it be? Who doesn't know all about it? . . .
that neighborly intimacy had to end in this, and it is truly a
blessing from heaven, because she is an angel, an *angelissimo*.
. . . Pardon the coinage, Bentinho, it was a means of accentu-
ating the perfection of that young lady. I thought quite the
contrary in the old days. I mistook childish ways for expressions of character, and did not see that this mischievous little
girl with the pensive eyes was the capricious flower of a sweet
and wholesome fruit. . . . Why didn't you tell me too what
others know, and here at home is more than guessed at, and
approved?"

"Does Mamma really approve?"

"Well? We spoke of this and she did me the honor of asking
my opinion. You ask her what I said to her, and in no un-

certain terms. Just ask her. I told her that she could not wish
for a better daughter-in-law—kind, discreet, talented, friend
of our family . . . fine housewife, and that is not half of it.
After the death of her mother, she took charge of everything.
Padua, now that he is retired, doesn't do anything but receive his pension check and hand it over to his daughter. It's
the daughter who parcels out the money, pays the bills, keeps
account of expenditures, takes care of everything, food, cloth-
ing, light—you yourself saw her all last year. And as for her
beauty you know better about that than anyone. . . ."

"But, really, did Mamma consult you about our marriage?"

"Actually, no. She was kind enough to ask me if Capitú
would not make a good wife. It was I, in my answer, who
spoke of daughters-in-law. Dona Gloria did not demur, and
even seemed to smile."

"Every time Mamma wrote to me she mentioned Capitú."

"You know how devoted they are, and that is the reason
your cousin gets more and more sulky. Perhaps now she'll
marry all the sooner."

"Cousin Justina?"

"Didn't you know? It's probably just gossip; but, well, Dr.
João da Costa lost his wife a few months ago, and they say
(I don't really know anything about it—it was the protonotary
who told me), they say the two of them are half inclined to
make an end of their widowhood between them, by getting
married. The chances are that there is nothing to it, but it's
not beyond possibility, although she always said the doctor
was a bag of bones. . . . Only—if she is a cemetery—" he commented with a laugh; and then, seriously, "I said that as a
joke. . . ."

I did not hear the rest. I heard only the voice of my inner
fairy, which kept repeating to me, but now without words:

"You will be happy, Bentinho!" And the voice of Capitú told me the same thing, in different words and so too that of Escobar; and they both confirmed José Dias' news from their own observation. Finally, my mother, some weeks later, when I went to ask her permission to marry, besides her consent, gave me the like prophecy, save for the editing proper to a mother: "You will be happy, my son!"

101. In heaven

LET US be happy once and for all, before the reader, half dead with waiting, picks himself up and goes for a walk. Let us get married. It was in 1865, an afternoon in March, and it happened to be raining.* When we reached the top of Tijuca, and our honeymoon nest, the sky held back the rain and lighted the stars, not only those already known but also ones which will not be discovered until many centuries from now. It was a great courtesy, and it was not the only one. Saint Peter, who holds the keys of heaven, opened its doors to us, showed us in, and after touching us with his staff recited a few versicles from his first Epistle: "Ye wives, be in subjection to your husbands . . . Whose adorning let it not be the outward adorning of plaiting the hair and of wearing golden lace, but let it be the hidden man of the heart . . . Likewise, ye husbands, dwell with them, giving honor unto the wife as unto the weaker vessel, and as being heirs together of the grace of life. . . ." Thereupon, he made a sign to the angels and they intoned a passage of the Canticle, in such unison that they would have given the lie to the hypothesis

* In Brazil the superstition is that a rainy marriage means a happy one.

of the Italian tenor if the performance had been on earth; but it was in heaven. The music went with the text, as if they had been created together in the manner of a Wagnerian opera. Then we visited a part of that infinite place. Don't worry, I do not intend to describe it; human language does not possess forms proper to so great a task.

After all, it may be that it was all a dream: nothing more natural for an ex-seminarist than to hear Latin and the Scriptures all about him. It is true that Capitú, who knew neither Scriptures nor Latin, got a few of the words by heart, like these for example: "I sat down under the shadow of him that I had long desired." As for the words of St. Peter, she told me the next day that she was for them wholeheartedly, and that I was the only lace and the only adornment that she would wear. To which I retorted that my wife would always have the finest laces in this world.

102. Wife

IMAGINE A clock that had only a pendulum and no face, so that you did not see the hours marked. The pendulum would go from side to side, but no outward sign would show the march of time. This was the week on Tijuca.

Now and then we returned to the past and amused ourselves by recalling our sorrows and calamities, but this too was a way of not emerging from ourselves. So we lived anew our long years of waiting, the adolescent years, the "informing" which appears in the first chapters, and we laughed at José Dias who plotted our separation and ended by rejoicing in our union. Once or twice we spoke of going down, but the

mornings set for it were always rainy or sunny, and we were
waiting for an overcast sky, which would not come.

Nevertheless, I found Capitú a bit impatient to leave. She
agreed to remain, but kept talking of her father and of my
mother, of their not having news of us, of this and that, until
we quarreled a little. I asked her if she was already bored
with me.

"Bored with you?"

"It would seem so."

"Must you always be a child?" she asked, taking my face
between her hands and bringing her eyes close to mine. "Did
I wait so many years to become bored in seven days? No, Bentinho, I said this, because it is really so, I believe that they
may be anxious to see us and are imagining some illness or
other, and I confess, for my part, that I would like to see
Papa."

"Well, let's go tomorrow."

"No, it must be on a cloudy day," she retorted with a laugh.

I took her at her laugh and at her word, but her impatience
continued, and we went down in the sun.

The joy with which she put on her wifely hat, and the
wifely air with which she gave me her hand to get into or out
of the carriage, and her arm to walk in the street, all showed
me that the cause of Capitú's impatience was the outward display of her new estate. It was not enough to be a wife within
four walls and a few trees; she needed the rest of the world
too. And when I found myself down there, treading the
streets with her, stopping, looking, talking, I felt the same. I
invented walks in order that people might see me, approve
me, envy me. In the street, many turned their heads curiously, others stopped, some would ask, "Who are they?" and
one of the wise ones would answer, "That is Dr. Santiago,

who was married a few days ago to the young lady, Dona
Capitolina, after a long childhood romance. They live in
Gloria, the families reside on Matacavallos." And both of
them, "What a figure!"

103. Happiness is a kindly soul

FIGURE IS vulgar; José Dias expressed it better. He was the
only person from down below to visit us on Tijuca. He
brought us hugs from the family, and words of his own which
were truly gems of music. I do not set them down here in
order to save paper, but they were delicious. One day he compared us to birds that had grown up under adjoining eaves
of the same roof. One may imagine the rest, the fledglings
try their wings and soar into the sky, and the sky widens to
hold them. Neither of us laughed; we both listened, moved
and persuaded, everything forgotten, beginning with that
afternoon of 1858. . . . Happiness is a kindly soul.

104. The Pyramids

JOSÉ DIAS divided himself now between my mother and
me, alternating the dinners of Gloria with the breakfasts of
Matacavallos. All went well. After two years of marriage, except for the great disappointment of not having a child, all
went well. I had lost my father-in-law, it is true, and Uncle
Cosme was not long for this world, but my mother's health
was good, ours excellent.

I was an attorney for several wealthy houses, and the cases

were coming in. Escobar had contributed greatly to my be-
ginnings in the law courts. He had intervened with a celebrated lawyer to have me taken into his office, and had
arranged some retainers for me, all of his own accord.

Besides, our family friendship had been made beforehand.
Sancha and Capitú, after they were married, kept up the
friendship begun in school; Escobar and I, ours of the seminary. They lived in Andarahy, and were always inviting us
there. Since we could not go as often as we would have liked,
we sometimes went there to dinner on Sundays, or they had
dinner with us. *Dinner* hardly expresses it. We always went
very early, right after breakfast, to enjoy the day to the full,
and only separated at nine, ten, and eleven o'clock, when
there could be no more. Now when I think of those days at
Andarahy and Gloria, I feel a regret that life and all the rest
are not as rugged as the Pyramids.

Escobar and his wife were happy. They had a little daughter. Some time later, I heard of an adventure of the husband's, an affair of the theater, some actress or dancer, but if
it was true, it caused no scandal. Sancha was modest, her husband hard working. One day when I expressed my sorrow to
Escobar at not having a son, he replied:

"Man, don't fret. God will send them when He will, and if
He does not send any, it is because He wants them for Himself, and it will be better that they remain in heaven."

"A child, one's own child, is the natural complement of
life."

"It will come if need be."

It did not come. Capitú asked for it in her prayers. More
than once I caught myself saying prayers and asking for it. It
was no longer as it had been when I was a child; now, I paid
in advance, like house rent.

105. Arms

FOR THE most part, all went well. Capitú loved fun and amusement. In those first days, when we went for a walk or to the theater she was like a bird out of its cage. She dressed with charm and modesty. Though she was fond of jewels like other girls, she did not want me to buy her many or costly ones, and one day she became so exercised about it that I promised not to buy her a single one more; but it was not a promise that I kept.

Our life was more or less placid. When we were not with the family or with friends, or if we did not go to some play or private party (and these were rare), we passed our nights at our window in Gloria, watching the sea and the sky, the shadow of the mountains and the ships, or people who passed along the beach. Sometimes, I told Capitú the history of the city, at other times I gave her hints on astronomy, amateur hints, while she listened, attentive and curious, but not always so much so that she did not nod a little. She had never studied piano but learned after our marriage, so quickly that she was soon playing in the homes of our friends. At Gloria it was one of our recreations. She sang, too, but not much and on rare occasions, for she had no voice. One day she realized that it would be best not to sing at all, and gave it up. She liked to dance, and would adorn herself with loving care when she went to a ball; her arms were . . . Her arms deserve a paragraph.

They were beautiful, and the first night she attended a ball with them bare, I do not believe they had their equal in the city—not even yours, my dear lady, which were then only those of a little girl, if they yet existed, but probably they were still in the marble from which they came, or in the hands of the Divine Sculptor. They were the most beautiful of the evening, so unrivalled that they filled me with a dizzy pride. I scarcely conversed with the other guests preferring to watch them as they wove in and out among other arms encircling other frock coats. It was different at the second ball: then when I saw that men did not stop staring at them, seeking them out, almost begging for them, when I saw men brush against them with their black sleeves, I was vexed and glum. I did not attend a third, and in this I had the support of Escobar, to whom I frankly confided my displeasure. He agreed with me at once.

"Sanchinha shan't go either, or she will go in long sleeves; the other seems to me indecent."

"Yes, but don't tell the reason; they will call us seminarists. Capitú has already called me that."

I could not keep from telling Capitú, however, of Escobar's approbation. She smiled and answered that Sanchinha's arms were not shapely; but she quickly gave in, and did not go to the ball. She went to other balls, but her arms were half clothed in some filmy stuff or other, which neither covered them nor entirely discovered them, like the sendal of Camões.

106. Ten pounds sterling

I HAVE already said she was thrifty or, if I have not, consider it said now. She hoarded not only money but also old useless things, such as are treasured for the sake of tradition, remembrance or old time's sake. There were some shoes, for

instance, some little flat slippers with black ribbons that
crossed on the instep and ankle—the last ones she had worn
before putting on lady's shoes. She brought them to the
house, and would occasionally take them out of the bureau
drawer, where they were kept, along with other old things,
saying they were remnants of childhood. My mother, who had
the same trait, loved to hear her talk and act like that.

As for her purely financial economies, I will cite one case,
and this will suffice. It happened to be on the occasion of one
of those astronomy lessons at Gloria. I must confess I sometimes made her nod a little. One night she was so lost in contemplation of the sea, it made me jealous.

"You aren't listening, Capitú."

"I? I'm listening."

"What was I saying?"

"You . . . you were talking about Sirius."

"Sirius, Capitú! It's twenty minutes since I talked about
Sirius."

"You were talking about . . . about Mars," she corrected
hastily.

Actually it was Mars, but it was clear that she had only
caught the sound of the word, not the sense. I became serious;
I had an impulse to rise and leave the room. Capitú knew
it, and became the softest, the most honeyed of creatures. She
took my hand, admitted she had been figuring, that is, adding
up some sums of money in an attempt to discover a certain
bit that was missing. It was a question of converting from
paper to gold. At first I supposed that it was a ruse to put me
in a good humor, but in a few seconds I was also calculating,
but with paper and pencil, on my knee, discovering her short-
age for her.

"But what pounds are these?" I asked when I finished.

Capitú looked at me and laughed, then replied that the blame for her telling the secret was mine. She got up, went to her room and came back with ten pounds sterling in her hand. They were what she had saved out of the money I gave her each month for expenses.

"All this?"

"It's not much, just ten pounds. It's what your miser of a wife could save up in several months," she concluded, making the gold tinkle in her hand.

"Who was the broker?"

"Your friend Escobar."

"How is it he didn't say anything to me?"

"It was only today."

"He was here?"

"A little while before you came home. I didn't mention it for fear you might suspect something."

I wanted to squander double the amount of the gold on some commemorative present, but Capitú stopped me. On the contrary, she asked my advice on what we should do with those pounds.

"They are yours," I answered.

"Ours," she corrected.

"Then you keep them."

The next day, I went to see Escobar at the warehouse, and laughed at their secret—his and Capitú's. Escobar smiled and said that he had been just about to go to my office to tell me. The little sister-in-law (he continued to give this name to Capitú) had spoken to him during our last visit to Andarahy, and mentioned the reason for the secrecy.

"When I told Sanchinha," he concluded, "she was dumbfounded. 'How can Capitú save money now that everything is so dear?' 'I don't know, child; all I know is that she saved ten pounds.' "

"Wait and see, perhaps she will learn to do it too."

"No, I don't believe so. Sanchinha is not a spendthrift, but she is not frugal either; what I give her does, but that's all."

And I, after several instants of reflection: "Capitú is an angel."

Escobar nodded assent but unenthusiastically as one who regrets he cannot say the same of his wife. That is how it would have seemed to you too, so sure is it that the virtues of those near us fill us with a kind of vanity, pride or consolation.

107. Jealousy of the sea

IF IT were not for astronomy, I would not have discovered Capitú's ten pounds so soon. But it is not on this account that I return to the subject; I do so that you may not imagine it was my vanity as a teacher which made me suffer from the inattention of Capitú and become jealous of the sea. No, my friend. I must explain to you that I had often had these fits of jealousy, wishing to know what might be inside my wife's head—not outside or above it. It is a known fact that the wandering thoughts of a person can be guilty, half guilty, a third, a fifth, a tenth guilty, since in the matter of guilt the gradation is infinite. The simple recollection of a pair of eyes is enough to fix other eyes that remember them and delight in imagining them. There is no need of an actual, mortal sin, or exchange of letter, simple word, nod, sigh or signal still more light and trifling. An anonymous man or anonymous woman who passes by at the corner of the street can make us

put Sirius inside Mars, and you know, reader, the difference
there is between one and the other in distance and in size, but
astronomy has these confusions. It was this that made me
turn pale, grow silent, and want to run out of the room, to
return God knows when—probably ten minutes later. Ten
minutes later I would have been back in the living room, at
the piano, or the window, continuing the lesson that had
been interrupted:

"Mars is a distance of . . ."

So little time? Yes, so little time, ten minutes.

My fits of jealousy were intense, but brief: in an instant
I would tear down everything, but in the same instant I
would reconstruct the sky, the earth and the stars.

The truth is I grew fonder of Capitú, if that is possible, she
more tender, the air more balmy, the nights more bright, and
God more God. And it was not, properly speaking, the ten
pounds sterling which did this, or the passion for economy
they revealed and of which I was aware, but the precautions
that Capitú took with a view to one day disclosing to me her
daily, thoughtful care. Escobar also became dearer to me. Our
visits grew more frequent, and our conversations more intimate.

108. A child

STILL, all this did not kill my longing for a child, however
sad a little shaver he might be, sallow and thin, but a child, a
child of my own body. When we went to Andarahy and saw
the baby daughter of Escobar and Sancha, familiarly, Capi-
tùzinha, to distinguish her from my wife, for they had given
her the same name at baptism, we were filled with envy. The

little girl was chubby and full of grace, talkative and inquisitive. The parents, like other parents, recounted her pranks and bright sayings, and at night as we returned to Gloria, we sighed forth our envy and mentally begged heaven to put an end to it. . . .

. . . Our envy died, our hopes were born, and the fruit of them was not long in coming to this world. It was not puny nor ugly, as the one I had prayed for, but a lusty boy, strong and beautiful.

As for my joy when he was born . . . I do not know how to tell it. I have never felt its equal, nor do I believe that there can be any joy comparable to it, nor one that distantly or closely resembles it. It was a dizziness and a madness. I did not sing in the street, out of natural shame, nor at home, so as not to disturb the convalescing Capitú. Neither did I fall to the ground, because there is a god that watches over new fathers. Outside, I lived with my mind on the baby; at home, with my eyes on him—observing him, marveling at him, asking him where he came from, and why it was that I was so wrapped up in him, and other nonsensical stuff, without words, but thought or fancied in delirium at every instant. Perhaps I lost a few cases in court through negligence. Capitú was tender toward both him and me. We clasped each other's hands and, when we were not gazing at our son, we were talking of ourselves, of our past and our future. The hour of greatest charm and mystery was the nursing hour. When I saw my son sucking his mother's milk, and all that union of nature for the nourishing and life of a being that had been nothing, but that our destiny declared should be, and which our constancy and love brought forth, I felt something I cannot express, nor will I try; actually, I do not re-

member, with any certainty, and fear that whatever I might
say would be obscure.

Excuse me from telling the minutiae. No need to tell of the
devotion of my mother, and of Sancha, who came and spent
the first few days and nights with Capitú. I tried to refuse
Sancha's kindness. She answered that I had nothing to do
with this: Capitú, before she was married, had come to take
care of her in Rua dos Invalidos.

"Don't you remember, you came there to see her?"

"I remember; but Escobar . . ."

"I'll come and have dinner with you and at night return to
Andarahy. A week, and it will all be over. It's easy to see
you're a father with only one trip to your credit."

"What about you? Where's the second?"

This is the way we used to joke among ourselves. Today,
withdrawn within my *casmurricity,* I do not know whether
this kind of language still exists, but it must. Escobar did as
he said: he would dine with us and return home at night.
Toward evening we would go down to the beach or to the
Passeio Publico—he given over to his calculations, I to my
dreams. I saw my son a doctor, lawyer, businessman; I placed
him in various universities and banks, and even accepted the
hypothesis of his being a poet. The possibilities of politics
were consulted and I was willing to believe that I had begotten an orator, and a great orator.

"It may be," commented Escobar, "no one would have
imagined to what heights Demosthenes would rise."

Escobar often went along with my childish dreams; he too
interrogated the future. It was he who spoke of the possibility of marrying the boy to his daughter. Friendship does
exist: it was in my hands as I shook those of Escobar on hearing him say this, and in the total lack of words with which I

thus signed the pact. The words came afterward, in a rush and refined by the heart, which was beating hard. I accepted his offer . . . and proposed that we work toward this end, by bringing them up in the same way and together, in a united and perfect childhood.

It was my idea that Escobar be the baby's godfather; the godmother ought to be and would be my mother. But the first part of my plan was changed through the intervention of Uncle Cosme, who, on seeing the child, said to him among other caressing words:

"Come, get a blessing from your godfather, you rascal." And turning to me, "That's a favor I'll not refuse; and the christening must take place quickly, before my illness carries me off for good."

I discreetly related the anecdote to Escobar, so that he would understand and forgive. He laughed and was not offended. He did more, he asked to have the christening breakfast at his place in Andarahy—and so it was. I still kept delaying the ceremony, on the chance that Uncle Cosme would succumb to his illness in the meantime, but it seems the illness was more troublesome than fatal. There was no help for it but to carry the baby to the font, where he was given the name of Ezekiel: it was Escobar's and I wished in this way to make up for the relationship which had been denied us.

109. An only child

WHEN THE last chapter began, Ezekiel was not yet begotten; when it ended he was a Christian and a Catholic. This one is destined to bring my Ezekiel up to five years of age, a lusty, handsome boy, with his clear eyes already restless as if they wished to make love to all the girls of the neighborhood, or almost all.

Now, if you consider that he was the only one, that no other came, certain or uncertain, dead or alive, a one and only, you can imagine the anxieties he caused us, the sleep he robbed us of, and the scares he gave us with teething and other crises, the least little fever, the whole common existence of children. No matter what, we flew to the rescue, according to the need and urgency—something it would not be necessary to mention but there are readers so obtuse that they understand nothing unless you tell them everything—and what's left over. Let us go to what's left over.

110. Childhood traits

WHAT'S LEFT over will devour many more chapters. There are lives which have fewer, and even so are complete and finished.

At five and six years of age, Ezekiel did not seem to belie the dreams I had had on the beach at Gloria. On the contrary, one glimpsed in him all possible vocations from loafer to apostle. Loafer is used here in the good sense, in the sense of a man who thinks and remains silent; he would withdraw, at times, within himself, and in this reminded one of his mother from the time she was small. Then again he would become excited and insist on persuading the neighbor girls that the sweets I brought him were real sweets. He did not do it until he was stuffed with them himself, but neither do apostles carry abroad the Good Word until they have it all in

their own heart. Escobar, the good businessman, was of the
opinion that the main cause of this propensity was perhaps to
invite the neighbor girls, by implication, to a like apostolate
when their fathers brought them sweets; and he laughed at
his own wit and announced that he would make him his partner when he grew up.

Ezekiel liked music no less than sweets, and I told Capitú
to pick out for him on the piano the song of the Negro *cocada*
pedlar of Matacavallos . . .

"I don't remember it."

"Don't say that! You don't remember that colored man
who peddled sweets, in the afternoons . . ."

"I remember a colored man who used to sell sweets, but I
have no recollection of the tune."

"Nor the words?"

"Nor the words."

My lady reader, who will still remember the words, provided that she has read me attentively, will be astonished at
such forgetfulness, all the more because those words will remind her of the voices of her own childhood and adolescence;
she may have forgotten a word or two, but not everything remains in one's head. That is what Capitú said in reply, and
I could not answer her. I did something, however, that she
did not expect. I ran to my file of old papers. When I had
been a student at São Paulo, I had asked a music teacher to
transcribe the tune of the pedlar-song for me. He had been
happy to do it (all I had had to do was hum it to him from
memory), and I had kept the little scrap of paper. I went to
look for it. In a few moments, I interrupted a ballad she was
playing with the bit of paper. I explained to her; she ran
over the sixteen notes on the piano.

The tune had a special, almost delicious savor, for Capitú.

She told her son the story of the pedlar's song and then sang and played it over and over. Ezekiel put the music to good use by asking me to disprove the text and give him some money.

He played at doctor, soldier, actor and dancer. I never gave him oratories; but wooden horses and a sword at his side suited him. I won't speak of the battalions which passed by in the street and which he ran to see; all children do it. But all children do not have eyes like his. In none have I seen the joyous excitement with which he watched the passage of the troops and heard the roll of the drums.

"Look, Papa! Look!"

"I'm looking, son!"

"Look at the leader! Look at the leader's horse! Look at the soldiers!"

One day he woke playing the cornet with his fingers on air. I gave him a toy trumpet. I bought him lead soldiers, pictures of battles that he pored over for hours on end, wanting me to explain a piece of artillery, a fallen soldier, or one with his sword upraised, and all his love was for the one with upraised sword. One day (ingenuous age!) he asked me impatiently:

"But, Papa, why doesn't he bring his sword down and have it over with?"

"My son, it's because he's painted."

"But why did he paint himself?"

I laughed at the mistake and explained that it was not the soldier who had painted himself on the paper, but the engraver, and I had to explain also what an engraver was and what an engraving was—the curiosity of Capitú, in short.

Those were the principal traits of childhood. One more and we finish the chapter. One day, at Escobar's place, he

came across a cat with a mouse in its teeth. The cat would not
release its prey and yet did not know where to run. Ezekiel
did not make a sound; he stopped, crouched, and kept looking. When we saw him so, all intent, we called to him and
asked what it was. He made a sign for us to be quiet. Escobar
surmised, "I'll bet it's the cat and he's caught a mouse. I
can't get rid of the mice in this place; they're the very devil.
I'll see."

Capitú also wanted to see what the boy was doing. I went
along. As a matter of fact, it was a cat and a mouse, commonplace event, without interest or charm. The only peculiar
circumstance was that the mouse was alive, kicking, and my
little son entranced. But the instant was short. As soon as the
cat saw more people, it prepared to run. The child, keeping
his eyes on it, again motioned us for silence, and the silence
could not have been greater. I was going to say religious; I
scratched out the word, but I put it in here once more, not
only to signify the totality of the silence but also because
there was in the action of the cat and the mouse something
akin to ritual. The only sounds were the last squeaks of the
mouse, and they were feeble; its legs scarcely moved, and
crazily. Somewhat disgusted, I clapped my hands to make the
cat run away. And it ran. The others did not have time to
stop me. Ezekiel was dismayed.

"Aw, Papa!"

"So! By now the mouse has been eaten."

"Yes, but I wanted to see it."

The other two laughed. *I* also found it funny.

111. Told quickly

I FOUND it funny, and I still find it so, in spite of the time
that has passed, the events that have occurred and a kind of
sympathy that I have for the mouse; it was funny. It causes
me no regret to say so. Those who love Nature as she ought
to be loved, without partial repudiation or unjust exclusions,
find nothing low in her. I like the mouse; I do not dislike the
rat. I have even thought of getting them to live together; but
I realize that they are incompatible. As a matter of fact, one
gnaws my books, the other my cheese; but it is a small thing
I forgive them; I have forgiven a dog for robbing me of my
peace under worse circumstances. I will tell the incident
quickly.

It was when Ezekiel was born. His mother was in a fever,
with Sancha hovering over her, and three dogs barked in the
street all night long. I tried to find the officer on the beat and
it was as if I had tried to find the reader, who has only just
now learned of this. Then I made up my mind to kill them. I
bought poison, had three meatballs made, and I myself in-
serted the drug in them. I went out into the night. It was one
o'clock; neither the patient nor her nurse could sleep because
of the deafening racket of the dogs. When they saw me they
ran off; two went in the direction of Flamengo Beach, one
remained a short distance away, as if waiting. I went toward
him, whistling and snapping my fingers. The devil still
barked, but trusting in my signals of friendship, he barked
less and less, until he stopped altogether. As I proceeded, he
came to me, slowly, wagging his tail, which is a dog's way of
smiling. I had already taken out the balls of meat and was

about to throw him one, when that special smile, gesture of endearment or confidence, or whatever it may be, immobilized my will. I stood there, somehow touched with pity, and returned the meatballs to my pocket. The reader, perhaps, will think that it was the smell of the meat which quieted the dog. I don't say it was not. I believe he was unwilling to ascribe perfidy to my gesture, and therefore placed himself in my hands. The result was that he went free.

112. Ezekiel's imitations

EZEKIEL WOULD not have done this. He would not have made poisoned meatballs, I suppose, but neither would he have rejected them. What he would have done, certainly, was go after the dogs with a volley of stones as far as his legs would carry him; if he had had a stick he would have used the stick. And Capitú was wild about this future warrior.

"He doesn't take after us, who like peace," she said to me one day, "but Papa was like that as a boy. That's what Mamma used to tell me."

"Yes, he's no sissy," I replied, "and I find only one little defect in him: he likes to imitate people."

"Imitate? In what way?"

"Imitate their gestures, their manners, their attitudes. He imitates Cousin Justina, he imitates José Dias; I've even noticed that he has a way of moving his feet like Escobar, and the way he uses his eyes. . . ."

Capitú looked at me thoughtfully, and finally said we should correct him. For the first time, she realized it was a bad habit in the boy, but it seemed to her that it was only

imitating for the sake of imitating, as many grown persons do
who adopt the manners of others; but in order that it might
go no further . . .

"We must not mortify him either. There is still time to correct him."

"Yes, I'll see. And didn't you do it too when you were
angry at someone?"

"When I was angry, I admit—a child's vengeance."

"Yes, but I don't like imitations in my family."

"And in those days did you love me?" I asked, tapping her
on the cheek.

Capitú's answer was a sweet, mocking smile, one of those
smiles that can never be described, and rarely painted. Then
she stretched out her arms and threw them over my shoulders; they were so full of grace that they seemed (an old
image!) a necklace of flowers. I did the same with mine, and I
was sorry there was no sculptor around to transfer the pose to
marble. Only the artist would win glory by it, that is certain.
When a figure or group comes out well, no one is concerned
about the model, but only about the work. It is the work that
endures. No matter; we would know that it was ourselves.

113. Third party claim proceeding

NOW THAT I speak of this, you will probably ask whether I,
who had been so jealous of her, did not continue to be
jealous in spite of the child and the passing years. Yes, sir, I
did—to the point where the slightest gesture tormented me,
a casual word, the urging of a simple request; often, indif-
ference alone was enough. I became jealous of everything and

everyone. A neighbor, a partner in a waltz, any man, young or old, filled me with terror and mistrust. It is certain that Capitú liked to be seen, and the most proper means to that end (a lady once told me) is to see also, and there is no seeing without showing that one sees.

The lady who told me this, I believe, had taken a fancy to me, and it was probably because she did not discover in me reciprocal affection, that she explained thus the boldness of her eyes. Other eyes sought me too, not many, and I shall say nothing about them; since, I confessed at the start that I was to have future adventures—but they were as yet, still in the future. In those days, for all the pretty women I met, not one could have received the smallest fraction of the love I had for Capitú. My own mother was not loved more than half as much. Capitú was all and more than all; I did not draw a breath, even when working, without thinking of her. We went to the theater; I remember only twice that I went without her, an actors' benefit and a first performance of an opera, which she did not attend because she felt ill, although she insisted on my going. It was too late to send the tickets to Escobar. I went, but came home at the end of the first act. I found Escobar at the front door.

"I wanted to talk to you," he said.

I explained that I had gone to the theater but had returned because I was worried about Capitú who had felt ill.

"Ill of what?" asked Escobar.

"She complained of her head and stomach."

"Then I'll leave. I came about that business of the claims." It was a third party claim proceeding. Something important had turned up, and, having dined in the city, he did not want to go home without telling me about it, but now he would tell me another time. . . .

"No, let us talk about it. Come on up. She may be better. If she is worse, you can leave."

Capitú was better and even feeling fine. She admitted to me that she had only had a slight headache, but exaggerated her suffering so that I would go out and enjoy myself. She did not speak cheerfully, which made me suspect that she was lying in order not to alarm me, but she swore it was absolutely true. Escobar smiled and said:

"My little sister-in-law is as sick as you or I. Let's get at our claims."

114. In which is explained the explained

BEFORE WE get at the claims, let us explain a point which has already been explained, though not fully. You have seen how I asked (Ch. 110) a music teacher of São Paulo to write down the tune of the Matacavallos pedlar's song. The thing is silly in itself and not worth a chapter, much less two. But there are matters such as this which furnish lessons that are interesting, if not agreeable. Let us explain the explained.

Capitú and I had sworn never to forget that pedlar's song. It was in a moment of great tenderness. The Divine Scribe knows the things that are sworn to in such moments—he who records them in the eternal books.

"Do you swear?"

"I swear it," she said, extending her arm tragically.

I put the gesture to good use by kissing her hand; I was still in the seminary. When I went to São Paulo and tried to remember the tune one day, I saw that I was losing it entirely. I succeeded in recalling it and ran to the teacher, who was kind enough to write it down on a scrap of paper.

It was in order not to be false to my oath that I did this. But
will you believe it, when I ran to my old papers, that night
in Gloria, I too no longer remembered the tune nor the text?
I pretended to be true to my oath, and that was my sin.
Forget! Anyone forgets.

Indeed, no one definitely knows whether or not he will
keep an oath. It rests with the future! For this reason our political constitution, in substituting for the oath the simple
affirmation, is profoundly moral. It put an end to a terrible
sin. To break one's word is still an unfaithful act, but anyone
who has more fear of God than of men, does not mind lying
once in a while, seeing that it will not put his soul in purgatory. Do not confuse purgatory with hell, which is eternal
ruin. Purgatory is a pawnshop which lends on all the virtues,
for high interest and short term. But the term may be renewed until, one day, one or two middling virtues pay for all
one's sins great and small.

115. Doubts upon doubts

NOW LET us get to the claims. . . . And why should we get
to the claims? God knows what a bother it is to write them
up, let alone tell about them. As for the new circumstance of
which Escobar had brought word, I will say what I told him
at the time: it was worth nothing.

"Nothing?"

"Almost nothing."

"Then it is worth something."

"As something to strengthen our case, it is worth less than
the tea that you are going to take with me."

"It's too late for tea."

"We'll take it quickly."

We took it quickly. Meanwhile Escobar looked at me suspiciously, as if he thought I rejected the additional claim in order to escape writing it up; but this suspicion conflicted with our friendship.

When he left, I mentioned my doubts to Capitú. She dissolved them into nothing with the fine art she possessed, a knack, a grace all her own, capable of dissipating the sorrows of Olympio.

"It must be the business of the claim proceeding," she concluded, "and if he came all the way over here at this hour, it means he is impressed with the case."

"You're right."

One word led to another, I spoke of other doubts. I was a well of them; they were croaking inside me like genuine frogs, until they stole my sleep at times. I told her I had begun to consider my mother somewhat cool and distant with her. But the fine art of Capitú was equal to this also.

"I have already told you what it is: the way of a mother-in-law. Your little mother is jealous. As soon as this passes and her longing returns, she'll be as she was. When she misses her grandson . . ."

"But I've noticed that she's cool with Ezekiel too. When I bring him to see her, she doesn't make as much fuss over him as before."

"Who knows, perhaps she isn't well."

"Shall we have dinner with her tomorrow?"

"Let's . . . No . . . Yes, let's."

We had dinner with my old mother. You could call her that now, though her locks were not all white nor wholly white, and her face was comparatively fresh: it was a sort of quinquagenarian youthfulness or luxuriant ancientness, take

your choice . . . But nothing melancholy! I will not mention the moistness of her eyes when we came and when we
left. She had little to say. And yet she was no different than
usual. José Dias spoke of marriage and its beauties, of politics, of Europe and of homeopathy; Uncle Cosme of his aches
and pains; Cousin Justina of the neighbors, or of José Dias
when he was out of the room.

When we left for home, it was night, we went on foot, discussing my doubts. Capitú again advised that we be patient.
Mothers-in-law were all like that; then there came a day and
they changed. As she spoke, her tenderness grew afresh.
Henceforth she became increasingly gentle with me. She did
not wait for me at the window, so as not to arouse my jealousy,
but when I set my foot on the step, there at the top of the
stairs, through the grillwork of the gate, I would see the
lovely face of my darling bride, as smiling as our whole childhood. Ezekiel was sometimes with her. We had accustomed
him to see our morning and evening kiss, and he would cover
my face with his little kisses.

116. Son of man

I SOUNDED out José Dias on my mother's changed manner.
He was amazed. There wasn't anything, there couldn't be
anything—or he wouldn't keep hearing such incessant praise
of "the beautiful and virtuous Capitú."

"Now, when I hear it, I too join the chorus; but at first I
was *most* humiliated. For one, like me, who had refused to
accept this marriage, it was hard to admit that it was a verita-
ble blessing from heaven. What a worthy lady the mischievous child of Matacavallos has become! It was her father

who kept us apart for a while, before we came to know each other, but everything turned out all right. Yes indeed, when Dona Gloria praises her daughter-in-law and sister . . ."

"Mamma?"

"Absolutely!"

"But why hasn't she visited us for so long?"

"I believe that she has been ailing with her rheumatism lately. This year has been very cold . . . Just think how miserable she must be—she who used to walk about the entire day, and who now is obliged to remain quiet, alongside her brother who has his affliction also . . ."

I wanted to observe that this reason explained the interruption of the visits, not the coolness when we went to Matacavallos; but, I did not carry my intimacy with our dependent that far. José Dias asked to see our "little prophet" (that is what he called Ezekiel) and made much over him as usual. This time he spoke in the Biblical manner (he had been leafing through the Book of Ezekiel the night before as I later learned), and asked him, "How goes it, son of man?" "Tell me, son of man, where are your toys?" "Would you like a sweet, son of man?"

"What's this son of man business?" asked Capitú sharply.

"It's the manner of speaking of the Bible."

"Well, I don't like it," she replied.

"You are right, Capitú," agreed the dependent. "You can't imagine how full the Bible is of crude and coarse expressions. I was speaking that way for the sake of variety . . . How are you, my little angel? My angel, how do I walk down the street?"

"No," interrupted Capitú, "I'm trying to break him of his habit of imitating people."

"But it's very funny; when he mimics my gestures, he seems

to be myself in miniature. The other day he happened to copy one of Dona Gloria's gestures so well that she gave him a kiss in payment. Come, how do I walk?"

"No, Ezekiel," I said, "Mamma said 'no.' "

I too found it an unpleasant habit. Some of the gestures were becoming habitual with him, like those movements of Escobar's hands and feet. Lately he had even caught the same manner of turning his head when he talked, and of letting it fall when he laughed. Capitú scolded. But the child was mischievous as the devil; we had scarcely begun to talk of something else, when he jumped into the middle of the room, shouting to José Dias:

"You walk like this, senhor."

We could not help laughing, I most of all. The first person to stop laughing, reprimand him and call him to her, was Capitú.

"I won't have it, do you hear?"

117. Friends and neighbors

AT THAT time Escobar had already left Andarahy and bought a house in Flamengo, a house which I saw there still, a few days ago, when I had an urge to test if the old sensations were dead or merely sleeping. I cannot quite tell because sleep, when it is heavy, confounds the living with the dead, except that the living breathe. I *was* breathing, but (perhaps because of the sea) with some difficulty. Finally I walked on, lit a cigar, and found myself in Cattete; I had gone up the Rua da Princeza, an ancient street . . . O ancient streets! O ancient houses! O ancient legs! We were all ancient, and, needless to say, in the worst sense; that is—old and done for.

Though the house is old, nothing has been altered. I don't
know but what it still has the same number. I will not tell
what the number is since I don't want you to go there and
ferret out the story. Not that Escobar still lives there, or even
lives. He died a short time later, in a manner which I will
describe. While he lived, since we were so close, we had, so to
speak, a single house; I lived in his and he in mine, and the
strip of beach between Gloria and Flamengo was like a private
right of way. It made me think of the two houses of Matacavallos, with their wall between.

A historian, who wrote in our language, I believe it was
João de Barros, puts into the mouth of a barbarian king certain gentle words, uttered at a time when the Portuguese
were proposing to establish a fort nearby. The king said that
good friends should remain far apart, not near, so as not to
rage against each other, like the waters of the sea that beat
furiously on the rocky cliff visible from where they were. May
the dead writer's shade pardon me if I doubt that the king
said any such thing, or even its truth. Probably the writer
himself invented it to adorn his text, and he was quite right,
because it is a handsome speech, truly handsome. And I believe the sea actually did beat against the rocks, as has been
its custom, since Ulysses and even before. But, as for the comparison being true, no, I do not believe that. Certainly there
are neighboring enemies, but there are also friends, close in
space as well as in each other's hearts. And the writer forgot
(unless, of course, it came after his time) the adage, "Far from
eyes, far from heart." Our hearts could not have been closer
together. Our wives lived, each in the house of the other. We
passed our evenings here or there, conversing, playing cards,

or gazing at the sea. The two youngsters passed their days, now at Flamengo, now at Gloria.

When I happened to remark that what had taken place between Capitú and me might also happen to them, the others all thought so too, and Sancha added that they were even getting to look alike. I explained:

"No, it's because Ezekiel imitates the gestures of others."

Escobar agreed with me, and suggested that sometimes children who are always together finally come to look alike. I nodded assent, as I usually did in matters in which I had no opinion one way or the other. Anything was possible. They were certainly very fond of each other, and it might have ended in marriage, but it did not end in marriage.

118. The hand of Sancha

EVERYTHING COMES to an end, reader. It is an old truism to which may be added that not everything that lasts, lasts for long. This latter part is not readily admitted; on the contrary the idea that an air castle lasts longer than the very air of which it is made is hard to get out of a person's head, and this is fortunate; otherwise the custom of making those almost eternal constructions might be lost.

Our castle was solid, but one Sunday . . . The night before, we had passed the evening in Flamengo, not only the two inseparable couples, but also the dependent and Cousin Justina. It was then that Escobar, as we stood talking in the window, told me that we must come back and have dinner there the following day; that it was necessary to discuss a family project, a project for the four of us.

"For the four of us? A *contre-danse?*"

"No. You'll never guess what it is, and I won't tell you. Come tomorrow."

Sancha's eyes did not leave us during our conversation in the recess of the window. When her husband walked away, she came to me. She asked me what we had been talking about. I told her, "about a project for something but I don't know what." She asked me not to say anything, and revealed what it was: a trip to Europe two years from then. She said this with her back toward the room, almost in a sigh. The sea pounded forcibly along the shore; and there was the suck of the undertow.

"We all go?" I asked finally.

"Yes, all."

Sancha raised her head and looked at me with so much joy that because she was such a friend of Capitú I would have liked to kiss her on the forehead. And yet Sancha's eyes did not ask for fraternal expansiveness—they seemed sultry and imperious, they said something quite different, and soon she moved away from the window, where I remained looking pensively toward the sea. The night was clear.

From my corner, I sought Sancha's eyes, near the piano: mine met hers on the way. They stood still, and remained facing each other, one pair waiting for the other to pass, but neither passed, just as happens on a narrow path when two stubborn travelers meet. Caution drew us apart; I returned to the view beyond the window. I began to dig into my memory. Had I ever looked at her with such an expression? I was not sure. I was sure of only one thing, that one day I thought of her as one thinks of the fair unknown who passes by; but suppose she guessed . . . Perhaps the simple thought shone through me, and she fled me then, vexed or shy, and now an irresistible urge . . . Irresistible: this word was like the padre's benediction at Mass, which each receives and repeats within himself.

"Tomorrow, the sea will be a challenge," it was the voice of Escobar, who was standing at my side.

"You intend to swim in that sea tomorrow?"

"I've gone in in worse, much worse. You can't imagine what a good wild sea is like. One must swim well, as I do, and have these lungs," he said beating his chest, "and these arms. Feel."

I felt his arms, as if I were feeling those of Sancha. This confession is painful for me to make, but I cannot suppress it; it would mean distorting truth. I not only had this idea—but also, feeling his arms, I found them thicker and stronger than mine, and I envied them; in addition they could swim.

As we were leaving, my eyes spoke once more to the mistress of the house. Her hand pressed mine, and lingered there longer than usual.

Modesty demanded then, as now, that I see in Sancha's gesture approval of her husband's project and thankfulness for it. It must have been that, but a strange current passing through my body, forced me to repudiate the conclusion I have just written. I still felt Sancha's fingers pressing mine, and mine hers. It was an instant of madness and sin. It passed quickly, and when I held Time's watch to my ear, I heard only the minutes of virtue and reason ticking away.

". . . A very lovely lady," were the closing words of a speech that José Dias had been making.

"Very lovely!" I repeated with feeling, which I moderated right away, and corrected myself: "Really, a beautiful evening!"

"As all those of that house should be," continued the dependent. "Out here, no; out here the sea is angry. Listen."

We heard the roar of the sea—as we had heard it from the house—the undertow was strong, and in the distance we could see the waves rise in great swells. Capitú and Cousin Justina, who had gone ahead, were waiting for us in one of the turns of the shore, and the four of us walked on together, conversing. But I was in no condition for conversation. There was no forgetting the hand of Sancha, nor the looks we had traded. Now I read this in them, now that. The Devil's seconds had got intercalated into the minutes of God, and the watch was thus alternately marking my perdition and my salvation. José Dias said goodbye at our door. Cousin Justina was to stay the night with us and leave the next day after breakfast and Mass. I retired to my study, where I stayed longer than usual.

The picture of Escobar, that I kept there, alongside the one of my mother, spoke to me as if it were he *in propria persona*. I struggled sincerely against the impulses I had brought from Flamengo; I cast from me the image of my friend's wife, and called myself disloyal. Besides, who could say there had been any intention of that sort in her goodbye gesture and in the previous ones? It could all be ascribed to her interest in our trip. Sancha and Capitú were such good friends that it would be an added pleasure for them to go together. Even if there had been some sexual intent, how could I be sure it was anything more than a swift flash of sensation, destined to die with night and sleep? There are pangs of remorse that spring from no greater sin and have no greater duration. I held fast to this hypothesis, and so made peace with the hand of Sancha, which I felt from memory within my own, warm and lingering, clasped and clasping. . . .

In all sincerity, I was uncomfortable, caught between a friend and temptation. It may be too that timidity had some-

thing to do with the crisis. It is not only to heaven that we owe
our virtues, but to timidity also—not to mention chance—but
chance is pure accident; the best source of virtue is heaven.
Still, since timidity comes from heaven, and heaven gives us
our moral complexion, the virtue which is daughter of timidity is, genealogically speaking, of the same celestial blood.
That is the way I would have reasoned, if I could have; but at
first I wandered without reason. It was not passion or love.
Was it caprice or what? At the end of twenty minutes it was
nothing, absolutely nothing. The picture of Escobar seemed
to speak to me; I saw his frank and simple attitude, shook my
head, and went off to bed.

119. Don't do it, my dear!

THE LADY reader, who is my friend and has opened this book
with the idea of relaxing between yesterday's cavatina and
today's waltz, would like to close it in a hurry now that she
sees we are skirting an abyss. . . . Don't do it my dear; I'll
wheel about.

120. Legal papers

THE NEXT morning I awoke freed of the abominations of
the night. I called them hallucinations, had coffee, looked
through the newspapers, and began to study some legal papers
—one of my cases. Capitú and Cousin Justina left for the nine
o'clock Mass at Lapa. The figure of Sancha disappeared entirely in the midst of the allegations of the opposing side,
which I had been reading in the documents, allegations which

were false, inadmissible, without support either of law or practice. I saw that it would be easy to win the case; I consulted Dalloz, Pereira e Souza. . . .

Only once did I glance at the picture of Escobar. It was a handsome photograph, taken the previous year. He was standing frock coat buttoned, left hand on the back of a chair, right hand on his chest, gaze far away to the left of the spectator. It had elegance and naturalness. The frame I had had made to order so as not to cover the inscription which was written below, not on the back: "To my dear Bentinho his devoted Escobar. 20-4-70." These words strengthened my thoughts that morning and beat off the recollections of the preceding evening. In those days my sight was good; I could read the inscription from where I sat. I returned to my legal papers.

121. The catastrophe

IN THE midst of them I heard hurried footsteps on the stairs, the bell ringing, then someone clapping his hands, and a knocking at the grilled gate—voices, everyone running to answer. It was a slave from Sancha's house who called me:

"To go there . . . Senhor swimming, Senhor dying."

That was all he said, or I did not hear the rest. I dressed, left a message for Capitú, and ran to Flamengo.

As I ran, I divined the truth. Escobar had gone for his customary swim, had ventured farther than usual despite the heavy seas, had been overwhelmed by the waves and drowned. The rescue canoes had been unable to do more than bring back his body.

122. The funeral

THE WIDOW . . . I will spare you the widow's tears, mine,
those of the others. I left around eleven. Capitú and Cousin
Justina were waiting for me, the one with downcast, stupid
look, the other little more than annoyed.

"Go keep poor Sanchinha company. I'll arrange for the
funeral."

That is what we did. I decided that the funeral should have
pomp and magnificence. There was a large attendance of his
friends—beach, streets, the Praça da Gloria, were all filled
with carriages, many private ones. Since the house was not
large, it could not hold everyone; many stood on the beach
discussing the accident, pointing out the place where Escobar
had met his death, listening to the tale of how the body was
brought in. José Dias also heard them speak of the business
affairs of the deceased, and express different opinions on the
value of his estate, though agreeing that his liabilities were
few. They praised the excellence of Escobar's character. One
or two discussed the recent Rio Branco cabinet: it was in
March, 1871. I have never forgotten the month or the year.

As I had decided to make a speech at the cemetery, I wrote
a few lines at home, and showed them to José Dias, who
thought them genuinely worthy of the dead man and of
me. He asked me for the paper, read the speech aloud,
slowly, weighing the words, and reaffirmed his first judgment. He spread the news around Flamengo. Several acquaintances came up to me and asked:

"Then we are to hear from you?"

"A couple of words."

It would be very few more. I had written them because I feared my emotions would prevent improvisation. In the tilbury in which I had ridden about for a couple of hours, I had done nothing but recall the days of the seminary, my intimacy with Escobar, our sympathies, our friendship, begun, continued, and never interrupted, until a stroke of fortune had separated forever two beings who had given promise of remaining united for many a long day. From time to time I had wiped my eyes. The driver had ventured two or three queries concerning my spiritual state, and getting nothing out of me, had continued to perform his office. When I returned home, I had put those emotions on paper; this would be my speech.

123. Eyes like the tide

FINALLY THE hour arrived for commending the soul to God and for departure. Sancha wished to take a last farewell of her husband, and the despair of that effort filled us all with grief and pity. Many men wept; all the women. Only Capitú, supporting the widow, seemed able to control herself. Consoling the other, she tried to pull her away. The consternation was general. In the midst of it, Capitú gazed down for a few seconds at the corpse, gazed so fixedly, with such passionate fixedness, that it was no wonder if tears sprang to her eyes, a few, quiet tears . . .

My own ceased at once. I stood looking at hers; she wiped them away in haste, glancing furtively around at the people in the room. She redoubled her caresses to her friend, and tried to take her away, but the corpse seemed to hold her too. There was a moment when Capitú's eyes gazed down at the

dead man just as the widow's had, though without her weeping or any accompanying words, but great and wide like the
swollen wave of the sea beyond, as if she too wished to swallow up the swimmer of that morning.

124. The speech

"COME, it is time . . ."

It was José Dias prompting me to close the coffin. We
closed it, and I grasped one of the handles; whereupon, the
final confusion began. I give you my word, when I reached
the door, saw the bright sunlight, all the people and carriages, the uncovered heads, I had one of those impulses of
mine which never arrive at execution: it was to throw the
box, corpse and all, into the street. In the carriage I told José
Dias to hold his tongue. At the cemetery I had to repeat the
ceremony of the house, unfasten the straps, and help bear the
coffin to the grave. You can imagine what this cost me. After
the corpse was lowered into the grave, the lime and the spade
were brought. You must know all about this, you have probably attended more than one funeral, but what you do not
know, and none of your friends can know, reader, nor anyone
but me, is the state I was in when I saw all those eyes on me,
the quiet feet, the attentive ears, and at the end of several
seconds of total silence, heard a vague whisper, questioning
voices, noticed looks, while someone, José Dias, said in my ear:

"Go on, speak."

It was the speech. They were waiting for the speech. They
were entitled to it; it had been announced. Mechanically,
I put my hand in my pocket, drew out the paper, and read

in a mad outpouring—not all, nor without halting, nor clearly; my voice seemed to go in instead of coming out, my hands trembled. It was not only the new emotion, that caused it, but the text itself, the memories of my friend, the confessed love and grief, the praise of his person and his worth; all this, which I was obliged to say and could hardly utter. At the same time, fearful that they would guess the truth, I strove to hide it. I believe that few heard me, but the general attitude was one of comprehension and approbation. The hands given me to shake were offered in fellowship. Some said, "Very fine! Well done! Magnificent!" José Dias thought my eloquence in keeping with the respect due the deceased. A man, who seemed to be a reporter, asked permission to publish the manuscript. It must have been my great perturbation that made me refuse such a simple request.

125. A comparison

PRIAM THOUGHT himself the most unfortunate of men for having kissed the hand of him who slew his son. It is Homer who tells the story, and he is a good author though he speaks in verse—but there are accurate narrations in verse, even in bad verse. Compare Priam's situation with mine. I had just praised the virtues of the man who had received, dead though he was, the gaze of those eyes. . . . It is impossible that a Homer would not have drawn a much more effective scene from my situation, or at least one equally good. And don't tell me that we lack Homers for the reason pointed out in Camões. No, senhor, we lack them, it is true, but it is because the Priams hide themselves in obscurity and silence. Their tears, if they

shed them, are wiped away behind the door so that their faces
may appear bright and clean. Their talk is rather of joy than
of melancholy, and all goes along as if Achilles had not slain
Hector.

126. Musing

A LITTLE distance from the cemetery, I tore up the speech
and threw the pieces out the carriage window, in spite of the
efforts of José Dias to stop me.

"It's no good," I said to him, "and as I might be tempted
to let someone publish it, now it's destroyed once and for all.
It's no good, it's worth nothing."

José Dias demonstrated at great length that the contrary
was true. Then he praised the funeral, and, for a finale, made
a panegyric on the dead man: a great soul, active mind, up-
right heart, friend, good friend, worthy of the very loving
wife that God had given him . . .

At this point of the speech, I let him go on talking to himself, and began to muse. My musings were so dim and confused that I could not find my way among them. In Cattete
I stopped the carriage, told José Dias to fetch the ladies at
Flamengo and take them home; I would continue on foot.

"But . . ."

"I want to make a call."

The reason for this was to finish my musing and take some
resolution that would be adequate to the moment. The carriage went faster than my legs; the latter might pause or not,
slacken their step, stop, go back over the road, and leave my
head to muse at will. I walked along and mused. I had already
compared Sancha's gesture of the previous evening with her

despair of that day; they were irreconcilable. She was truly
a most devoted widow. Thus the illusion created by my vanity vanished completely. Would it not be the same in Capitú's
case? I tried to reconstruct the scene: her eyes, the attitude
in which I had surprised her, the gathering of people which
would naturally constrain her to conceal if there were anything to be concealed. What appears here in logical and de-
ductive order had been a hubbub of ideas and sensations, as
a result of the jolting carriage and the interruptions of José
Dias. Now, however, I reasoned and recalled, clearly and
well. I concluded inwardly that my old passion still darkened
my vision and deluded me as always.

As I arrived at this conclusion, I also arrived at the door
of my house, but I turned and went back up Rua do Cattete.
Was it the doubts that worried me or the need that I felt to
worry Capitú with my prolonged absence? Let us say it was
both reasons. I walked a good stretch, until I felt calmer, and
then headed home. The clock in a bakery was striking eight.

127. The barber

NEAR MY house there was a barber who knew me by sight.
He loved to play the fiddle, and his playing was not as bad
as it might have been. As I passed he was executing some
piece or other. I stopped on the sidewalk to listen (anything
is an excuse to a heart in agony). He saw me and went on
playing. He did not wait on one customer, and then another,
who had come there despite the hour and its being Sunday,
to entrust their faces to his razor. He lost them without losing
a note; he was playing for me. This attention made me go

frankly to the shop door and look straight in at him. At the back, the chintz curtain which shut off the interior of the house was raised and a young brunette appeared, bright dress, flower in hair. It was his wife. I believe that she had noticed me from inside and came to thank me with her presence for the honor I did her husband. If I am not mistaken, she even said as much with her eyes. As for the husband, he was now playing more fervently. He did not see his wife, he did not see the customers. He glued his face to the instrument, his soul passed into the bow, and he played and played. . . .

Divine art! A crowd was gathering. I left the door of the shop and walked toward home. I let myself in and went noiselessly up the stairs. I have never forgotten the incident of this barber either because it was linked to a grave moment of my life, or because of this maxim, which compilers may take out and insert in their school books. The maxim is that we are slow to forget the good deeds we do, and really never forget them. Poor barber! he lost two beards that night, which were the bread of the next day, all in order to be heard by a passer-by. Suppose now that this passer-by, instead of going on, had remained at the door to hear him and make love to his wife—then, no doubt, all bow, all fiddle, he would have played desperately. Divine art!

128. A handful of events

AS I was saying, I went noiselessly up the stairs, pushed open the gate, which was slightly ajar, and came upon Cousin Justina and José Dias playing cards in the little sitting room close by. Capitú rose from the settee and came to me. Her face was now serene and clear. The others paused in their game, and we all talked of the accident and the widow. Capitú blamed Escobar for his recklessness, and did not conceal the sadness her friend's grief caused her. I asked why she had not stayed with Sancha all night.

"She has a great many people there. Even so, I offered to stay, but she refused. I also told her it would be best for her to come here and spend a few days with us."

"She refused that too?"

"That too."

"And yet the sight of the sea must be painful for her, every morning," pondered José Dias, "and I don't know how she will be able . . ."

"It will pass. What doesn't?" put in Cousin Justina.

And as we began an exchange of words around this idea, Capitú left the room to see if her son was sleeping. In passing the mirror, she stopped to arrange her hair, so leisurely that one would have thought it affectation if one had not known she was very fond of herself. When she returned her eyes were red. She told us that when she saw her son sleeping, she thought of Sancha's little daughter, and the widow's sorrow. And, without caring about the visitors or noticing whether a servant happened to be around, she threw her arms around me and told me that if I wished to think of her I should first think of my own life. José Dias pronounced the phrase "very beautiful," and asked Capitú why she had never written poetry. I tried to turn it into a joke, and thus we finished the evening.

The next day I was sorry that I had torn up my speech—not that I wanted to publish it but it was a remembrance of the deceased. I thought of recomposing it, but all I could remem-

ber were disconnected phrases that made no sense when I
joined them. I also thought of writing another, but it would
be difficult now, and might be recognized as false by those
who had heard me at the cemetery. As for gathering up the
bits of paper thrown into the street, it was too late. They
would have already been swept away.

I made an inventory of my souvenirs of Escobar: books, a
bronze inkwell, an ivory-headed cane, a bird, Capitú's album,
two Paraná landscapes, and others. He had received some
from me too. We used to exchange memories and gifts such
as these on birthdays, or for no particular reason. All this
made my eyes grow dim. Then came the day's papers: they
gave an account of the accident and of the death of Escobar,
of his education and his commercial ventures, his personal
qualities, the regard of the business world, and they also
spoke of the property he had left, of his wife and his daughter.
All this was on Monday. On Tuesday the will was opened:
it named me substitute executor; the first place went to his
wife. He did not leave me anything, but the words that he
wrote me in a separate letter were sublime in their expression
of friendship and esteem. This time Capitú wept copiously;
but quickly composed herself.

Will, inventory, all took place almost as quickly as told
here. After a short time, Sancha retired to the home of her
relatives in Paraná.

129. To Dona Sancha

DONA SANCHA, I beg you not to read this book; or, if you
have read thus far, abandon the rest. You have only to close
it; better still, burn it, so that it will not be a temptation to

you to open it again. If, in spite of the warning, you are
determined to continue to the end, the fault is yours; I will
not be responsible for the pain you are about to receive.
What I have already inflicted on you by describing the gestures of that distant Saturday—is all ended, seeing that events,
and I with them, gave the lie to my illusion; but what is to
come now cannot be erased. No, my dear, read no further.
Go on growing old, without husband, without child, as I
do and it is still the best that one can do after youth is gone.
One day we will go from here to the gate of heaven where
we shall meet again, renewed like the new green plants in
spring,

> "Made new—as trees are brought to life again
>   With their new foliage—purified." *

The rest, in Dante.

130. One day

ONE DAY Capitú wanted to know what made me so silent
and gloomy. She suggested Europe, Minas, Petropolis, a series
of balls, a thousand of those remedies prescribed for the
melancholy. I did not know how to answer her; I declined the
diversions. Since she insisted, I replied that business had
been going badly. Capitú smiled to cheer me. And what if
it had? It would improve, and until then her jewels, objects
of any value, would be sold, and we could go and live in
some alley. We would live quietly, forgetting and forgotten;
later we would rise to the surface again. The tenderness with
which she said this would have moved a stone. But *I* was not
moved. I answered drily that there was no need to sell any-

* Translation of Lawrence Grant White (N. Y.: Pantheon Books, 1948).

thing. I remained silent and gloomy. She proposed a game
of cards or checkers, a walk, a visit to Matacavallos; and, as
I would have none of them, she went into the living room,
opened the piano and began to play. I availed myself of her
absence to take my hat and leave.

. . . Pardon me, but this chapter ought to have been pre-
ceded by another, in which I would have told an incident that
occurred a few weeks before, two months after Sancha had
gone away. I will write it. I could place it ahead of this one
before sending the book to the printer, but it is too great a
nuisance to have to change the page numbers. Let it go right
here; after that the narration will proceed as it should right
to the end. Besides, it is short.

131. Anterior to the anterior

THE TRUTH was that my life was once again sweet and placid.
The law paid me well enough. Capitú was more beautiful.
Ezekiel was growing up. We were entering the year 1872.

"Have you noticed that Ezekiel has an odd expression
about the eyes?" asked Capitú. "I've seen only two other people with the same expression, a friend of Papa's and poor
Escobar. Look, Ezekiel, look straight, there, look at Papa—you
needn't roll your eyes, there, there. . . ."

It was after dinner. We were still at table. Capitú was
playfully teasing her son, or he her, or each the other, for
they were truly very fond of each other—but actually, he was
even fonder of me. I drew closer to Ezekiel; I found that
Capitú was right. They were Escobar's eyes, but they did not
seem odd to me for that reason. After all there are probably

not more than a half-dozen expressions in the world, and many resemblances occur naturally. Ezekiel did not understand, he looked in startled amazement from her to me, and finally jumped up and threw his arms around my neck:

"Let's go for a walk, Papa?"

"Presently, my son."

Capitú, unmindful of either of us, was staring at the other side of the table. But when I told her that for beauty, Ezekiel's eyes resembled his mother's, Capitú smiled and shook her head with an air I have never found in another woman, probably because I never loved the others half as much. People are worth the value that our affection sets on them, and it is from this that we get the adage, "Ugly is fair to a lover." Capitú had half a dozen gestures that were unique on this earth. This one went straight to my heart—which explains why I ran to my wife and darling, and covered her face with kisses. But the second incident is not fundamentally necessary to the comprehension of the last chapter nor of those to follow. Let us stay with Ezekiel's eyes.

132. The sketch and the color

NOT ONLY his eyes, but the remaining features also, face, body, the entire person, were acquiring definition with the passage of time. They were like a rough sketch that the artist elaborates little by little. The figure begins to look out at you, smile, throb with life, almost speak; at length the family hangs the picture on the wall in memory of what was and can be no longer. In this case, it could be and was. Habit helped conceal the change; nevertheless, the change occurred.

It happened not in the manner of the theater, but like the day, which appears slowly, so slowly that at first a letter can scarcely be read, and then, behold, the letter may be read in the street, in the house, in the study, without opening the windows; the light filtering through the Venetian blinds is sufficient for distinguishing the words. I read the letter, uncertainly at first, though not all of it; later I was able to make it out more surely. True, I refused to read it, shoved the paper into my pocket, ran home, shut myself in, refused to open the blinds, even closed my eyes. When I opened my eyes again, letter and writing were clear—the message crystal clear.

Escobar emerged from the grave, from the seminary, from Flamengo; he sat at table with me, welcomed me on the stairs, kissed me each morning in my study or asked for the customary blessing at night. All this repelled me; I endured it so as not to be revealed to myself and to the world. But what I could conceal from the world I could not conceal from myself —I was closer to myself than anyone. When neither mother nor son were with me, my desperation was extreme, and I would vow to kill them both, suddenly or slowly—slowly, so as to transfer into their dying, all the moments of my dulled, agonized life. When I returned home and saw waiting at the head of the stairs the little child so devoted to me, I would be disarmed and would defer the punishment from day to day.

I shall not record here what passed between Capitú and me during those dark days; such a record would be too repetitious. Now, so long after the events, I would be unable to recall them without omissions or weariness. But I shall relate the most significant thing. The most significant thing was that the storms had now become continuous and ter-

rible. Before discovering that evil land of Truth, we had had
other storms, but of short duration—before long the sky
would be blue, the sun bright and the sea smooth, and we
would again unfurl our sails, and they would carry us to the
fairest islands and coasts of the universe before another squall
blew down everything, and we lay to, waiting for another
calm; it would not be slow in coming, nor would it be doubt-
ful, but rather complete, near at hand, and sure.

Forgive these metaphors; they savor of the sea and of the
tide which brought death to my friend, my wife's lover,
Escobar. They savor also of Capitú's eyes, eyes like the tide
when the undertow is strong. And so, though I have always
been a landsman, I tell this part of my life as an old sailor
recalls his shipwreck.

The only thing lacking between us now was the final word.
We read it, however, in each other's eyes, vibrant and decisive. Whenever Ezekiel approached, he only drove us
apart. Capitú suggested placing him in a boarding school,
from which he would only come home week ends. It was difficult for the little boy to accept this situation.

"I'll go with Papa! Papa must go with me!" he shouted.

And it was I who took him, one Monday morning. The
school was in old Lapa Square, not far from our house. I went
on foot, taking him by the hand; my same hands had taken
away the other's coffin. The little boy accompanied me, crying and asking questions at every step . . . Would he return
home? . . . When? . . . Would I come to see him? . . .

"I will."

"You won't come, Papa."

"Yes, I will."

"Swear it, Papa!"

"Of course."

"Papa, you didn't swear to it."

"I swear it."

I brought him there and left him. The temporary absence did not eliminate the evil, and all Capitú's artful attempts to attenuate it were to no purpose: I grew steadily worse. The new situation itself aggravated my torture. Ezekiel was no longer constantly present; but his return on week ends— either because I was no longer accustomed to him or because time was completing the resemblance—was the return of Escobar, only more alive and noisier. After a while, even the voice seemed the same. On Saturdays I avoided dining at home and would not return until he was asleep; but there was no escaping him on Sundays as I sat over newspapers and legal work in my study. Ezekiel would enter, boisterous, expansive, smiling and full of love, for the little devil kept growing fonder of me. I, on the contrary, now felt an aversion, an aversion I could scarcely conceal from Capitú and the others. Since I could not completely hide my state of mind, I kept out of his way as much as possible. Either I would have work which obliged me to lock my study door, or on Sundays go out and I would promenade my secret misery through the city and its environs.

133. An idea

ONE DAY—it was a Friday—I could endure no more. A certain idea, which took black form within me, opened its wings and began to flap from side to side, as ideas do when they wish to be free. That it was Friday, I believe, was chance, but it could also have been design. I was brought up in terror of that day. I had heard ballads sung at home, ballads from the plantation and the old country in which Friday was a day of foreboding. Still, as there are no almanacs in the brain, it is probable that the idea would not have beat its wings except for its need to get out and breathe the air of life. Life is so beautiful that even the idea of death must be born before it can be realized. You must already understand. Now read another chapter.

134. Witches' Sabbath

THE IDEA finally freed itself from my brain. It was night, and I could not sleep, however much I tried to shake it from me. Yet no night ever passed so swiftly. It began to grow light. And I had thought it no more than one or two o'clock. I went out, intending to leave the idea at home; it accompanied me. Outside, it had the same dark color, the same tremulous wings, and though it flew, it was as if fixed, and I carried it on my retina—not that it hid external objects from me, but through it they were paler than usual, and fleeting. Nothing remained.

I do not much remember the rest of the day. I know I wrote some letters, bought a substance, which I shall not name in order that I may not awaken the desire to try it. The pharmacy has failed, it is true; the owner became a banker—his bank prospers. When I found myself with death in my pocket I felt as if I had just drawn the grand prize—no, greater joy; for a lottery prize fades away, but death does not. I went to my mother's house to say farewell, but under pretext of paying a visit. Whether it was really so or an illusion, everything there seemed better that day: my mother less sad, Uncle Cosme unmindful of his heart, Cousin

Justina of her tongue. I passed an hour in peace. I even considered relinquishing my project. What would I need in order to live? Never leave that house again, or engrave that hour within myself. . . .

135. Othello

I DINED out; went to the theater in the evening. They happened to be playing *Othello,* which I had never seen or read. I was familiar only with its theme, and rejoiced at the coincidence. I watched the Moor rage because of a handkerchief —a simple handkerchief!—and here I furnish material to be considered by psychologists of this and other continents, since I could not escape the observation that a handkerchief was enough to kindle the jealousy of Othello and fashion the most sublime tragedy of this world. Handkerchiefs have passed out of use; today one must have nothing less than sheets, at times it is not sheets but only shirts that matter. These were the vague and muddled ideas that passed through my mind as the Moor rolled convulsively and Iago distilled his calumny. During the intervals between the acts I did not leave my seat. I did not wish to risk meeting someone I knew. Most of the ladies remained in the boxes, while the men went out to smoke. Then I asked myself if one of these women might not have loved somone who now lay quiet in the cemetery; and there came to me other incoherencies, until the curtain rose and the play went on. The last act showed me that not I, but Capitú ought to die. I heard the prayers of Desdemona, her pure and loving words, the fury of the Moor, and the death he meted out to her amid the frantic applause of the audience.

"And she was innocent!" I kept saying to myself all the way down the street. "What would the audience do if she were really guilty, as guilty as Capitú? And what death would the Moor mete out to her then? A bolster would not suffice; there would be need of blood and fire, a vast, intense fire to consume her wholly, and reduce her to dust, and the dust tossed to the wind, in eternal extinction. . . ."

I roamed through the streets the rest of the night. I had supper, it is true, a trifle, but enough to live on till morning. I saw the last hours of night and the first hours of day. I saw the late strollers and the first sweepers, the first carts, the first noises, the first white streaks of day, a day that came after the other and would see me depart never to return. The streets I roamed seemed to flee from me of themselves. I would never again contemplate the sea beyond Gloria, nor the Serra dos Orgãos, nor the fortress of Santa Cruz, and the rest. There were not so many people on the street as on weekdays but there were quite a number off to tasks they would do again; but I would never do anything again.

I reached home, opened the door very slowly, climbed the stairs on tiptoe, and let myself into my study. It was almost six. I took the poison out of my pocket, sat in my shirt sleeves and wrote one more letter, the last, directed to Capitú. None of the others were for her. I felt the necessity of writing some word which would leave her remorseful for my death. I wrote two versions. I burned the first, thinking it too long and diffuse. The second contained only what was necessary, clear and brief. It did not remind her of our past, nor of the struggles we had had, nor of any joy: it spoke only of Escobar and of the necessity of dying.

136. The cup of coffee

MY PLAN was to wait for my morning coffee, dissolve the drug in it and gulp it down. Meanwhile, I had not wholly forgotten my Roman history, I remembered that Cato, before he killed himself, read and reread a book of Plato. . . . I did not have Plato by me; but an odd volume of Plutarch which related the life of the celebrated Roman would suffice to occupy the little remaining time. To imitate him in all points, I stretched out on the settee. Nor was it only for the purpose of imitating him; I had to arouse in myself the same courage, just as he had required the thoughts of the philosopher to die intrepidly. One of the evils of ignorance is being without this remedy at the final hour. There are many people who kill themselves without it, and expire nobly; but I believe more people would put a term to their days if they could find this sort of moral cocaine in good books. Nevertheless, as I wished to avoid all suspicion of imitation, I remember distinctly that in order that the book of Plutarch might not be found beside me and mentioned in the newspapers, along with the color of the trousers I was wearing at the time, I planned to put it back in its place before drinking the poison.

The butler brought the coffee. I rose, put away the book, and went to the table where the cup of coffee stood. They were already stirring in the house; it was time to make an end of myself. My hand trembled as I opened the paper wrapping of the drug. Even so I was courageous enough to empty the substance into the cup and begin to stir the coffee, my eyes wandering, my thoughts on the innocent Desdemona. The play of the evening before was obtruding itself upon

the reality of the morning. But the photograph of Escobar
gave me the courage I lacked: there he was, with his hand on
the back of the chair, gazing into the distance. . . .

"Let us make an end of this," I thought.

As I was about to drink, I reflected whether it would not be
better to wait for Capitú and the boy to leave for Mass;
I would drink it then, that would be better. This settled, I
began to pace the study. I heard Ezekiel's voice in the hall, I
watched him come in and run to me, shouting, "Papa! Papa!"

Reader, at this point there was a gesture that I will not
describe because I have completely forgotten it, but, believe
me, it was beautiful and tragic. Practically speaking, the
appearance of the little boy made me retreat until I knocked
against the bookcase. Ezekiel threw his arms around my
knees, perched on tiptoe as if he wanted to climb up and
give me the usual kiss, and kept repeating as he pulled at
me, "Papa! Papa!"

137. Second impulse

IF I had not looked at Ezekiel, it is probable that I would not
be here writing this book, because my first impulse was to run
to the coffee and drink it. I went so far as to lift the cup, but
the little boy was kissing my hand, as he always did, and the
sight of him, as well as the gesture, gave me another impulse
which it is painful for me to record; but, oh well, let everything be told. Let them call me assassin if they like; I am not
the one to gainsay them or contradict them. My second impulse was criminal. I bent down and asked Ezekiel if he had
already had coffee.

"Yes, Papa; I am going to Mass with Mamma."

"Have another cup, just a half-cup."

"And you, Papa?"

"I'll ring for more. Go on, drink it!"

Ezekiel opened his mouth. I brought the cup to his lips, with such trembling that I almost spilt it, but ready to pour it down his throat in case the taste or the temperature was repugnant to him—for the coffee was cold. . . . But I felt something, I do not know what, that made me draw back. I set the cup on the table, and found myself wildly kissing the child's head.

"Papa! Papa!" exclaimed Ezekiel.

"No, no, I am not your father!"

138. Enter Capitú

WHEN I raised my head, I was looking straight at Capitú. Here is another stroke which smacks of the theater, and yet it is as natural as the first one, seeing that the mother and son were going to Mass, and Capitú never left the house without speaking to me. By now it was a brief, cold word; and usually I did not even look at her. She always looked, and waited hopefully.

This time, as I faced her, I do not know whether my eyes deceived me, but Capitú appeared livid. There followed one of those silences which can, without exaggeration, be called an age. Such is the extension of time in great crises. Capitú regained her composure, told her son to go outside, and asked me for an explanation. . . .

"There is nothing to explain," I said.

"There is everything to explain. I don't understand your tears, nor Ezekiel's. What took place between you?"

"Didn't you hear what I said to him?"

Capitú answered that she had heard weeping and the murmur of voices. I believe that she heard everything clearly, but to admit it would mean losing the hope of silence and of reconciliation. Therefore, she denied hearing and admitted only seeing. Without relating the episode of the coffee, I repeated to her the words at the end of the last chapter.

"What?" she asked, as if she had not correctly heard.

"That he is not my son."

Capitú's stupefaction, and the succeeding indignation were both so natural they would confuse the finest eye-witnesses of our courts. I have heard that there are such available for all kinds of cases—question of price. I do not believe it, particularly since the person who told me this had just lost a suit. But, whether or not there are witnesses for hire, mine was genuine. Nature herself took the stand in her own behalf, and I would not care to doubt her. Thus, without marking Capitú's words, her gestures, the pain that racked her, or anything, I repeated the words I had twice spoken, with such resoluteness that she wilted. After several moments she said to me:

"This unjust abuse can only be explained by sincere conviction; and yet you, who were so jealous of the least gesture, never showed the slightest shadow of distrust. What has given you this idea? Tell me," she continued, when I made no reply, "tell everything. After what I have heard, I can hear the rest—it can't be much. What has now given you such conviction? Come, Bentinho, speak! Send me away, but first tell me everything."

"There are certain things one does not say."

"Which one does not leave half said; but now that you have said half, say all."

She sat in a chair near the table. She may have been a trifle confused; her bearing was not that of an accused person. I begged her once more not to insist.

"No, Bentinho, either tell the rest, so that I may defend myself—if you think that there is any defense possible for me, or I beg you for an immediate separation; I can endure no more!"

"The separation is a foregone conclusion," I retorted, seizing upon her words. "It would have been better to part with half words or in silence; each would leave with his own hurt. Seeing, however, that you insist, senhora, here is what I can say, and it is everything."

I did not say everything. I could scarcely allude to the affair with Escobar without mentioning his name. Capitú could not help laughing, a laugh which unfortunately I cannot transcribe. Then in a tone half ironic, half melancholy,

"And even dead men! Not even the dead escape your jealousy!"

She fastened her little cape and stood up. She sighed, I believe she sighed, while I, who would have liked nothing better than her complete justification, uttered some words or other to this purpose. Capitú looked at me disdainfully, and murmured:

"I know the reason for this: it is the chance resemblance . . . The will of God must explain everything . . . You laugh? It is natural; in spite of the seminary, you do not believe in God; I believe . . . But let's not speak of this. It is best to say no more."

139. The photograph

TRUTHFULLY, I was on the brink of believing myself victim of a grand illusion, a phantasmagory of hallucination; but the sudden entrance of Ezekiel shouting, "Mamma! Mamma! it's time for Mass!" restored me to a sense of reality. Capitú and I, involuntarily, glanced at the photograph of Escobar, and then at each other. This time her confusion was pure confession. They were one; there must have been some photograph of Escobar as a little boy which would be our little Ezekiel. With her lips, however, she confessed to nothing; she repeated her last words, pulled away her son, and they went off to Mass.

140. Return from church

NOW THAT I was left alone the natural thing was to drink the coffee. Well, no, senhor; I had lost my taste for death. Death was one solution; I had just hit upon another, so much the better for not being final: it opened the door to reparation, if necessary. I did not say *pardon,* but *reparation,* that is, justice. Whatever may have been the reason for the act, I rejected death, and awaited Capitú's return. It was more delayed than usual; I began to fear that she had gone to my mother's, but she had not.

"I confided all my bitterness to God," Capitú said to me on her return from church. "I heard within me the answer that our separation is inevitable, and I am at your disposal."

Her eyes, as she said this, were masked, as though watching for a gesture of refusal or of delay. She was counting on my weakness or on my uncertainty concerning the paternity of the boy, but it was all to no avail. Could it be that there was a new man within me, the creation of new and strong pressures? If so, it was a man scarcely hidden beneath the surface. I replied that I would think it over, and we would do as I decided. To tell you the truth, it had all been thought over and decided.

In the meantime, I had recalled the words of the late Gurgel that time at his house when he showed me the portrait of his wife, which resembled Capitú. You must remember them; if not, reread the chapter. I do not place the number of it here, because I no longer remember which it is, but it cannot be far back. They come down to this: there *are* these inexplicable resemblances. . . . Later in the day, and on other days, Ezekiel came to see me in the study, and the child's features were a clear image of him who was dead, or perhaps I was paying more attention to them. Pell-mell, there rushed to mind vague, remote episodes—words, meetings and incidents, in all of which my blindness saw no wrong and my old jealousy had been lacking. Once when I found them alone and silent, a secret that made me laugh, a word of hers when she was dreaming, all those recollections now poured upon me in such a rush that they left me dizzy. . . . And why did I not strangle them that day, when I turned away my eyes from the street where two amorous swallows were treading on the telegraph wire? Within, *my* swallows trod air, eyes tangled in eyes, but so cautiously that they were disentangled on the instant, with a gay and friendly word for me. I told them of the love episode of the swallows outside, and they thought it amusing. Escobar declared that, for his part, it would be better if the swallows, instead of treading on the telegraph wire, lay roasted on the dinner table. "I have never eaten their nests," he continued, "but they must be good, if the Chinese invented the dish." And we went on talking of the Chinese and of the classics that mention them, while Capitú, avowing that we bored her, went about her tasks. Now I remembered all this, which then seemed nothing.

141. The solution

HERE IS what we did. We picked up and went to Europe, not for a pleasure trip, nor to see anything, new or old. We went straight to Switzerland. A governess from Rio Grande, who went with us, remained as companion for Capitú and to teach Ezekiel his mother tongue; he would learn the other things in the schools of that country. My life thus adjusted, I returned to Brazil.

After several months, Capitú began to write to me; I replied briefly and coldly. *Her* letters were submissive, without hatred, perhaps even affectionate, and toward the end full of longing; she begged me to come and see her. I sailed a year later, but I did not go to see her, and I repeated the voyage, with the same result. On my return, those who remembered her asked for news, and I gave it to them as if I had been staying with her. Naturally, the trips were made with a view to giving this very impression, and deceiving opinion. One day, finally . . .

142. A saint

YOU UNDERSTAND that if José Dias did not go with me on these trips to Europe, it was from no lack of willingness on his part. He stayed as companion to Uncle Cosme, who was almost an invalid, and to my mother, who had grown old suddenly. He too was old, though hardy. He would go aboard to see me off, and the words that he said to me, his gestures with a handkerchief, the very eyes that he wiped, were such as to move me also. The last time he did not go aboard.

"Come on. . . ."

"I can't."

"Are you afraid?"

"No; no, I can't. I'll say goodbye now, Bentinho. I don't know if you will see me again; I believe that I am about to go to the other Europe, the eternal one. . . ."

He did not go right away; it was my mother who embarked first. Look in the Cemetery of São João Baptista for a tomb without a name, with only this to mark it: *A saint*. It is there.

I had this inscription made after some difficulty. The sculptor thought it peculiar; the superintendent of the cemetery consulted the vicar of the parish; the latter ponderously explained to me that saints are on the altar and in heaven.

"Pardon me," I interrupted, "but I don't mean to say that this grave holds a canonized woman. My idea is to convey by this word an earthly definition of all the virtues that the deceased possessed in life. This is so much so that, since modesty was one of them, I desire to preserve it for her posthumously, by not inscribing her name."

"Still, the name, the filiation, the dates . . ."

"Who will care about dates, filiation, or even names, after I am gone?"

"You mean to say that she was a sainted lady, is that it?"

"Just so. If Protonotary Cabral were alive, he would confirm what I am telling you."

"I do not question the truth of it, I hesitate only as to the formula. Then you knew the protonotary?"

"I did. He was a model padre."

"Good canonist, good Latinist, pious, and charitable," continued the vicar.

"And he possessed some social gifts," said I. "I used to hear them say at home that he was a notable backgammon player. . . ."

"He had a way with dice!" gently sighed the vicar. "The throw of a master!"

"Then you think? . . ."

"Seeing that there is no other meaning intended, nor could any other be possible, yes, senhor, it is permissible. . . ."

José Dias sat in on this conference, with great melancholy. At last, when we went away, he spoke harshly of the padre, called him meticulous. The only excuse he found for him was his not having known my mother—neither he nor the other men of the cemetery.

"They didn't know her. If they had known her, they would insist on carving *saint of saints*."

143. The last superlative

IT WAS not José Dias' last superlative. He had others which I'll not bother to record here. I will skip to the last, the best of them all, the sweetest, one which made death a fragment of life. He was now living with me. Though my mother had left him a little remembrance, he told me that, with or without the legacy, he would not be separated from me. Perhaps he was hoping to bury me. He corresponded with Capitú. He asked her to send him a picture of Ezekiel, but Capitú delayed sending it from post to post until he no longer asked for anything, unless it might be the heart of the young student. He asked her not to forget to tell Ezekiel about the old friend of his father and of his grandfather, who was "destined by heaven to love the same blood." It was thus he prepared to care for the third generation, but death came before Ezekiel. The illness was swift. I had intended to send for a homeopath.

"No, Bentinho," said he, "an allopath will do; one can die in any school. Besides, those were the ideas of my youth, and time has taken them away. I return to the faith of my fathers. Allopathy is the Catholicism of medicine."

He died serene, after a short agony. Shortly before, he had heard us say the sky was beautiful and had asked us to open the window.

"No, the air might do you harm."

"What harm? Air is life."

We opened the window. As a matter of fact, the sky was blue and clear. José Dias raised his head and gazed out. After several instances, he fell back murmuring, "Most beautiful!" They were the last words he uttered in this world. Poor José Dias! Why should I deny that I wept for him?

144. A tardy question

SO MAY all the eyes of friends that I leave in this world weep for me, men and women; but it is not likely. I am forgotten. I live at a distance, and go out seldom. And I did not really tie together the two ends of my life. This house in Engenho Novo, although it reproduces the one in Matacavallos, does little more than remind me of the old house, and that, more as a result of comparison and reflection than of sentiment. But I have already said this.

You will ask why, when I had the old house itself, in the same ancient street, I let them tear it down and came and reproduced it here. The question ought to have been asked at the beginning, but here is the answer. The reason is that, immediately after my mother died, I wished to move back there, but I first made a long visit of inspection lasting for several days, and the whole house disowned me. Outside—the great aroeira and the pitanga tree, the well pool, the old bucket and the washing-place—nothing knew me. The casuarina tree was the same one that I had left at the far end of the estate, but the trunk, instead of being straight as in the days gone by, now had the air of a question mark: probably it was startled by the intruder. I gazed about, searching some thought that I had left there, and I did not find one. On the contrary, leaves and branches began to hum something I did not immediately understand, but I believe it was the song of youthful mornings. Beneath this sonorous and jovial music, I also heard the grunting of the pigs, a kind of concentrated chorus of philosophic scoffing.

It was all strange and hostile. I let them tear down the

house, and later, when I came to Engenho Novo, I decided
to make this reproduction according to the directions I gave
the architect, as I related above in its proper place.

145. The return

WELL, it was right in this house that one day, as I was dress-
ing for breakfast, I was brought a card with the name:

EZEKIEL A. de SANTIAGO

"The gentleman is here?" I asked the servant.
"Yes, senhor. He is waiting."
I did not go immediately. I made him wait some ten or
fifteen minutes in the living room. Then it occurred to me
that it would be proper to show a certain amount of surprise
and joy, run to him, embrace him speak to him of his
mother. His mother—I believe I have not yet mentioned she
was dead and buried. She was: she reposes there, in the old
country, in Switzerland. I put on the rest of my clothes in
haste. As I left the room, I assumed a fatherly air, something
between mild and brusque, half Dom Casmurro. When I
entered the living room I found the young man with his
back to me, looking at the bust of Massinissa painted on the
wall. I came on cautiously, not making a sound. Nevertheless,
he heard my step and whirled round. He knew me from my
pictures, and ran toward me. I did not stir hand or foot; he
was neither more nor less than my old youthful companion
of the seminary of São José, a little shorter, less heavy, and,
except for his coloring which was vivid, the same face as my
friend. He was dressed in modern clothes, naturally, and his

manners were different, but the general aspect reproduced
him who was dead. He was the self-same, the identical, the
true Escobar. He was my wife's lover; the son of his father.
He wore mourning for his mother; I too was in black. We
sat down.

"You are no different from your latest pictures, Papa," he
said to me.

The voice was Escobar's; the accent was French. I told him
that I was really very little different from what I had been,
and I began a series of questions in order to have less to say
and thus dominate my emotion. But this in itself brought
animation to his face, and my classmate of the seminary kept
rising more and more from the cemetery. Here he was before
me, with the same laugh, and greater respect; in short, the
same affability and the same charm. He was anxious to see
me. His mother had spoken often of me, praising me extraordinarily, as the finest man in the world, and the most
worthy of being loved.

"She was beautiful in death," he concluded.

"Let us have breakfast."

If you think that the breakfast was bitter, you are mistaken.
It had its tedious moments, it is true. At first it pained me
that Ezekiel was not really my son, that he did not complete
me and continue me. If the young man had taken after his
mother, I would have ended by believing everything, all the
more easily because he seemed to have left me the evening
before. He recalled his childhood, scenes and words, his going
to boarding-school . . .

"Do you still remember, Papa, when you took me to the
boarding-school?" he laughed.

"Of course, why shouldn't I?"

"It was in Lapa Square. I was desperate, and you never

once stopped, Papa, pulled me along at every step, and with my little legs . . . Yes, senhor, if you please."

He held out his glass for the wine that I offered him, took a sip and went on eating. Escobar used to eat that way too, with his face in his plate. He told me about his life in Europe, his studies, particularly those in archaeology, which was his love. He spoke of antiquity with passion, ran through the story of Egypt with its thousands of ages without getting lost in the figures; he had his father's head for mathematics. Although the idea of the other's paternity was already familiar to me, I did not enjoy the resurrection. At times, I closed my eyes in order not to see gestures, or anything, but the rascal talked and laughed, and the dead man talked and laughed through him.

Since there was no recourse but to be with him, I played the father in earnest. The idea that he might have seen some photograph of Escobar, that Capitú had thoughtlessly taken with her, never occurred to me, or if it did, did not persist. Ezekiel believed in me, as he believed in his mother. If José Dias had been alive, he would have found him the spit and image of me. Cousin Justina wished to see him; but, as she was feeble, asked me to bring him to her. I knew that relative. I believe her desire to see Ezekiel was with a view to verifying in the young man the sketch she had found, perhaps, in the child. It would be a last treat; I intercepted it in time.

"She is very ill," I told Ezekiel, when he asked to see her; "any emotion might cause her death. We'll see her when she is better."

We never went. Death took her within a few days. She rests in the bosom of the Lord, or where you will. Ezekiel saw her face in the coffin and did not recognize it, nor could he, so

changed was it by the years and death. All the way to the
cemetery, things kept coming back to him—a street, a tower,
a stretch of beach; and he was all happiness. This is what
happened each time he came home at the end of the day: he
would tell me of the memories that kept returning to him, of
the streets and houses. He was amazed that many of them
were the same ones he had left behind, as if houses died
young.

At the end of six months, Ezekiel spoke to me of a trip to
Greece, Egypt and Palestine, a scientific trip, a promise made
to some friends.

"Of which sex?" I asked with a laugh.

He smiled, slightly annoyed, and answered that women
were such creatures of fashion and of the day, that they would
never understand a ruin of thirty centuries. It was two classmates from the university. I promised to furnish the resources, and gave him then and there an advance on the
money needed. I told myself that one of the consequences of
the stolen love of the father was that I gave money for the
son's archaeology. I'd rather have given him leprosy. . . .
When this idea flashed through my mind, I felt so cruel and
perverse that I grabbed the boy and would have hugged him
to my breast, but I drew back; then I gazed into his eyes as
one does with a true son. His answering look was tender and
grateful.

146. No leprosy

THERE WAS no leprosy, but there are fevers throughout all
these lands of men, whether old or new. Eleven months later,
Ezekiel died of typhoid fever and was buried in the vicinity

of Jerusalem, where the two university friends set up a tomb
for him with this inscription, taken from the Prophet Ezekiel,
in Greek: "Thou wast perfect in thy ways." They sent me
both texts, Greek and Latin, a sketch of the grave, an account
of the expenses, and the rest of the money that he had taken
with him—I would have paid triple never to have seen him
again.

As I wished to verify the text, I consulted my Vulgate and
found it was correct, but there was a complement to it:
"Thou wast perfect in thy ways, *from the day that thou wast
created*." I stopped and asked this unspoken question: "When
would have been the day of Ezekiel's creation?" No one answered me. Here is one more mystery to add to the many
others of this world. Despite everything, I ate a good dinner
and went to the theater.

147. The retrospective exhibition

YOU ALREADY know that my soul, however lacerated, did not
remain in a corner like a pale, solitary flower. I did not permit it that color, or lack of color. I lived the best I could, and
not without the company of women to console me for the
first one. Caprices of short duration, it is true. It was they
who would leave me, like people who go to a retrospective
exhibition and either get tired of looking, or the light in the
gallery fades. Only one of these visitors had a carriage waiting
at the door and a liveried coachman. The others went mod-
estly *calcante pede,* and if it was raining, it was I who went
for a cab and helped them in, with profuse farewells and
more profuse recommendations:

"Do you have the catalog?"

"Yes, I have it; till tomorrow."

"Till tomorrow."

They never returned. I would stand at the door waiting, I would go to the corner, look up and down, consult my watch, and see nothing, nobody. Then, if another visitor appeared, I would give her my arm, we would go in, I would show her the landscapes, the historical paintings, the genre paintings, a water color, a pastel, a *gouache,* and she too would grow weary, and go away with the catalog in her hand. . . .

148. Well, and the rest?

NOW WHY is it that none of these ladies of my caprice made me forget my heart's first love?—Perhaps because none had her eyes like the tide, or the eyes of a sly, oblique gypsy. But this is not, properly speaking, the rest of the book. What remains is to discover whether the Capitú of Gloria was already within the Capitú of Matacavallos, or if this one was changed into the other as the result of some chance incident. If Jesus, son of Sirach, had known of my first fits of jealousy, he would have said to me, as in his Ch. IX, vs. 1: "Be not jealous of thy wife lest she set herself to deceive thee with the malice that she learnt from thee." But I do not believe it was so, and you will agree with me. If you remember Capitú the child, you will have to recognize that one was within the other, like the fruit within its rind.

Well, whatever may be the solution, one thing remains and

it is the sum of sums, the rest of the residuum, to wit, that my first love and my greatest friend, both so loving me, both so loved, were destined to join together and deceive me. . . . May the earth rest lightly on them! Let us proceed to the *History of the Suburbs*.

Contents